The Life and Opinions of the Housecat Hastings

together with excerpts from his visionary masterpiece *The Kibble*

by Harrison Bae Wein

Derwood
Press

"The Life and Opinions of Housecat Hastings," by Harrison Bae Wein. ISBN 978-0-9911119-0-9 (Softcover); 978-0-9911119-1-6 (eBook).

Library of Congress Number: 2013919853

Manufactured in the United States of America.

Illustrations by Natalie Ewert.

Cover design by Bryan Ewsichek.

This book is dedicated to my muse, Hastings,

and to my wife and family.

Kittenhood

You may wonder, my fellow felines, how I came to be the cultured, erudite housecat that sits here now typing these words. It all began when Buddy, for reasons I still don't fully understand, decided to take a scrawny, diffident little kitten under his paw and become my mentor. However, if I were asked to pinpoint the specific turning point of my life, it would be with the sudden and unusual death of our corpulent, eccentric caretaker. When Martha drew her last breath, she set my life on a course none, and least of all I, could have anticipated. Admittedly, it was largely our fault that she died in the first place.

The irony in the situation was that Buddy and I, not Martha, had been marked for death that night. Knowing this, we had already planned our escape from her cat-filled apartment. However, as I crunched my dinner distractedly I heard Buddy mutter my nickname under his breath. "Trombone," he said, "don't look now, but they're making their move." I glanced over my shoulder and almost choked on my kibble.

"I told you not to look," he grumbled.

There were at least a dozen toms creeping toward us—all at least twice my size. They were led by a fleshy gray male with a torn ear and raw wounds scarring his face and flank. Buddy himself had inflicted these wounds the night before on my behalf. With a sinking heart, I realized that we had little chance of getting out of this predicament alive.

"What are we going to do?" I whispered to Buddy, trying to keep the panic from my voice.

1

"Sharpen your claws on the sidewalk."

"Huh?"

"That means get ready to fight for your life," he said in a firm, low voice. He then quickly spat out my instructions, "When I say, 'go,' we turn and face them together. If they surround us, we stand flank to flank, facing opposite directions. Slash anything that comes near. Don't stop fighting as long as you can still twitch a whisker." Then he bravely turned around to face them, his dark, muscular form braced low for the fight.

I was paralyzed with fear. My muscles simply would not move.

"What are you waiting for?" Buddy hissed over his shoulder. "Get ready."

Just then, we heard a groan from the other room and the squeak of bedsprings. "Carlota, are you still here?" Martha called.

Carlota, the maid, had already left, but Buddy immediately saw our opportunity. "Run!" he shouted, and leaped over the food bowls. I followed, but fell short and landed among the bowls, scattering them and spraying kibble everywhere as I tumbled onto my side.

I quickly regained my footing and looked around. Buddy was barreling his way through the crowd that was watching from the sidelines. Our assailants were streaming around the scattered food bowls, closing in on me. I took off after Buddy, my paws slipping on the smooth floor as I scrambled through the gap he'd cut through the spectators.

Martha ambled into the room looking for Carlota, and Buddy darted behind her legs for protection. I tried to copy his slick dodge around her legs but instead slid straight ahead and into her thick ankles.

"What's going on here?" Martha shouted, looking down at me. The herd was close behind me, roaring with meows of rage. Sinking my claws into Martha's slippers for leverage, I pitched myself to Buddy's side. He winked at me as he unsheathed his claws.

The attacking throng quickly descended upon us. Our ears were filled with their war cries, which were soon joined by Martha's panicked scream. We slashed at any fur within our reach, our paws blurring with the desperate fury of our defense. Martha's legs, as thick as tree trunks, protected us on one side, and Buddy and I made a valiant stand, flank to flank, defending each other's backs.

Within seconds, however, their sheer numbers overwhelmed us. Their oncoming bodies pinned us against Martha's thick, pasty flesh. I felt myself being crushed, the air squeezing from my lungs. Martha was crying for help.

Suddenly, I felt the rubbery cushion at my back begin to give way. I started to fall backward, and then we heard a huge thud behind us as we tumbled over on top of each other.

The room fell silent. We righted ourselves and stared, one and all, at Martha. She lay on her substantial belly in her floral, sky-blue housedress, gasping for air with her mouth wide open and a surprised look in her eyes.

The scarred gray male who had led the attack went up to her face. He began to nuzzle her nose, but quickly jumped back when her legs and arms twitched. Her mouth relaxed, spittle leaking from its corners, and her eyes seemed far away. Her gelatinous body twitched again, and then she was still.

Buddy looked at me in shock. Even he hadn't expected this.

The kitties rushed over and immediately began to scold the toms. They considered Martha to be one of the greatest cat caretakers of all time. "Look what you've done," one of them lamented. "What's going to happen to us now?"

What, indeed? we all wondered. The fight was clearly over, however. We had bigger things to worry about. Buddy and I had narrowly escaped death, but none of us had any idea what was in store for us now.

Martha's husband Steven found us together in a vigil in the kitchen when he got home. The brawl was all but forgotten. He did a double-take, then frowned and muttered in the same mild-mannered tone he always used, "You finally did yourself in, didn't you, Martha?"

* * * * * * * * * *

Had you seen me back then, my dear readers, you would have judged me to be one of the least equipped to survive the trauma and uncertainty that was to come, much less to become the thriving, handsome cream orange tabby that now writes these words for your benefit.

I started out, in fact, the very smallest of my litter. The world is a treacherous place for any newborn kitten, as you well know, but it is even more so for the runt of the litter. Like most kittens, I never knew my father, and my mother paid me little mind. I was the smallest, I was the weakest, and my mother quickly decided that there was little to gain in investing her time and milk in me. It was a coldly rational decision, and I don't harbor any resentment toward her for it.

There were countless cats in Martha's apartment, with more seemingly born every time you turned around. Martha had no children, few relatives and even fewer friends. We housecats were the center of her world. She decorated with cats, read books about cats, watched documentaries about cats and in general talked both to and about cats in a manner that I now recognize as distinctly unhealthy.

Martha spent her days leaning back on a stack of fluffy pillows in her king-sized bed, watching television and lording over a teeming mass of multicolored fur. Aside from getting up to go to the bathroom, she rarely left her bed and never, to my memory, ventured out of the apartment at all.

It is true that we were generally free to do as we pleased in Martha's catopia, but of course there was little to do. For a small, newborn kitten like myself, it was quite a terrifying place. The older cats bickered and fought constantly, stumbling over each other to get into bed and gain the affections of our caretaker, and perhaps even win a taste of the rich fatty foods she so adored. We kittens tried hard to stay out of their way, hiding under the furniture and generally learning how to blend into our surroundings. I very quickly learned the art of not being noticed. My goal in life was to leave no impression and, in fact, no one ever seemed to notice I was there.

And yet, despite what sounds even to myself in retrospect a terrible situation, I cannot say that I was unhappy. It is a curious fact of life that, when we are young, almost no matter how bad our situation, we know no better, and therefore accept our lot in life without further thought. I could not say I was a happy kitten, but nor can I claim to have been miserable. I lived as I lived, and I was.

* * * * * * * * *

That all changed when I was perhaps three months old. I was sitting in a corner of the bedroom on a sunny afternoon, watching the jostling on Martha's bed from a safe distance. I remember how I longed to grow strong and daring enough to join the melee up there, for that was all I knew to aspire to back then. It was at that moment that I heard a gruff voice muttering beside me, "That woman should get her butt off the bed once in a while and take a walk around the block."

"Huh?" I asked, and turned to find the notorious Buddy but a few pawsteps away. Buddy was a brawny, imposing tom with dark gray and black stripes. A former street cat, he was widely considered to be the toughest of the tough in our overcrowded little apartment. Everyone was scared of him and stayed out of his way. I hadn't been around when Buddy first came to the apartment, of course, but rumor had it that, on his very first day there, Buddy had murdered a tom who crossed him, sinking his teeth into the offending tom's neck and holding it, allowing the blood to stream out and down his throat until he felt the life completely drained from his victim.

"Buddy," I gasped.

"Yeah, you know me. Congratulations."

Trembling with fear, I turned my eyes down from him as a sign of respect, expecting him to simply walk away and leave me be, but he didn't. "Look at her; she's killing herself," he said, shaking his head. "Now, we've got no choice but to sit here trapped in this apartment. That fat mole woman has no excuse. She needs to get out and live a little."

I looked up at Buddy for more of an explanation, but he had already begun to walk away. I longed to chase him to ask him what he meant, but I was too frightened to follow.

I'd never before heard so much as a word that challenged the way I thought about our lot in life. All I knew was that we were born into what we were born into, and that was that. I expected to live my entire life in that apartment, as we all did, in Martha's catopia.

But Buddy's seemingly insignificant comment started me thinking: What else was there? If we did have a choice, what would we choose to do? Would we stay in the apartment like Martha? Or would we go outside and roam free?

After a contemplative night camped along the wall under the sofa, riding out the night's usual chaotic activity with a couple of other scared kittens whose names I would never know, I spotted Buddy on the living room window sill basking in the morning sun. I'd never done anything so daring before, but something deep within compelled me to muster my courage and talk to this scariest of toms. It took several attempts for my tiny legs to successfully jump up there, but I clutched at the window sill with my claws and eventually scrambled up to join him. Buddy was asleep and presumably unaware of my presence, but I was trembling like a mouse in a mouth as I approached him.

Suddenly, one of Buddy's eyelids lifted. "What are you doing on my window sill?" he asked in a sleepy but nonetheless threatening drawl.

"I...I...," I stammered, "I wanted to talk to you."

"Yeah?" he asked, opening both eyes. "What about?"

"You said something yesterday."

"Oh yeah, I remember you, Squirt."

"My name's not Squirt."

Buddy laughed. I didn't know what I'd said that was so funny. I wanted to correct him about my name, but didn't actually have anything to offer as a substitute. Martha never bothered to give most of us names because there would have been no possible way for her to remember them all. A few of us did have names—like Buddy, the notoriously flatulent Frankie and a few others who stood out in unique ways. I wasn't one of those. But by my whiskers, the one thing I knew for sure was that my name wasn't Squirt.

Buddy was still laughing, and with all my pent up nervousness at confronting this legendary tom, I thought I was going to cry. A loud meow of frustration escaped me.

"Well, burn my catnip," he said, bemused at my display. "Maybe your name's Trombone, with that meow."

"I don't know what my name is!"

Buddy observed me as I tried to calm myself down by licking my forearms, fully aware that he could slash my face and send me to the ground with one swipe if he chose. "Why, you don't know anything, Trombone, not even your own name," he said. "What do you want to be talking to someone like me for?"

I mustered my courage and looked up at him. "What you said, about Martha and how she should get out and live..."

"Yeah?"

"Well," I began, struggling to express all the questions that had been running through my head all night, "what is there out there?"

He studied me, considering whether I was worth explaining it to. "Ah, you wouldn't understand," he decided, resting his head back down on his paws and closing his eyes.

Like all cats, I had my pride, and it gave me the dose of courage I needed to challenge even this most intimidating of toms. "Why not?" I asked.

Buddy raised one eyelid a bit to look at me, then closed it again and continued in a tired voice,

"You've lived all your life here. You don't know anything else. You've never even been outside."

"I've been to the veterinarian," I corrected him.

"That doesn't count. You're soft. You're all soft. You don't understand the world outside."

"Well, what's it like?"

He opened his emerald eyes and fixed me with a cold stare. "It's brutal. Dog eat dog. Dog eat cat. Cat eat mouse. No," he concluded, shaking his head, "you wouldn't survive a day out there, Trombone."

"It sounds scary," I shivered.

"It is," he agreed, then sat up to look down at the bustle of the street far below. "But it's awesome," he added.

"It is?"

"Yeah," he said, gazing dreamily out the window. "There's nothing like the thrill of survival out there. Chasing mice, foraging for food, finding that perfect spot to catch the sunlight. It's exhilarating. It's real."

"Wow."

"We're not even cats in here. We're cuddly wuddlies. You," he stressed, pointing a paw at me, "are a cuddly wuddly."

Indeed, Martha called us that all the time. I'd never thought anything of it before.

"The woman is pitiful," Buddy decried, nodding his head toward the bedroom, "watching the lives of other people on television for hours, laughing at their stupidity, crying at their sorrows, giving advice they can't hear and banging her pillows in frustration when they don't listen. She never does anything herself. Her maid does the housework. Her husband brings

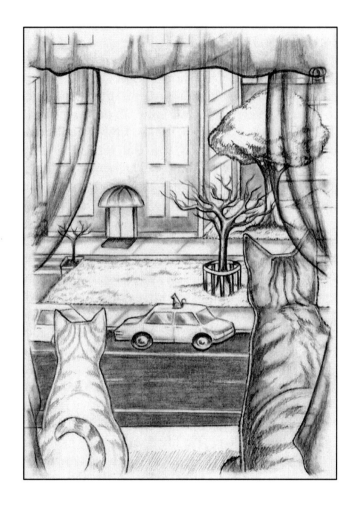

What is there out there?

the food. She hides from life. And she forces the same on us, Trombone. In this place, your brain rots as fast as a dead bird on a black tar roof."

"Well, why don't we escape?" I asked, excited by his passion.

"I've tried," he said wistfully, looking down to the street again, his face almost touching the window, whiskers bending against the glass as if they were trying to push it away. "You can't do it. The doors are too heavy for us. Only people can open them. And even if you can get out of this apartment, there's only a long hallway out there. Then if you make it to the elevator, only people can reach the buttons to make it move. But face it, you can't even get out of this apartment in the first place without them knowing about it. It's hopeless."

"Nothing's hopeless."

"Wise words," Buddy said, lying down again and closing his eyes, "for idiots." At the time, I wasn't familiar with such linguistic tricks. I stood there dumbfounded. "Now leave me alone and stop bothering me, would you?" he said, waving a paw to dismiss me.

I had little else to say, but I didn't go away. Filled with angst and excitement by what Buddy had just told me, I sat there and watched the street below while he slept. He lifted an eyelid to spy me a couple of times, but he didn't chase me away.

I left Buddy eventually, scared that he would wake up and slash me to get rid of me. I spent the day wandering around on my own as usual, looking for good places to nap and carefully avoiding any fights. But I thought a lot about what Buddy had said. I wondered if I would ever know the taste of freedom he so relished.

The day before, I'd never so much as given the world outside our little home a single thought, but now I suddenly longed to know what it was like. My young, naive mind imagined roaming free with Buddy, having him teach me all that he knew.

* * * * * * * * * *

The next time I spoke with Buddy, it wasn't I that started the conversation. To this day, I still don't know why Buddy chose to take me under his paw. Perhaps he saw me as a pupil, or was just lonely for company. In any case, that evening I was packed among the other cats in the typically rough jostling for a spot near the food bowls. There was some pushing to my right, but I thought nothing of it until I heard a gruff voice beside me say, "I used to eat real food, not this processed junk." I recognized Buddy's voice and turned to see him spit his partially-chewed kibble back into the bowl. He stared down at the pile with disgust.

"Hey, don't spit in the food," a white tom on his other side said.

Buddy turned toward him, and though I couldn't see the expression on Buddy's face, I could clearly see the fear swelling in the white tom's eyes. He abruptly backed away and went to find another spot to eat his meal.

"How do you do that?" I gaped in astonishment.

"Come on," he nodded to me. "Let's take a walk."

I quickly left off eating and followed him out of the kitchen and into the living room. He jumped up to the same window sill he'd been on that morning. I followed, but needed several tries before I'd successfully jumped and clutched my way up there with him. He was already sitting, and I sat down to face him, saying nothing as I tried to catch my breath.

"They're all scared of me," he said with some satisfaction. "All I have to do is look at them."

"Is it true," I huffed, "what you did to that tom when you first got here?"

Buddy looked out the window. The sun was going down, casting a melancholy light on the street below. The street lamps were already on and many of the cars had their lights on, too. "It's true," Buddy said, "but it's not what you think."

He stared down at the street for some time without speaking. I wasn't sure if he intended to continue his story, but I was eager to hear more of it. "What happened?" I prompted him.

Buddy turned back to me and sighed. "When the super caught me out back, I was used to roaming free, being by myself, going where I wanted and doing what I wanted. I protested all I could, but he caught me by surprise and he knew how to handle a cat by the scruff. I was helpless. I don't know why he thought I'd want to join Martha's menagerie here, but he did. She said she'd take me in, even though I made it very clear I didn't want to go with her. They thought my meowing was cute," Buddy hissed disdainfully, his whiskers twitching with anger.

He turned his head to carefully survey the room. There were a few scattered cats lounging about on their own, but none appeared to be listening to him. He resumed, but more quietly, "To suddenly get trapped in here with all these cats, thrown into all this chaos, it can push you over the edge. I was mad. And I'll tell you, Trombone, though I probably shouldn't: I was scared, too. I was sure they were going to gang up and kill me, and so I had to do something fast to make an impression. When that first cat challenged me, I thought I had to kill him to set an example.

"Killing him was no problem," Buddy continued, casually starting to lick a paw. He stopped and explained, "I was a street cat, Trombone. These toms in here have no idea how to fight. I made it as quick and painless for him as possible. He really shouldn't have picked a fight with me in the first place."

"And you let the blood go down your throat like that until he stopped moving?"

Buddy laughed deeply. "No," he said, "that part was a little embellishment. I spread that rumor myself—and who's going to argue with me? It's a nice deterrent."

"Yuk."

"Yeah, well, death's not pretty."

"And Martha never knew what happened?" I asked eagerly.

"Well, I cleaned myself off before Martha could catch me. I know she suspected it was me, but she could never be sure. As for the other cats, they've left me alone ever since. They're all scared to even come near me. Except for you, that is." He looked at me curiously. "Now why is that, Trombone?"

"I don't know." I shrugged my shoulders. "You talked to me first."

"I wasn't really talking to you."

"I thought you were."

"Well," he said, "maybe there's something different about you, Trombone. Maybe you've got some guts, unlike the rest of these pussies. Or maybe you're just delusional."

I didn't even know that what word meant. All I knew was that I found Buddy fascinating and I was determined to stick with him as long as he would let me.

* * * * * * * * *

I began to follow Buddy wherever he went, and he tolerated me as good-naturedly as his rugged demeanor would allow. The others quickly came to see us as a sort of team. Young and experienced kitten that I was, they of course considered me little more than Buddy's sidekick. Nevertheless, any association with such a respected, feared tom like Buddy was exhilarating and empowering for an unsure kitten like myself. Before, I had barely registered in anyone's mind. Had I suddenly disappeared, no one would have noticed it at all, much less bothered to ask,

"Whatever happened to what's his name with the orange coat?"

Now, all the other cats knew who I was. I began to strut around just like Buddy, turning from them with a studied arrogance, mimicking the look of disdain that Buddy wore on his grim gray and black face.

But along with the new attention that I garnered, resentment came my way as well. Buddy was widely feared, of course, but I was not. "Who do you think you are, so high and mighty?" I recall being asked at one point. I arched my back, lifted my tail and walked away without giving an answer. Such was my behavior in those days of naive hubris.

It had been only about two weeks since Buddy had taken me under his paw when I let my growing confidence go to my head and got into my first real catfight. As young kittens in our very first weeks of life, we had had endless harmless tussles, but this was quite a different thing altogether.

Buddy and I had gone to join in the usual jostling over the food bowls after Carlota had filled them for dinner. We were separated, but there was nothing unusual about that in the frenzy to get at the fresh kibble. As I pressed forward to get my fill, I noticed two imposing toms conspiring to block my way: one with an orange and black tortoiseshell pattern on his fur and the other a light gray.

I meowed loudly, thinking they would immediately make way for me. Instead, they answered with long, deep and threatening guttural hisses. I moved to the left, and the tortoiseshell moved to bar my way forward. I moved right, and the gray one did likewise.

"Get out of the way," I ordered.

"Why don't you go get your buddy to help you, little kitty?" the tortoiseshell mocked.

"Yeah, your buddy Buddy," the gray one taunted.

At that, Frankie ambled forward, turned his rear to me and flatulated directly in my face. I bravely stood my ground and tried not to betray any emotion, but it was such a noxious smell at those close quarters that I involuntarily gagged. The three of them burst out in mocking laughter.

I took the opportunity to run around them and over to the food bowls. I lowered my head to take a bite, hoping that, having had their fun, they would forget about me. But they had no intention of letting me get away so easily.

"Now that wasn't nice," the tortoiseshell said, turning around and unsheathing a claw.

"Definitely a bad move," the gray one agreed, circling behind me.

"And you're eating from my bowl," Frankie said in that buzzy voice of his. That cat was so obsessed with food, even in a brawl his threat centered around food. It was a wonder he could still walk, with that pendulous belly almost touching the ground.

Seeing no choice, I turned to face them, my heart pounding as it never had before, the blood roaring in my ears. The two approached me slowly from opposite sides, with Frankie following close behind. I raised my tail and hissed instinctively.

I knew I was no match for them. Not only were there three of them, but I still had many weeks to grow. All three of them were absolute hulking masses of heavy housecat flab that had only to pin me down to end our fight. But I knew everyone was watching. I had to prove my courage, whatever happened.

Tortoiseshell was the first to swipe at me, and his move was quicker than I expected. He boxed my ear and knocked me down sideways into a bowl of kibble. Gray was on top of me in an instant, slashing at me with his claws. Panic struck me and I slashed frenziedly, flailing my paws both to parry and strike in an uncoordinated mess of defense.

Suddenly I heard a shout beside me. "Yeehaw! I've been itching for a good fight! Bring it on!" Buddy had come to help. "Get up, Trombone," he said, offering me a paw. "Let's even the odds here a bit."

"We've no bone to pick with you, Buddy," the tortoiseshell said nervously.

"Well, you just picked it, pussy," Buddy snarled. With that, he lunged at the tortoiseshell and slashed his face with a quick swipe of the paw. The gray one moved to attack, but Buddy was faster than him, too, lunging and biting his neck, then tossing him to the side.

Inspired, I jumped onto Frankie's shoulders and caught him completely by surprise, sinking my claws into his solid tan coat. He tried to shake me off, but I bit into his scruff and held on for dear life as he thrashed back and forth with all his might.

Realizing I wasn't going to let go so easily, Frankie fell onto his side and rolled over until he had me pinned against the floor. He pressed his weight down, squeezing the air out of me until I finally let go. He then got up as fast as he could, which with all the extra weight he was carrying around, took some time. Nonetheless, I was so winded that I barely got up in time to face him again. However, Frankie promptly retreated, glancing nervously behind him until he was out of sight.

I was very satisfied with myself until I turned around and realized that it wasn't I that had put the fear in Frankie's heart, but the vision behind me. The gray tom was lying bloody and moaning on the floor, with several deep slash marks down his flank and a badly torn ear. Buddy was standing over him like a lion, his front paws on his shoulders to hold him still. He scanned the room with a vicious, challenging expression.

I was stunned by the amount of damage Buddy had done in so little time. "Where'd the other one go?" I asked him, shaking and flush with excitement.

"He ran away like a frightened kitten," Buddy sneered. "By the way, nice job, Trombone. You showed real spirit there."

"I didn't really hurt him."

"Yeah, but you stood up for yourself. Three on one, that's not fair. You did good."

The gray gave a large cry of pain as Buddy shifted his weight off of him. Then we heard Martha's groan and the squeals of bedsprings from the other room. "Let's get out of here," Buddy said. He bolted from the room, and I followed.

We watched from the living room as Martha found the injured cat, got a towel to roll him onto and then took him back to her bedroom to tend to his wounds. Once she was out of our sights, Buddy led me away from the other cats who were watching the spectacle, and we jumped up to our windowsill.

"This is the endgame," he said under his breath. "Our kibble's cooked."

"Why?" I asked, confused. "We just won."

"For now. But look, Trombone, they're going to want their revenge. They're going to plot against us after this, and there's no telling how many they'll get to help. They'll wait a day, maybe two, maybe a hundred. But they'll get us. We're marked now."

"But I don't understand," I cried. "You killed a cat before and it kept all the rest of them away. Now you're saying that hurting one of them is going to make them attack us?"

Buddy nodded. "And kill us," he added. "Back then, they were sizing me up, trying to figure out who I was. So I showed them, and they left me alone. This time I don't have the mystique of the unknown. Three of them ganged up on you already. Cats don't like to cooperate, Trombone, but they can be united by a common enemy. That enemy is us," Buddy said heavily. "Now that everyone's seen them humiliated, they'll tell them they have to cooperate, because there's no knowing who we'll attack next. Others will join them out of fear. I'll wager we'll be facing up to a dozen next time, maybe more."

"Great Bastet!" I exclaimed, evoking the feline god. "What are we going to do?"

"I don't know, Trombone. I'm going to have to teach you to fight like an alley cat, I guess. We're going to have to make a stand."

"Let's run away," I pleaded.

"A break?"

I nodded eagerly.

He shook his head. "I told you already, Trombone, we can't get out of here. It's impossible."

"Nothing's impossible," I insisted.

He considered for a moment. "You remember what I told you the last time you said something like that?"

"Yes," I said bashfully. "Wise words for idiots."

"Yeah, well, maybe you were right after all, Trombone. It sure is worth a try."

* * * * * * * * * *

Buddy told me to stick close to him that night in case there was any trouble, and I was happy to comply. The other cats tracked our every move with utter hatred in their eyes. We realized it was only a matter of time before they made their move. With only two of us, it was highly unlikely that we would be able to triumph in any sort of skirmish. Escape was our only way out.

I must admit to you, my feline friends, that the prospect of freedom frightened me almost as much as all those marble eyes constantly following our movements. Despite Buddy's romantic descriptions of the outside world, the thought of life on the street was terrifying to a kitten who'd never before felt pavement on his paws. Visions tormented me of being lost in a maze of narrow streets, hiding behind garbage cans to avoid gangs of vicious alley cats and stray dogs slobbering with hunger as they sniffed out my scent.

But I could see no alternative. I tried to will myself to look forward to becoming a successful stray under Buddy's tutelage. I would do all right, I told myself, if I just stuck with my friend out there.

"Our only hope is out the door," Buddy said on the windowsill late that night. "Now, Martha never goes out. Carlota watches us too carefully. The way I see it, we've got to do it when Steven gets home." Buddy paused to scan and make sure no one was sneaking up on us, as he'd been doing ever since our skirmish.

"Go on," I prompted him, anxious to hear his plan.

"We slip out quietly so he doesn't see us. We wait by the elevator, slip in when the door opens, then slip out downstairs, and freedom is just a sprint across the lobby."

"How are we going to slip out without him seeing us?"

"As soon as he opens the door, we bolt. Maybe he won't even care and just let us go."

This was my opportunity to tell him about an idea that had come to me soon after we'd first spoken of escaping. "What about the garbage chute?" I suggested eagerly. "When Steven or

Carlota takes out the garbage, we can go underneath the bag and sneak along beside them without them even seeing us. Then we can escape down the chute."

Buddy thought about it for a second. "Not bad," he considered. "I've seen the setup, when I ran out the door one day. I'm not sure if we can open that metal door to get into the chute." He put his paw on his chin as he recollected the scene in his mind. "But still, there's no door to that room, so we could hide and wait. When someone goes in to throw out their garbage and opens the chute, we jump, slash them if they try to grab us, and just take the ride down. Yeah," he said, brightening. "It just might work, Trombone. You're really learning to think outside the litter box."

I smiled, flattered by the compliment.

Buddy put his paw on my shoulder and fixed my eyes with a somber expression. "Are you sure you're ready for this, Trombone?" he asked steadily.

"I'm ready," I assured him.

In truth, I was anything but certain.

* * * * * * * * * *

We watched Carlota eagerly the next day, tracking her moves every bit as closely as the other cats tracked ours. We were determined to seize any opportunity that presented itself to us, no matter the risk. But Carlota never took out the trash. She opened the door a sliver and slipped through the opening to leave for the day without ever giving us a chance to follow. We sighed as the locks clicked, resigned to wait for an opportunity to escape that evening with Steven.

I remember anxiously going over our plan in my mind as we walked back to the food bowls for dinner. And that was when they attacked. The rest I have already recounted for you.

After Steven came home to find his wife on the kitchen floor, he made a phone call and soon there were all sorts of official people about. The front door was opening and closing regularly.

"Let's make our break now," I urged Buddy amid the commotion.

Buddy nodded sternly. "Exactly what I was thinking," he said as he turned away from the admittedly fascinating activity around Martha's enormous carcass. He led the way to the liquor cabinet by the front door, a large dark wooden affair that we could easily hide behind. We waited there, our hearts beating in anticipation of an opportunity.

It was only a matter of a minute or two before it arrived. Buddy dashed out as soon as the door opened, and I followed in close pursuit.

We immediately ran into a thick forest of legs. Countless people were gathered there, standing around and gossiping about what was going on inside Martha and Steven's apartment. I skidded to a stop, overwhelmed by all the noise and the obstacles before me.

"Run, Trombone," Buddy hissed over this shoulder as he sped toward the garbage chute.

I shook off the shock and followed. With each pair of legs I dodged and left behind me, I felt a greater freedom and independence. "We're doing it," I thought to myself with exhilaration. "I can't believe we're doing it. We might really get out of this place." The thrill was intoxicating.

But it was not to last. I was about three quarters of the way there when I was unexpectedly plucked off the ground by the scruff. Still swinging from the momentum of my escape run, I lashed out in protest but to no avail. As Buddy had warned me, the super—the building superintendent, that is—knew how to handle a cat. Smelling of grease and sweat, he ambled down the corridor to the apartment, holding me aloft with his rough hand so that I swung helplessly past the bemused people as they snickered at me. He rang the bell, leaving me hanging like a piece of meat at the butcher.

When Steven answered the door, the super hoisted me even higher. "Looks like you got a runaway," he declared, and I heard someone laugh derisively behind me.

"You better lock him up," Steven said, stepping aside.

"You got another one out there, too," the super said as he brought me inside.

"Could you catch him for me?"

"Sure. No problem."

They threw me into Martha's bathroom and shut the door before I was even back on my feet. For the next few moments, dear readers, I paced that cramped space in utter turmoil. On the one paw, I anxiously hoped that Buddy, for his sake, had executed our plan without me and been able to escape. On the other, I had become quite dependent on the old tom and didn't want to lose him. My heart was torn.

It wasn't long, however, before Steven opened the door again and the super thrust the furiously struggling form of a dark gray and black striped tom into the bathroom with me. I must admit to feeling a surge of relief at seeing my dear friend again. I cried out, rushing to greet him as the door slammed shut again.

"Don't touch me, Trombone," Buddy snapped, batting me away in fury.

Rebuffed, I retreated behind the toilet, my tail down between my legs. Buddy tried repeatedly to jump up onto the high, thin window sill over the bathtub but could not get a grip on the ledge. He made one last desperate jump but failed yet again. "We're never going to get out of this hell hole!" he shouted up at the window in frustration.

His head down, Buddy came out of the bathtub and curled up in the middle of the light blue tile floor, too depressed to say another word, too forlorn to even cry.

For my part, I daren't make a sound. I feared Buddy might take his frustration out on my slight, vulnerable little figure. I cowered in fear and despair behind the toilet, wondering what would become of us as I tried to calm my trembling.

* * * * * * * * *

Night was soon upon us, and the apartment quickly cleared of all the commotion that had overtaken it. Steven opened the bathroom door to let us out, and I followed Buddy silently through the bedroom and into the open living room. Buddy jumped up onto his window sill, but I decided to keep my distance and stayed on the floor beneath it.

The doorbell soon rang. When Steven answered the door, a woman we had never seen before came inside without a word. She was younger than Martha and considerably thinner; maybe three or four of her could fill the space Martha did. She wore brightly colored clothes and thick, shiny jewelry. She and Steven embraced after he closed the door and they kissed each other long and hard on the lips.

"What happens now, sugar?" she asked in a loud, buzzing voice.

"Well," he said, "first we have to get rid of all these goddamned cats."

* * * * * * * * * *

They came the next morning to carry us away. It was well past breakfast time when they arrived. We'd been given nothing to eat since Carlota had left the night before. Some had waited by the door in the morning for her usual arrival, but she never came. As we grew hungrier, Frankie and some others tried in desperation to meow at Steven for food, but the louder their meowing the louder his swearing at them, and they eventually gave up altogether.

I made sure to stay close to Buddy all morning, despite the fact that he hadn't spoken to me once since our failed escape attempt. While all of us shared a similar terror over our plight, that didn't mean that we felt a sense of camaraderie. I could never be quite certain that the animosity the others had held toward me before might not reemerge at the most unexpected time.

When the cat catchers came in with their stacks of wire metal carriers, we all quickly realized what was happening and scattered. I followed Buddy under Martha and Steven's bed and we shrank into the broad, dark shadow there, hoping we wouldn't be noticed. Unfortunately, we very soon saw work boots surrounding us on all sides. The men abruptly poked us out with sticks and, when we bolted, grabbed us with their thick gloves. They promptly stuffed us into the carriers, two to a cage. Buddy and I were among the first to be caught. We were confined together, to my relief, but Buddy barely looked at me.

The men unceremoniously stacked our carriers by the living room door and went about chasing more of our companions. The cats around us cried and hissed in despair, poking and pulling with their claws at the grids of thin metal bars, but Buddy said nothing. There was a quiet fury in his expression that was most unsettling. I was too afraid of him to express any of the turmoil that churned in my own belly, and so I sat quietly at the back of the carrier, wondering what was going to happen to us next.

"Good riddance," Martha's husband scoffed to his girlfriend as they stood beside us watching the people in blue overalls chase his wife's beloved companions around the living room. "I never did like any of them."

"You really let your wife have anything she wanted," the woman mused.

"Well, I loved her once. I really did."

"I hope you pamper me the same way, sugar."

"Don't worry," he said tenderly, putting his arm around her waist. "I will."

Soon after, the cat catchers lifted us up and carried us into the hallway. The fear that then welled in my poor youthful little heart, my fellow felines, was more than I can describe. "Buddy," I cried as the carriers were piled near the elevator.

"Oh, don't worry kid," Buddy reassured me in a tired, resigned tone. "You'll be fine."

He said no more. We all fell into a hushed silence as the fear and uncertainty overwhelmed us. They piled us into the elevator, where we soon felt our rapid descent. If I believed in literary devices such as metaphors I might here point out that it was a metaphorical descent we were taking as well as a literal one.

Downstairs, the people pointed and stared as our cages were stacked up in the bright white marble hallway. We were then put out on the sidewalk, where more people pointed and stared. We tasted the fumes of trucks and buses in the cold bite of the fall wind, shivering as much from our fear as from the cold. Finally, they stacked us up into the rear of a dark, rank truck.

The ensuing trip jarred us about so much that several of us, myself included, would surely have regurgitated had Steven or his young new female friend bothered to give us any food to eat that morning. After being thrown about for a seemingly interminable period of time, the back door finally opened and we were stacked in a muddy, deserted yard. We weren't there long, however, before they brought us inside into a large, putrid room reeking of soiled litter boxes, cleaning fluids and pure feline fear. Cold metal cages lined the room's walls. I could barely breathe for the terror that gripped me then.

We were placed two to a cage barely longer than our outstretched bodies. Buddy and I were thankfully kept together, so at least I had his company. I almost moved to throw my paws around him in thankfulness, but Buddy was sulking so darkly in the corner by himself, it was clear he was not in the mood for such emotional displays.

A terrifying cacophony of barking from outside the room soon monopolized my attention. This, my feline friends, was my very first exposure to the canine world. As one wave of noise would die down, another dog would suddenly call out, "Help me!" or "Pick me!"—I could scarcely tell which with that shrill racket. The other beasts would soon join in until the sound was near deafening. I overheard one of my fellow captives say that it was exponentially louder when you were actually in the room with them, and I prayed that such a thing would never happen to me.

A brief conversation ensued among the cats, during which I learned that it is a well-established fact that dogs are quite stupid and their society operates solely on the principles of fear and intimidation. I shivered at the thought of ever meeting one of these base, disgusting creatures face to face.

We cats said little else in our humiliation. We were too afraid and ashamed, our spirits quashed by our imprisonment. Some of the older cats seemed particularly nervous, although no one said why out loud, and their anxiety stalked through our cages like a pack of stealthy wolves.

"This is all your fault, Buddy," one of them called out. "We're gonna get you for this."

"You've got the mind of a dog and the body of a bird," Buddy shot back at him—as terrible an insult as I've ever heard. There was a collective gasp at his strong words, and no one said anything more.

Workers came by to give us food and water; visitors came to gawk. Buddy, gradually thawing toward me, explained that these latter were seeking to adopt us and bring us home. "Be as cute as you can, Trombone," he advised me. "You want to get out of here as fast as you can. I don't have much of a chance, but you're still young enough."

"What do you mean, you don't have much of a chance?" I asked.

"No one wants to adopt an older cat," he said firmly, his voice so despondent that I thought it best not to press him to explain further.

The dark days dragged on, the barking dogs haunting my every moment. I was plagued by nightmares in which I encountered one. Few of us were adopted, but many were taken out for "visits," brief supervised encounters in a small pen with prospective adopters. Although it seemed like years to my young mind, it was in fact a mercifully few days before I caught the eye of a tall, big-boned young woman with blond hair, who dragged her thin, frumpy husband over to the cage and said, "This is the kind of coloring I was looking for. Isn't he cute?"

"I guess so," he said, then added uncharitably, "for a cat."

"Let's visit with him."

"If you say so," he shrugged.

They left and were gone for so long that I thought they had changed their minds. But a shelter worker finally came to get me.

"Give it your best," Buddy reminded me as the worker took me from our cage. "Make them think you love them more than anything else in the world."

I followed my mentor's advice, arching my back gracefully, rubbing my cheeks against them, closing my eyes and purring the most soothing sound a human ever heard. The gambit worked. They decided to adopt me right there and then.

They put me back in the cage and, standing before us, started discussing the terms of my adoption. As I listened to them, my heart swelled with panic. I realized they weren't even entertaining the idea of adopting Buddy. I was about to be separated from my beloved mentor forever. I couldn't conceive of how I could live without his steady paw guiding me.

They left us for some time, during which I was seized with hysteria. Buddy did his best to calm me, but I was inconsolable. I barely remember what we said, only that I was blind with panic.

When the worker came to take me away, I howled and stretched my paws out to my dear friend and mentor. I was lifted and shoved into a cold cardboard box on the floor. I tried to scramble out, but her strong hands held me down.

"There's nothing you can do for me now," Buddy said wistfully as she folded the top of the box. "I'm just glad you're getting away, Trombone. Enjoy your new home and don't even think about me."

They lifted me up and carried me away.

In the clutches of that overwhelming despair, I neglected to do what I wish to this day I had: to thank Buddy from the bottom of my heart. The kitten that the Winkelmans put into their car that day may have seemed nothing more than an average frightened, inexperienced kitten—a little smaller and perhaps a bit cuter than the others, if I might say so myself. But unbeknownst to them, and even to me, I was already very different from the other cats they had left behind, for I had been touched by Buddy's greatness. He had planted something inside me. He'd taught me to dream about a life beyond what I knew, to strive for something more than what I had. Few of us cats ever even think about anything beyond what is right before our eyes—and that, I declare, is a felinous shame.

But at the time, of course, I had no clue that there was, or ever would be, anything special about me. I was just a scared little kitten, ripped from everything I knew and terrified of what lay before me.

Upbringing

Trapped in a dark, cramped cardboard box with only a few small air holes, I was bounced and jostled dreadfully in the back of the Winkelman's car as they drove me to their home on Forest Drive. At first, I quaked with fear, but soon it was anger that began to take hold of me. I fumed at the unfairness of our lot, so often subject to the most frivolous of human whims. This woman picked me, she said, because I had the coloring she was looking for! Did she pick her husband because of his careless frumpiness? Or perhaps because of his pockmarked face? I think not.

My anger bubbled and bubbled, and finally boiled over completely. I scratched and clawed at the box's air holes in blind fury. I threw my shoulders against its sides, I rammed it with my head, but it was all to no avail. I finally sank down, defeated. As I was jostled and thrown about, my nausea rising at the constant movement, I resigned myself to the fact that I would never see my dear friend Buddy again. But more than that, I would never make my own decisions. I would never have control of my life. Such is a captive cat's lot, and the realization of it as I sat cowering in that cardboard box plunged me into despair. I pitied myself, dear reader, and I am not ashamed to admit that I broke down and cried for the rest of my journey.

We finally reached the Winkelman's home. They brought the box inside, put it down on the floor, and then proceeded to discuss the finer points of introducing me into their home as I waited to be released. I was somewhat taken by a natural curiosity about my new situation and tried to peep out of the holes, but I couldn't discern much.

From the conversation I overheard, it soon became apparent to me that my new caretakers had never cared for a cat before. Their questions were endless. Should they carry me around? When should they let me out of the room? Where should they keep my litter box? Great Bastet! Humans must always make things so complicated. Just open the box, fling wide all the doors and allow me to investigate. What is difficult about that?

They finally opened the box, but they limited my explorations to an appallingly small room on that first day, leaving me alone and stopping in periodically to ask me if I was getting used to my new home.

"Get used to it?" I meowed at them in frustration. "I can't even get out of this room!"

Despite my sullen mood, I aggressively explored that small room and marked its contents for my own. It had a large white laminated desk with an armless, black cushioned chair and a sleek plastic box with a small TV-like screen that they called a computer. I did not know at the time what it was; Martha and Steven had never owned such a thing.

The novelty of this fairly limited space, however, wore off quickly. The more frustrated I became by my new caretakers' dimness and the louder I meowed at their stupidity during their brief visits, the cuter they seemed to think I was. This, as you might imagine, angered me even more. Humans cannot understand one word we say, despite their supposed intelligence, in contrast to our quite comprehensive understanding of their language.

My new caretakers did administer all sorts of pleasant rubbings and soothing words and, as I listened to their conversations, I realized that they weren't deliberately trying to frustrate me, but rather were following some misguided advice concerning the wisdom of a gradual introduction into their home. I thus decided to take matters into my own paws.

That evening, I waited by the door for one of their visits, and the next time it opened I whipped past their legs and bolted down the hallway. It was a short, dark space, not at all like the long, nearly endless corridor with all those other doors outside Martha and Steven's apartment, and before I knew it, before the man had even said, "Hey, he's out," I was in what I later learned they called the dining room. It was dominated by a fairly large table surrounded by several chairs, somewhat like what Martha and Steven had called the "dining area" in their apartment, at the far end of the living room, but in a sleeker style with a lighter color wood.

The two humans were right on my tail. The man turned on the lights in the room and the woman said, "Poor guy. He looks scared," which was, I might add, a slanderous misinterpretation of my state of mind. I was startled by the sudden burst of light, but my disposition at the time was one of confidence and a readiness, born of despair and frustration, to take on any new challenge with which I was confronted. I had already recognized that my new caretakers were simple but harmless and would likely be able to tend to my needs quite satisfactorily. My situation had clearly improved from my previous one, trapped in a cramped, tiny cage within a dank, fetid room in the company of dozens of other cats. Thus, I was anything but "scared."

My disorientation at the sudden bright light, however, enabled them to scoop me up and bring me back to that accursed computer room. They sat with me and tried to interest me with all sorts of manufactured trinkets, but I shunned them, strutting around proudly as if they weren't there.

While many of the details from that unfortunate day of well-intentioned imprisonment have mercifully faded into the mists of memory, I am constantly reminded of one. "So you really like the name Hastings?" the man, Howie, asked the woman, Alicia.

"Yes," she said. "I think we should go with Hastings. He's Hercule's companion. What do you think?"

Howie turned to me. I was marking up the leg of a desk with my cheek. "What do you think, little guy?" he asked. "Do you like 'Hastings'?"

Hastings? I thought. What kind of name is Hastings? Buddy, Buster, Max, Sam, Rocky—those are good names for a tom. But Hastings? "No way!" I meowed emphatically.

They laughed heartily. "I guess he likes it," Alicia said.

"I guess so," Howie agreed.

I meowed again in frustration.

"I guess he really likes it," Howie chortled.

It would behoove humans not to guess so much but to actually listen to what we of the feline species have to say. In this respect, human arrogance is unmatched by any other species on the planet, except perhaps for the pigeon. In any case, from henceforth my name was to be Hastings, whether I liked it or not. It was just one of many indignities I had to endure that first day.

But shed no tears for me, my dear reader. I was not to be cribbed, cabined and contained for long. The next time they opened the door, I sprinted out once more, this time past the dining room and into what they called the living room. This, I quickly observed, contained a low couch, an "entertainment center," as they call it, and most importantly, the exercise bicycle which was later to provide me with such amusement in the swatting of Howie's legs as he tried to pedal.

It seems somehow unfair that Howie and Alicia should win the upper hand at the very moment I was making such observations of my surroundings, but that is what happened. They caught me again. Nevertheless, after enduring my third consecutive escape not long afterward, they finally began to understand that a cat like myself with such an exemplary sense of curiosity simply cannot be contained for long, so they finally admitted me free access to my new home.

Having secured my freedom, I was now able to execute a complete and thorough exploration.

However, I did not deem it crucial to do so immediately. The precedent had been set, a fact which satisfied me in itself. I wandered briefly into my new caretakers' bedroom, an action which seemed to provide them much amusement, but then I returned to the computer room in order to close my eyes and plan the major explorations which I would undertake the following day. It had been a trying week, and now that I was finally assured of my safety, I needed some rest.

* * * * * * * * * *

I awoke early the next morning, refreshed and ready to explore my new home. My first impression was that, in contrast to Martha and Steven's apartment, Howie and Alicia's home was cluttered and untidy, with too much furniture for such a modest-sized house. The bed was unmade, with books and magazines messily piled on the floor on either side. There was an unordered pile of magazines by the toilet as well, and more on the table in the living room. Books spilled out of bookcases in both the living room and computer room.

And much more than reading material was out of place, dear readers. Bottles of lotions, barrettes and hair bands were tossed across the dresser in the bedroom, computer disks and pens were loosely scattered across the computer desk, and shoes lay strewn around the floor by the front door.

Let me say also that I quickly detected the distinct odor of dog. Dogs had lived in the house before, and a canine smell remained there still. It is an established fact that once a house hosts a dog, it forever hosts the dog's odor.

One notable characteristic of my new home was that there were many large, wonderful windows through which I could observe the lauded outside world. The first thing I noticed upon looking out from one was how low to the ground I was. The house stood alone, unattached to any others, and therefore the windows provided broad vistas of both the front and the rear. At the front of the house, I could watch the quiet, tree-lined street from wide ledges on the windows in either the computer room or the dining room. Through a large sliding glass door in the living room, I could observe the wooded area behind the house. There, I was to discover a multitude of birds, squirrels, rabbits, opossums and other wildlife.

It was when I began to explore the living room more thoroughly, however, that I received what was, at that time, the surprise of my life.

"Well, hello there!" someone said.

I jumped to what must have been nearly the ceiling. "Who said that?" I asked breathlessly, looking around.

"Up here," the low, warbly voice called.

I looked around and saw behind me a large metal cage sitting upon a black trunk. I hadn't noticed it before in my explorations, despite the unpleasant smell that was emanating from it. It was an obvious thing to investigate, but in my excitement and curiosity concerning the general layout of the room I had somehow overlooked it. I leapt up on the couch and climbed onto the arm for a better view of the cage.

"Greetings!" the thing inside said in a most amiable tone. "Terribly sorry to startle you like that. I didn't know how else to get your attention."

It was a strange creature, an oval mound of smooth, dark brown fur about my length but somewhat wider (remember, I still had more to grow at that time), with a tan diamond right in the middle of its forehead. I had never seen anything like it and was wary of its intentions.

"Hello," I answered courteously but without any true warmth. I wisely wanted to assess what kind of strange creature I was conversing with before displaying any true friendliness toward it.

"Welcome to our home," the creature said. It had a low, soothing, almost hypnotic voice.

"What are you?" I asked.

"Why, I'm a guinea pig, of course."

"A guinea pig? What's that?"

"Well, *I'm* a guinea pig. Why don't you take a good look at me?"

"Hmmm," I said with suspicion. "Where do you come from?"

"From the vivarium."

"What's that?"

"It's a store where they sell reptiles, like lizards and snakes."

"I'm still pretty young, but I've seen reptiles on TV, and you don't look at all like a reptile to me."

"Oh, you can't mistake me for a reptile," he laughed. "No, I was bred to be eaten by reptiles. They called me 'alternative snake food.'"

"Snake food!" I cried in horror.

"Why yes. I was meant to be snake food, it's true. Howie and Alicia rescued me when I was a mere six weeks old. Howie had come in to look at the snakes, but Alicia wouldn't agree to buy one. They decided to bring me home instead. It's doubtful I would have made it much longer than that if they hadn't so heroically saved my life."

I stared at him in bewilderment, wondering what purpose this nearly formless brown furry mound on a carpet of soiled shredded wooden bits could serve. "What do you do?" I finally forced myself to ask.

"Is that an existential question or a practical one?"

The question made no sense to me at the time, of course. I suppose it must have shown on my face, for he continued, "If you're asking what I do with my days, I generally sit in my home in quiet contemplation. What else is there to do?"

I was unsure how to answer his question, or even whether it warranted an answer. "I'm a cat," I said proudly.

"I can see that," he said. "Have you got a name for yourself?"

My dignity was instantly deflated at the thought of revealing my new name. "My name was Trombone before I came here," I said despondently, "but now they say it's Hastings."

"Hastings," he cried, "why that's a capital name! Just capital!"

"Hastings isn't a cat name," I said petulantly.

"Of course it is," he assured me. "And I think it's quite unique and wonderful."

"So what's your name?" I asked.

"My name is Hercule," he said proudly. "A distinctive name for a distinguished guinea pig. It is a pleasure to meet you, Hastings," he added with a bow of his head.

I didn't know any social graces at the time and had no idea that I was supposed to say the same. I was too concerned with my own situation to think about this strange creature's feelings, anyway. "Do you like it here?" I asked him.

"Oh, yes. This is a wonderful home. Howie and Alicia are wonderful people. They see to your every need, and are quite kind and affectionate."

"But they keep you in a cage," I noted, eying the intimidating metal wire that enclosed him.

"Cage?" he exclaimed, his low, warbling voice suddenly transformed to a steeply rising, piercing high pitch. I was to find later that this occurred whenever Hercule was upset or excited. However, just as quickly as the pitch could rise, it could revert to its previous soothing manner. "That is one way to look at it, I suppose," he resumed, his voice back to its low purr. "But I prefer to see it as a comfortable home. It's everything a guinea pig could want. I have plenty of hay, plenty of food and plenty of water. I have all the time I need for the quiet contemplation I love so dearly. And I have fresh fruits and vegetables every night. Those are most delicious!"

"Yuk."

"What?" he exclaimed in that rapidly rising pitch. Then, his voice suddenly back to its low, soothing tone, "You don't like fresh fruits and vegetables?"

"No way," I said proudly, imagining that Buddy would never approve of them.

Hercule considered for a moment, then said, "I didn't think any creature would ever turn down a fresh carrot or a slice of apple."

"Well, now you've met one," I informed him.

"Indeed, I have," Hercule acknowledged. "But Hastings, tell me, why the melancholy face? Aren't you happy here in your new home?"

I looked at him with a bit of surprise. I hadn't been aware of being melancholy until he'd mentioned it. Now that he had, I recognized that despite all the stressful excitement of my new situation, thoughts of my good friend and mentor Buddy still plagued my mind. "Buddy is still back there at the shelter, Hercule. I wish there was something I could do to help him."

"Buddy is your friend?'

I nodded, my eyes suddenly welling. I tried hard to keep myself from crying.

"Oh, I am sorry, Hastings my boy. I remember that feeling after my rescue from the vivarium. It is a truly terrible thing to cope with."

I shook my head sadly. "He said something to me that I didn't understand. He said he was old and didn't have much of a chance."

"Oh dear."

"What?"

"Well, what he meant was that he was likely going to be put to sleep."

I breathed a sigh of relief. "That's good," I said. "I usually sleep more than half the day, at least. I find it very refreshing."

Hercule shook his head. "No, my young friend. Not that kind of sleep. The other kind of sleep, the one where you don't wake up."

"Wow," I said. "People do that, I know, but not cats. Sometimes Martha would sleep for hours after Steven left for work."

"No," Hercule insisted patiently. "I mean, the sleep where you never wake up, ever."

"Never?" I asked, suddenly horrified.

"Never," Hercule confirmed.

I stared at him for what must have been a full minute. At first I couldn't believe what he'd just told me, but I reluctantly acknowledged to myself that the guinea pig must be right. I stood up in shock and began to wander away. I needed to be alone to process this horrible news.

"See here, my boy," Hercule said as I left him, "if you need to talk to anyone about this, my door is open to you at all times."

"Thanks," I muttered distractedly, and slunk away to find a spot beneath a chair in which to hide.

* * * * * * * * *

Howie and Alicia tried to coax me out of my funk that day, and their persistent enthusiasm almost managed to break my lugubrious mood.

They were able to lure me several times into a practice hunting session with a most ingenious device consisting of some beads on a string that they flung hither and thither with a plastic rod. But despite their best efforts, all I could muster were brief bursts of energy.

By the next day, it was clear even to them that there was something wrong with their new feline companion. I slunk about, hid under furniture and showed interest in little beyond food, water and only the occasional hunting practice.

The following day, they surprised me by seizing me without warning and forcing me into a plastic carrier. They took me to the car and quickly drove away.

"Oh no," I moaned. "Now they'll bring me back to the shelter and put me to sleep just like Buddy because I didn't express happiness for being in my new home!"

But my fears were ungrounded. It turned out to be a trip to the great veterinarian Dr. Ernest Choi. My new caretakers seemed familiar with Dr. Choi, and they chatted amiably about me as he performed his brief examination. I quickly took somewhat of a liking to him based on his confident but gentle handling of me.

"He seems a bit depressed to me," Alicia said.

"Well, that's normal," Dr. Choi said. "He's in a new home and has to get used to his new surroundings. Right, Buddy?" he said to me, scratching me behind the ears and causing me to close my eyes.

It took a moment for his words to register. *Buddy?* I thought. He'd called me Buddy. I realized with a pleasurable chill that he had sent me a secret signal. This Dr. Choi somehow knew about Buddy. As the humans chattered on, I sat there marveling at how he could know something like that.

One thing I did know was that I could trust this man. As the three of them finished their conversation, Dr. Choi rubbed my head and reassured me, "You're going to like your new home. They're good people."

I took comfort in those soothing words in the days that followed. If Dr. Choi believed that Howie and Alicia would provide me with a good home, I knew I could have confidence in that judgment.

* * * * * * * * * *

Despite Dr. Choi's assurance, it was difficult for me to regain my former joie de vivre, no matter how hospitable my new home. I had left behind what was inarguably a dangerous, hostile environment, but yet I still felt its loss. I missed Buddy the most, of course, but I discovered that I also missed the constant presence of the masses that had before assured my anonymity. Buddy's bitter view of apartment life had certainly clouded my opinion about it, but that bustling life had been all I knew and I found that I missed it. The weight of my solitude bore down on me oppressively, like a human holding you down when she's trying to clip your claws.

Howie and Alicia continued to tempt me with their manufactured trinkets. I played along from time to time, but they could assuage my deep sorrow with such distractions for no longer than a few minutes at a time.

"Look here, my boy," Hercule said to me as I sat near him on the arm of the couch one afternoon, "you can't linger in the past like this. Sighing and moping all around the place, that's no way to live."

"I'm OK."

"The past is merely a construct in your mind, my dear Hastings. It can have only as much relevance as you allow it."

I stared at him in puzzlement. "What?"

"You're letting it get to you, my boy. You must make yourself stop thinking about it."

"How can I make myself stop thinking about it?" I cried. "It's all so unfair."

"Life is not fair, my dear cat," he answered. 'But who ever told you it would be? Whoever it was has done you a great disservice. Fairness is a human concept. People themselves do a miserable job of it, from what I understand, and it doesn't apply to us at all."

"Are you trying to make me feel better?"

"See here," Hercule tried again, "if you were confronted by a dog in a dark alley, what would you do?"

The sound of their powerful barks in the shelter had given me such a great fear of these creatures that even the thought of this scenario made me instantly shiver.

"Would you slouch down on the ground and just let him eat you without trying to run or fight?" Hercule asked.

"No, of course not."

"Well, that's precisely what you're doing now."

"I'm not in a dark alley with a dog," I pointed out.

"No," he cried in frustration, his voice rising to a squeak, "it's a metaphor."

"A met and a four?"

"No, a metaphor," he enunciated slowly. "It's when something represents something else."

"Well, why don't you just say the other thing, then?"

He sighed. "Let me try saying it another way. The past is over."

"Of course it is."

"Precisely! Yet you still let your mood be influenced by what has already happened. It no longer bears any relevance to your life."

"How can you say that? Buddy may be dead by now."

"I understand that, Hastings."

"No, you don't understand," I insisted. "How could you possibly understand?"

"I've lost friends too, Hastings. We all have. It's part of being alive."

"Friends like Buddy?" I asked indignantly.

Hercule said heavily, "When Alicia and Howie rescued me from the vivarium, my feline friend, I wasn't alone in that cage."

I felt a horrible shock at this revelation. "You weren't?"

Hercule shook his head. "My litter mates and close friends Petunia, Peony, Pansie, Geranium and Daisy—we were all in there together. It was a cramped little plastic box that barely allowed us room to move about. The food was never fresh and the water festered in the bottle until we finished every last drop. I remember how that last bit was always such a challenge. Someone had to drink it to get them to refill the bottle, but it tasted so dreadful. We would draw bits of straw to see who would have to do the nasty deed. But we had accepted our fate and come to terms with it, in a way. It is very rare for anyone to rescue alternative snake food. We lived with little hope."

"What happened to them?" I asked solemnly.

He shook his head sadly. "They're all gone now. I'm quite certain of that. The chance of someone else rescuing them was virtually nothing."

"But how do you live with it?" I asked.

"Oh, I was upset at first, but I've learned to come to terms with it, Hastings. I now recognize that certain things in this life are simply out of our control. We may be sad about things that have happened, and we may regret things we ourselves have done, but we must learn to treat the past as the fiction it truly is."

"Fiction?" I asked incredulously.

"Why, yes, fiction. Once a moment in time has passed, it becomes but an inner working of our brain's imagination, little different from fiction. In fact, many individuals have such distorted remembrances of the past that their memories can really more accurately be described as fiction. I prefer to make no distinction myself. The present is all that is truly real to me. Of the three states of time—past, present and future—the present is the only one in which we are currently living. Therefore, I find it is best to pay attention to the present."

"But what do you do when you see your friends in your head when you're falling asleep or waking up or eating dinner by yourself? How can you stand it knowing they might not even be alive anymore?"

"It's a cruel world we live in, my dear Hastings. A very cruel world. We must first accept that. For all the comforts of our lives, there are certain hard, immutable truths: We are born, we live, we die. Those are beyond our control. We must try to enjoy the rest as best we can."

"You seem so happy, even when you're talking about death," I said angrily.

He shrugged. "I suppose I would rather be happy and enjoy my life while it lasts than be perpetually and incurably sad. I find that your course takes too much effort."

"I want to be happy too," I said defensively, "but look at what's happened to me. I have no choice."

Hercule shook his head. "Yes, do look at what's happened to you, Hastings. You are the lucky one. You have a roof over your head, food and water in your bowls and people to take care of your every need. It took me some time before I got over the loss of my friends, Hastings, but I was able to do it and so will you. Be master of your thoughts. Don't let them control you. My philosophy is: Take control of the present and learn to accept what has happened in the past."

I sighed. "I wish I could think like you."

"Many creatures do," he said. "Many creatures do, my dear cat."

Tired of his musings, I leapt down from the couch without further comment and looked about for a suitable shaded spot in which to properly indulge my psychic wounds.

* * * * * * * * *

Dear readers, I could not simply accept my situation. I raged against the walls that confined me and, inspired by my plan with Buddy, soon resolved to escape. I didn't think for a second what life might be like outside those walls. I didn't consider how I would survive without Buddy's guidance. All I knew in my blind anger and frustration was that I wanted out.

One morning not long after my arrival, I hid beneath one of the dining room chairs and bolted between the humans' legs as soon as they opened the front door to leave.

Yes, my friends, at that moment I was free. Finally, free.

I was also instantly seized with panic. The strays among you may mock me to hear this, but as I have set out to write an honest history for you, I must describe the overwhelming rush of fear that overtook me as I paused in that front yard, a clear blue sky above me instead of a roof, patchy grass under my paws rather than carpet and the rustling sound of the wind in the leaves coming from every direction. The sights and sounds that greeted my senses at that moment of presumed triumph were like nothing I had ever experienced. My senses were overwhelmed.

Keep in mind, my fellow felines, that I had never been outside of human housing, save for temporary transportation in a carrier, during which times I was distracted by too many other things to take much note of my surroundings. Had Buddy been there to guide me that day, I would doubtless have followed him to freedom without hesitation.

But I had no one to hold my paw. I hesitated, overcome with fear and indecision, and Howie easily caught up to me, scooped me up and carried me inside, cruelly disparaging my stupidity all the while.

They shut the door behind me and left me alone in the dining room. I sat on the carpet licking the strange earthy taste off of my paws. The comfort that the warm, quiet security of the indoors then brought to me made me anguish over whether I really had the temperament and fortitude to live alone as a stray.

I thought long and hard that afternoon while gazing wistfully out the windows at the world outside. It was on that day that I gradually reached the conclusion that, like it or not, unless someone like Buddy came along again to show me the way, I was—and therefore likely always would be—a housecat.

The idea saddened me somewhat, yet it also unexpectedly brought me a sense of relief. It was the relief that comes from finally beginning to develop a true sense of who you are—or, at the very least, of who you aren't.

* * * * * * * * * *

Lest you judge me too cruelly, my fellow felines, rest assured that my resignation did not mean that I was content to merely accept my life as a housecat. Nevertheless, over the next few days, I could not help but acknowledge the comfortable circumstance in which I found myself. I was fed twice daily, in the morning and at night, and if my caretakers were late in providing my meal I glared at them in a most intimidating manner until it was clear to them that they must tend to me without further delay.

I had the house to myself for most of the day, and they usually retired to their bedroom by eleven o'clock at night, leaving the entire house at my disposal again until the next morning. There were all the usual amenities of a well-stocked cat home and more than enough space for one of modest needs such as myself. Howie and Alicia made the effort to entertain me quite often back in those early days with various hunting games. They dangled beads on a string before me and provoked me to leap higher into the air than I ever thought I could. They also had a fake mouse on a stick which I enjoyed chasing for sport.

There were other mentally stimulating objects as well, such as a ball perched atop a spring protruding from a small board. This behaved wonderfully unpredictably when you swatted at it. There was also a round donut with a ball in it that raced around in a circle when you stuck your paw inside to bat it about. But perhaps most intriguing were the games of my own design that I played directly with my caretakers without any of these extraneous accessories. For example, while they slept they moved their feet under the sheets in quite sporadic and erratic patterns, providing me with a most excellent form of pouncing practice until they awoke and chased me away.

While Martha's home required no interaction with humans whatsoever if one did not wish it, relationships with Howie and Alicia, in one way or another, were simply unavoidable. Alicia would often swoop me up unexpectedly and hug me tight, burying my head in her ample bosom and slowly suffocating the life out of me. She greatly enjoyed lifting me into her lap as she sat down to watch TV on the couch. I would, of course, get up and walk away as soon as she released me, but however silly she was, I did find myself developing something of an affection for this bright, effusive woman who clearly cared for me.

Howie, on the other hand, took little interest in me and I little in him. He presented more of a challenge for me than Martha's husband Steven ever had, if only because I was the one and only cat in this new household. Howie took to proclaiming that I was Alicia's cat so often that it became my moniker in his personal lexicon: "Your cat coughed up a hairball in the dining room," "Your cat is ripping up the carpet again," and so on. He clearly disdained me, and I him.

I soon came to understand that Howie left all of the decisions in their life to Alicia, claiming a stake in nothing, and rarely disagreeing with her or even expressing any opinion at all. He reserved for himself only the right to make snide, critical remarks about the things he left for his wife to decide.

My interactions of most note with Howie took place in the early mornings. Howie fancies himself a fiction writer and, although he leaves the house each workday morning for what he refers to with bitterness as his "real job," he often wakes up early to write on the computer before he gets dressed. It was in these early hours of the morning—and only then, mind you—that I somewhat appreciated his company. I often sat with him and watched what he was doing with curiosity, sometimes rubbing my scent on him but more often than not just looking out the window as I often did, trying to imagine what life would be like outside—a fiction of my own design, I suppose—and enjoying the presence of another living creature in those early morning hours. Howie paid little attention to me, greeting me when I followed him into the computer room and perhaps once in a while rubbing the fur between my ears distractedly, but otherwise I barely seemed to exist for him.

I paid Hercule little mind in those early days. I felt at the time that I had little reason to interact with what I mistakenly viewed as a lesser creature. I left him to himself in his cage and spent most of my time alone in quiet contemplation.

I had but one job in my new home, I believed, and that was to mark everything of value with my exclusive scent. Whereas there were countless cats to contend with in my former home, I was able to mark this entire abode without fear of competition. The process took endless hours of rubbing against various objects—a project, I need not explain, that was to continue my entire time there; no self-respecting housecat can let such a responsibility slide for even a moment, save to enjoy a little time bathing in the sun or something of that nature.

I soon considered Howie and Alicia's house my own. It was an imperfect home, no doubt, but my home nonetheless.

* * * * * * * * * *

One of the greatest difficulties of being the sole feline resident in a human household is that establishing the proper balance of power between cat and caretaker is your sole responsibility. My early days in my new home were spent largely in developing methods to ensure that there was an appropriate such balance.

Indeed I cannot, much as I now love my dear friend Hercule, endorse the guinea pig credo of passive subservience. It is undignified and ill suited for the distinguished feline. Sometimes it absolutely sickens me to see Hercule nuzzling Howie's knuckles so tenderly when the latter sticks his pink, furless hand into his cage. It is degrading for him to behave in such a manner in order to receive a simple treat.

"But wait!" a human reading this, if there ever is one, might say. "Is it not true that you yourself often rub yourself against your caretakers in a most tender fashion? All you cats do this. Is that not the same thing?"

But this is not the case. We are marking the human as our own, just as a person might put a name tag on a piece of clothing or write their name on the inside cover of a treasured book. We cannot be responsible for human misinterpretations of our actions, can we, my fellow felines? While they may perceive our rubbing as just as much a sign of affection as a pig's nuzzling, the important point is that it is not.

Whatever a human believes to be his or her relationship to a cat, it is important for us not to forget that a human can never be our "owner," as they call it. They are our caretakers. We are living, sentient beings and can be owned no more than one human can own another. Ownership is for inanimate objects without free will. We felines have a natural will that is often fiercer than that of the very humans who persist in the belief that they own us. As such, we must never behave as property and mistakenly bolster the human view of our role in their households. They are, in fact, at our disposal, and our mark is a signal to other cats who they may encounter outside that these caretakers are taken and accounted for.

A successful housecat must assert a certain amount of control and dominance over his owner. I, for example, have on occasion bitten Howie's neck while he was asleep—gently so as not to hurt him in any way, but enough to alert him to how vulnerable he is. I also often employ the method of darting between his legs while he is walking, particularly when he is on the stairs. I move swiftly and quietly like the wind, causing him to stumble over me. It is a clear reminder to him that I have the power to send him tumbling down the stairs if I so chose.

One method that I developed and used on Howie very early on, and that I recommend for use on anyone who is a so-called dog-lover, is what I call the belly trap. The method derives from the most uncanny habit those ridiculous canines have of rolling on their backs when they are happy and exposing their very vulnerable bellies so that humans may rub them. This humiliating behavior renders them vulnerable to any sort of horrific attack, and is a clear sign of subservience. Humans love when dogs do this, and respond by laughing and rubbing the dog's belly vigorously. The rest of the animal world, needless to say, finds these exchanges nothing short of embarrassing. Nevertheless, the sophisticated cat may use such behavior in a sophisticated, mocking, ironic fashion.

The belly trap is performed as follows: Roll on your back like a dog and pretend that you would like your belly rubbed. No human can help but be tempted by such an offer, but the smart ones will resist. Howie took the bait when I first tested him. As soon as their hands touch your precious belly, use both your claws and your teeth to teach them a most violent lesson. Then flip over and run away before they have collected themselves for a response. Believe me, my fellow felines; you will have plenty of time to escape, for they will be quite surprised by your vicious response to their condescending behavior.

There are other manipulative tools at a cat's disposal besides aggression, of course. I have mentioned that humans seem to believe we are displaying tenderness when we are simply marking them with our scent. Marking a human is always a good bet when you need something from one, whether food, water or the cleaning of a litter box.

But there is an even better way to endear yourself to a human when endearment is necessary. Here, for those young or less socialized cats who are unfamiliar with the method, I will now describe what is perhaps the greatest weapon in the arsenal of feline behavior. I learned this trick in my very first home by observing other cats whose names I can't begin to remember. The method is most effective in securing the sympathies of a human for a period of days, if not longer. It is called the cat hat. No human can resist the cat hat. It is absolutely guaranteed to bring a human under your control.

Approach the human while they are lying in bed. It is fine if they are sleeping; the cat hat will affect both a deeper sleep and a subconscious connection with you. Jump up on the bed and climb onto their pillow. Lie down just above their head, positioning yourself so that the length of your belly—or your back, if you are averse to the thought of touching your precious belly skin against a human—rests against their head much like the item of clothing they call a hat. Humans find this contact against their head most agreeable, particularly on cold winter nights. It also, I might add, brings you benefit in that their heads emit a great deal of heat and warm the belly to aid in digestion.

It is a good idea to purr loudly as you employ the cat hat. If they are asleep, it will gently wake them to alert them to the special honor they are receiving. Humans, like all creatures, consider the purring of a cat quite soothing. I find it is almost hypnotic for them, allowing you to exert a great deal of control over their wills for some time afterward.

If you have a particularly difficult case—if, for example, your caretaker has threatened to take you back to the pound, you may, while employing the cat hat, use your paws to gently mark the fibers of their hair with your scent. They will likely believe that you are "playing" with their hair when you do this. Humans can never resist the tranquilizing effect of having their hair "played" with. And you receive the benefit of a remarkably large surface area of fibers to carry your scent.

So, you see, dear readers, even in those early days my young mind approached problems with a rational detachment. I systematically discovered how to manipulate the sentiments of the human beings I lived with. The lessons I learned have helped me ever since, and I hope that they will help you as well in your own endeavors.

* * * * * * * * * *

I had not been settled long into my new home before I began to notice the scent of the woman begin to change in a most disagreeable manner. My initial protests were of a vocal nature, bit these were greeted only with laughter. Of course, it is impossible to make these humans understand even the clearest of messages. I therefore began to use other means to express my displeasure. Whenever I caught her in the short enclosed hallway outside the bedrooms—a space from which she could not escape—I made it abundantly clear to her through a quite emphatic use of my teeth and claws (albeit carefully controlled so as not to cause any damage beyond some minor scratches) that I did not approve of whatever it was she was planning.

"Why does this crazy cat keep attacking me?" she asked her husband repeatedly.

"Maybe he senses you're pregnant," he answered one day, finally providing an explanation for what was causing this change I sensed in her. She was producing another human to add to their family! I had observed the phenomenon of pregnancy among the cats in Martha and Steven's household, and it seemed a most unpleasant process, the worse aspect of which was that it brought yet more kittens into the home. What a new young human could bring to a home, however, was completely unknown to me and quite unsettling.

Extremely dissatisfied with this unwelcome news, I increased the intensity of my attacks in the hallway in order to emphasize my disapproval. Alicia's avoidance maneuvers grew slower as her belly grew larger, making my stratagems increasingly easier to execute. Yet my message would not get through to her. We became quite frustrated with each other—she with my behavior and I with her ignorance. Eventually, I simply abandoned all hope of communicating the reason for my displeasure with her.

Aside from the woman's unpleasant aura, there was little change in the household that affected me directly during this time. The remaining open spaces in their home became further cluttered with various human baby paraphernalia: crib, bassinet, stroller, bouncy chair, changing table and so on and so forth. As the open floor space diminished, the humans had an increasingly difficult time traversing it, bumping their shins, tripping and cursing the lack of space. For an agile, lithe cat such as myself, however, it was little trouble to navigate such obstacles, and so these changes affected me very little.

The one significant change for me during that period was that Howie gained the exclusive responsibility of changing my litter box. Alicia promised him that she would return to performing her share of the task when her pregnancy ended, but to this day that promise was never fulfilled. I heard her explain at the time that she was worried about the possibility of catching a disease from me—an accusation which offended me greatly. I certainly harbor no disagreeable diseases and I, like Howie, see this explanation primarily as an excuse for absolving herself of an unwanted responsibility that should, in fact, be an honor. I am sure that there are many humans who would love to clean the litter box of an outstanding feline such as myself. I must say that this attitude brought my opinion of Alicia down considerably.

Overall, however, I had become quite content in my new home by the time the weather grew colder outside and we headed into my first winter on this earth. I did not realize that the windows would not be opened regularly for many months, and that eventually I would start to feel like a prisoner there. The situation would improve significantly with the arrival of spring, of course, but since I was young and naive, I was not to realize this for some time. For a while during the heart of that first winter, I despaired that the world had cooled forever, and that I would never again enjoy those open windows that brought the fresh breezes from outside. Closed tight for weeks on end, the house every day smelled more intensely of dog as the odors seeped slowly from the walls and floors, and of the pregnant Alicia, who emitted her own strange musty odor of pregnancy.

Hercule was the one who informed me about the seasons, and about how spring would bring back all the beautiful grass and flowers and trees. He had seen it happen twice already, he told me to my great relief.

Hercule became a close friend during that long and lazy period of expectation as we waited for the weather to improve and for the baby to be born. Incidentally, neither of us had any idea that it took so long to produce another one of these human creatures. New members of our species and the others we knew of were produced in a matter of weeks or at most a couple of months; this suggested to me a clear inferiority of the human species.

Although I came to know Hercule better during this period, he puzzled me no less. I simply could not understand his ready acceptance of his confinement. He rebutted me quite forcefully when I suggested to him that it might be a somewhat degrading situation for a distinguished guinea pig such as himself to be locked in a cage.

"You've got the situation all wrong, my boy," he said. "I'm the one in control here."

I was taken aback. "That's not what it looks like to me."

"The humans are at my every beck and call," he insisted.

"They are?"

"Why yes, of course. The next time they're cutting carrots or some other such scrumptious vegetable or fruit," he said, making me cringe at the thought of eating such a thing, "watch how I can get them to come to me."

And indeed, when Howie was cutting a cucumber that night, Hercule put up an infernal racket, that most undignified ascending squeak of his repeated so rapidly that it sounded like a car alarm.

"OK, OK," Howie called from the kitchen, and within moments was opening the door to Hercule's cage to give him a generous sample.

"Now do you see, my dear boy?" Hercule said to me triumphantly, standing over his chunk of cucumber. "Things are not always as they seem. This is the perfect home for a guinea pig, and I'm perfectly comfortable here. In fact, I couldn't possibly be happier."

"I see," I said, but the arrangement struck me as inherently undignified. I said nothing further to him on the subject, as I was not willing to sully my newfound friend's happiness in any way, but I knew I could never live as he did. I had enough trouble accepting confinement in something as large as a house.

I suppose, therefore, that I am quite fortunate not to have been born a guinea pig.

* * * * * * * * * *

One day I happened upon Hercule's cage, wherein he was busily engaged in the most bizarre activity. He was collecting the small brown tubes of poop scattered around the floor of his home and piling them up into a conical hut at the center of his cage.

"What are you doing?" I asked, taken aback.

Hercule, deep in concentration, hadn't noticed my skillfully silent approach, and he jumped several inches into the air in surprise at the sound of my voice. It is fortunate he wasn't near his creation at the time, or he might have toppled right into it. "By George!" he exclaimed, his voice rising to a squeak, "you scared me, Hastings!"

"Who's George?" I asked.

"Never mind that. What's your game, sneaking up on me like that?"

"I was just dropping by to see what you were doing."

"Look here," he said angrily, "you disturbed my artistic trance."

"Artistic trance? What's that? And what's that?" I asked, nodding toward the fecal structure with not a little tinge of disgust. It must be said, when we cats expel the content of our bowels into our litter boxes, we don't collect them and pile them up into little huts in the middle of the living room. What we do, as you well know, my friends, is bury them as deeply as possible and try not to think about them anymore.

"I am busy with my art," Hercule said proudly.

"Art? It looks like poop to me."

Hercule sighed. "It would seem like that to you, wouldn't it?" he said, "since you're still young, uncultured and very naive."

"What kind of art is that?" I exclaimed. "Art is a painting on the wall. That's poop."

"This is art," Hercule insisted. "It is just art of a different sort. This is an art of nature, of order and organization."

"I don't get it."

"Look at this sculpture," he said excitedly, presenting the thing to me with his tiny paws. "What do you see?"

"A pile of poop."

"No," he squealed, then quickly resumed his soothing tone. "You see symmetry, order, beauty."

"If you say so."

"I do."

"Do you do this every day, Hercule?"

"I do," he nodded.

"Why didn't I notice it before?"

"Well, from what I've seen, you're usually napping in a patch of sunshine for most of the day. That seems to be your most intellectually stimulating activity."

"Oh, it is," I agreed.

"I busily work away every afternoon while the humans are gone, developing ways to represent the order and beauty of nature in the simple objects around me. I find it to be a meditative art that soothes and strengthens the mind."

"Aren't you worried they'll catch you?"

"Oh, no, no, no," he said. "At the slightest hint of their return, I scatter my materials."

"And just ruin it?" I asked in shock.

"Of course, my dear Hastings. One must not covet one's art. Art is a reflection of life. There will always be more to capture and reflect upon."

From that moment on, I always made sure to visit Hercule's cage in the afternoons to see his creations. He seemed able to find an infinite number of patterns and structures to represent. Some of his works were quite amazing. Their grandiosity and symmetry could be breathtaking. His poop cone, for example, proved to be more than a mere pile of fecal matter. It was unsealed at the top, and its dark, hollow interior was, as

Hercule explained to me, a metaphor for the unknowable soul we all possess. Other structures included a grand and radiant sun made of Timothy hay laid upon his bedding, and a flimsy, uneven wall made of food pellets and poop—nourishment and excrement together to symbolize the deceptively fragile nature of our seemingly robust lives. Every day brought a new surprise from Hercule's cage, and his limitlessly creative work gave me a thorough education in the finer and deeper points of true art.

I at the time had no art of my own, no means of self-expression whatsoever beyond the simple hunting games I played with my caretakers. Not that these were completely unfulfilling—no cat could possibly resist the pleasures of swatting at those beads in a mesh tube, for example. Nevertheless, a curious and rich intellectual mind such as my own needs more variety and stimulation than that afforded to me at the time. Unfortunately, I had little idea how to even go about looking for true meaning and purpose in life. As the winter wore on, I began to feel lost, buffeted about like a dandelion seed in the wind.

Hercule noted my increasingly lackadaisical mood and encouraged me to enrich myself somehow, to be creative. However, an initial attempt at defecating outside my litter box and arranging the putrid feces convinced me that my means of expression could not be the same as Hercule's.

As time went by, I grew more frustrated and began to release this frustration on my caretakers in vigorous albeit harmless attacks (for I knew where my kibble came from). In response, they took to squirting me with water guns, locking me in the bathroom and hurting my sensitive ears with sharply backed reprimands. These methods of theirs worked, for the most part. I became very hesitant to take out my frustrations in this manner. Yet I had little other release.

It was clear that I desired more from life. That desire was becoming more and more a demand I could not ignore. But what could I do about it, dear readers? I would not begin to solve this problem for some time.

* * * * * * * * * *

It was the coming of spring that rescued me—at least for the moment, bringing a general shift in my mood and a new friendship to be forged.

During that long winter, I had begun from my window perch to observe with increasing interest the activities of the tomcats outside. There was one tom in particular who seemed to dominate the others. He was a gaunt, pure white cat—fairly small, actually—with green eyes and rippling, sinewy muscle. By watching him and the others as they hissed, chased each other and occasionally engaged in all-out feline combat, I was able to learn the laws of feline real property and territorial dispute resolution, which basically amounts to: finders-keepers, losers scram unless you can force me off this plot through fear, intimidation or force.

This white cat guarded his territory, which included our small front yard, quite diligently, practicing a no-tolerance approach with the other toms. His rash bravery inspired me tremendously. I delighted in watching him stalk his prey, creep slowly along the ground—particularly in fresh snow, where he could blend in perfectly with the soft white blankets covering the front yards—and then appear seemingly from nowhere to pounce with abandon, frightening his victim into a panicked flight. Surprise, fear and intimidation were his arsenal, and he used them wisely to secure what he claimed for his own. He was not averse to a claw or bite mark on his beautiful coat, or even a half-chewed ear if it meant that he had once more established his dominance and his claim to our section of Forest Drive.

The kitties adored him and mewed all over him, and for this, of course, I greatly admired him. He soaked up their attention, circling and sniffing them, rubbing cheeks with them and often retiring to the small patch of forest behind our house with them for privacy. Watching this white cat day after day, I thought that Buddy would likely have taught me to live just as the white cat did. I wondered if there was even a remote chance that this tom might consider guiding my paw as Buddy had intended to.

The white tom certainly began to notice me. He seemed bemused at my attention to his exploits and he actively encouraged my interest, presumably flattered by my admiration. Many a time, just before arching his back and puffing his tail to hiss threateningly, or crouched to the ground, creeping slowly up behind an unsuspecting tom that had wandered into our territory, he would pause to glance up at me and wink.

Despite these sporadic amusements, the dreary season seemed to my young mind to go on forever. I could not conceive that it could ever end, however strong Hercule's assurances. But the weather eventually began to warm, and the windows were opened for me to enjoy the fresh awakening sounds and smells of nature that filled the outdoor air.

I was thrilled by the extraordinary richness of the new life that emerged around us. The scents of the spring buds, of grass being cut, of the rain falling on sunbaked sidewalks—all filled me with joy. I longed to look more closely at those blossoming flowers I spotted in the neighbors' yards from a distance. We felines do not see the color red as humans do, but I am convinced that the world must look even more glorious through our blue and violet colored lenses than it does for humans or any other creature on earth. As beautiful as this all seemed from my window perches, however, I longed to examine these marvels of nature up close in all their glory.

I often called out to the creatures outside to ask them how it felt to be free—the opossums skulking about, the raccoons forever looking for food, the busy, frenetic squirrels and even the insects—but none seemed to notice me at all, save the deer. And let me tell you, my feline friends, it is best not to talk to these creatures at all. They are perpetually depressed. One injured deer, limping severely on a rear leg, acquiesced to talk to me once when I called to him through the screen door in the back.

"What happened to you?" I asked, wondering if the white tom could have inflicted this kind of damage.

"A car," he moaned, his head hung low.

"You were hit by a car?" I gasped.

"Yes. He avoided me at the last minute, unfortunately, and spared my life."

"Surely you mean fortunately?"

"No, I wanted it to hit me."

"Wanted it to hit you? But why? It's spring. The world is just coming to life again."

"What world?" he asked, raising his head to look at me, his eyes red and watery. "They take more of our world away from us every day to build their gargantuan homes. We can't find food anymore. They just took down our favorite patch of forest, where we used to race. Soon there'll be nowhere left to go at all. We'll have only their decorative flowers and bushes for food, and only their small yards to run across. Tell me, what kind of life is that, little cat?"

"I've heard my caretakers talking about you deer in the roads. They don't think you're very smart because you keep running in front of cars."

"Not very smart?" he gave a sad laugh, then winced in pain from accidentally shifting weight onto the injured leg. "No, we usually plan it very carefully. We do it at night most of the time. It's well known that humans don't see well at night and, since there's less traffic, they also tend to drive faster. There are two methods you can use," he lectured. "You can try waiting until the last minute and bolt in front of them, but that can get you just a glancing blow sometimes. A better method is to pick a spot around a curve and wait right in the middle of the street for those bright headlights that will deliver you from your misery. They say it's best to look directly into the lights to fix yourself to the spot and keep from panicking."

"But it didn't work for you?" I craned my head to look at his injured leg.

He shook his head sadly. "I couldn't wait. I bolted in the daylight. I just couldn't take it anymore," he said, shifting his weight slightly and wincing once more in pain. "I should have planned it better. I'm going to have to finish this tonight."

"Well, good luck." I said for lack of anything better to say.

"Thanks," he muttered and limped away from me into the forest in our backyard.

As I watched him leave, I resolved not to talk to any more deer. They were too depressing to bear. Perhaps, I thought, I should just stick to my own species.

* * * * * * * * * *

I had been diffident about trying to communicate with the white tom, fearing that he might not want to talk to me. But after that encounter with the deer, I gathered my courage.

The next time I saw him chase another tom out of our front yard, I called out, "Hey, you,"

He took his time watching the other tom run away. I didn't even think he'd heard me at first. I was thinking of calling out again, but then I noticed him spying me out of the corner of his eye. He sized me up for a moment, then sauntered over to the sparse flower bed beneath the window. "Yeah, what?" he asked in a quick, buzzy voice when he'd reached me.

Suddenly I realized I had no idea what to say. "I like watching you," I said dumbly, not wanting to let the opportunity pass.

He sat down and eyed me with suspicion. "Don't you have anything better to do in there?"

"Of course I do," I said defensively.

I doubt that," he contradicted me. "They really do a number on you in there, don't they?"

"What do you mean?" I asked.

"Keeping you inside like that, it's against your nature."

"It's not too bad."

He shook his head with pity. "A tomcat needs to run wild, to fight with other cats and scrounge in garbage cans for food. That's real life, not sitting around bored on a human's lap."

"I don't sit in anyone's lap!"

"Right," he dismissed my point with sarcasm. "What's your name, anyway?"

"Hastings."

"Hastings? What kind of a name is that?"

"It's from a book."

"A book," he scoffed. "People and their books. They think they're more important than what's going on around them. Well, at least it's not a TV show," he said. Then he repeated my name in ridicule. Hearing it from his mouth, I couldn't help but argue with his assessment.

"Well, what's your name?" I asked to change the subject.

"It's Mo," he declared. "You remember that." And then he turned to walk away.

"I will," I called after him through the metal screen. "I will remember it."

I wanted to talk to him more, but he had already spotted another acquaintance and was trotting away to meet him.

* * * * * * * * * *

My conversation with Mo had rattled me, so I decided to talk to Hercule about it. I found him in the midst of another creation. A tall, narrow tepee-shaped structure made out of hay stood at the center of his cage. At the moment I approached, he was studying his hay bale, carefully trying to select which stalks to add next to the still fragile structure.

"Can I talk to you, Hercule?" I asked.

"Of course, my friend," he answered, turning from the hay bale to give me his attention. "What's troubling you?"

I promptly told him all about Mo and my conversation with him.

"Oh, those tomcats don't have the faintest idea what they're talking about, Hastings. They have a very skewed view of the world. But then, I suppose they have to."

"Why is that?"

"Why, they don't have the luxuries we do. Most of them never will. It's too late for them, you see. Who will take Mo in and pamper him like we're pampered? They need to believe, for their own survival, that our life really isn't as good as it seems. So they make up reasons to look down upon it."

"So you mean he really wants to be a housecat?"

"Of course he does, deep down. Wouldn't you, if you were in his shoes?"

"I don't know," I said skeptically.

"Well look here, my boy, would you rather be sleeping outside in the freezing cold? Would you rather be getting your food from garbage pails, eating the things people throw away? Would you rather have cuts and scratches all over your body, and half your ear torn off in somebody else's mouth?"

"I guess not," I admitted, "but it seems like so much fun out there."

"That's because you're not out there, you see. The food is always tastier in the other cage."

"Huh?"

"That's an aphorism."

"Metaphors and aphorisms. I don't understand anything you say sometimes. Why don't you just say what you mean?"

"All right, Hastings, all right. My point is that we often think others have a better situation than ourselves. It's in our natures. It's what drives us to strive for better things in life. That's what drives you to want to be outside."

"So you're saying that if I were out there, I'd think it was better in here."

"That's precisely what I'm saying."

"And therefore," I extrapolated, "I'll never be happy with my life, because I'll always think that someone else has it better than I do."

"Good, Hastings! Now you're learning to use your critical thinking skills. But that's quite a somber conclusion you've drawn. I was heading toward a somewhat different endpoint."

"And that is?"

"Well, you see, I believe that the mind is transcendent. Once we understand our true natures, we can use the power of our wills to overcome its less, shall we say, desirable aspects."

"But Nature is so powerful," I observed. "Look at the way it's changing everything outside."

"That's true, my boy, but the world of flowers and trees is a different matter altogether from the world of the mind. Reason and passion and creativity are some of the greatest forces on Earth. Once you understand your own nature, you can bend it to your will and surpass the limited sort of happiness to which your natural instincts could lead you."

Hercule's argument was just so many words to me at the time. I sighed longingly. "I still think I'd be happier outside these walls, Hercule. There's something inside me that tells me I should be out there."

"Listen to that voice, my friend," he advised. "Hear what it has to say. But then make sure you remember your comfortable window perch, your neat litter box and your reliable supply of food. You'll come to realize that not everything your nature tells you is always for your own good."

"You may be right," I admitted. "It makes perfect sense. But it still feels wrong to me."

* * * * * * * * * *

In light of Hercule's explanation, I did not take Mo's scorn toward me to heart. In fact, I took my place at the window the very next day to watch out for him. To my delight, when he passed by and spotted me there, he came over on his own and quickly proved himself to be more friendly than he had at first let on.

From that day, I always looked forward to Mo's sporadic visits. He was even more erratic in his schedule than most felines, disappearing for days on end and then just popping up as if nothing had happened. As the weather improved, we often conversed through the screen at the back of the house when my caretakers slid open the glass door. My caretakers derived much amusement from watching us as we stretched to our full heights and kneaded the screen with our paws.

"Look at what they're doing," Alicia would say with amusement.

"Yeah, poking holes in our screen," Howie would answer sardonically.

But my cynical caretaker was wrong. Our intent was not to make holes. Mo regaled me with his heroic adventures. I was enchanted by these incredible narratives, which, in retrospect, did somewhat strain credulity. Once, he said, he'd faced down a pack of red foxes single-handedly, using his superior climbing skills to quickly jump on their backs, slash them and then flee up trees repeatedly until they were so cut up and frustrated they left him alone. Another time, he said, he'd scared a whole family of opossums to death when he caught them eating from his food bowl on the back porch of his caretaker's house.

Most of Mo's tales, however, involved beautiful kitties in distress. These stories always ended with the two producing litters together. One I remember in particular was how he'd made a daring rescue of a beautiful black kitty kidnapped by an old woman who kept hundreds of cats in her garbage-strewn little house. The smell inside had been so bad, Mo had thrown up three times and yet he'd still been able to bring her to safety. She became passionately devoted to him and, after she had fully recovered from the ordeal, they made three litters together.

"Three litters," I exclaimed. "Wow!"

"Oh, yes," Mo said proudly. "I've sired a thousand and one kittens now. No matter what happens to me, I'll know I'll live on in my offspring. A car may crush me, a tom may slice me in two, but the world can never forget me now."

"I'd like to sire lots of kittens, too!" I exclaimed.

"Well, I don't think you can, Hastings," he said, signaling toward my rear with a tilt of his head.

"What do you mean?"

"I mean you're not capable."

"What are you talking about, Mo?"

"Didn't you get *the operation*?"

"What operation?"

Mo sat down like a human, legs splayed, and displayed his ta-tas to me. "See down there?" he said.

I sat down likewise and looked at my nether region.

My dear readers, this betrayal was too much to bear! I knew instantly when it had happened. My caretakers had left me one night with Dr. Choi a few weeks after my initial visit with him. I had trusted him completely, of course, and so had not worried very much when he did something that made me extremely sleepy. When I awoke, I had an aching in my loins that abated only after many naps. I had thought at the time that it must have been a necessary medical procedure, performed for my own long-term benefit.

"That mouse!" I cursed.

"Whoa! There's no need for that kind of language, Hastings. Who are you talking about?"

"Doctor Choi!"

"It's not the doctor's fault. Don't blame him. He does what your caretakers pay him to. You should blame them."

And blame them I did, my friends. But what could I do? I attacked Howie's legs, but he locked me in the bathroom and threatened quite seriously to take me back to the shelter. I was thus compelled to repress my anger. Combined with Alicia's ever-expanding belly and the offensive smell that accompanied it, my discontent was growing nearly unbearable.

I now recognize that this operation might not have been as sinister as I had thought at the time. On the contrary, it may have played quite a significant role in making me the superior cat I am today. Many male cats become obsessed to distraction by certain biological urges, as Mo's preoccupation with kitty conquests illustrates. In order to become a cat of a truly superior intellect, one must be able to disengage one's mind from the tethers of the physical. In consenting to neuter me, perhaps Dr. Choi was in fact bestowing upon me a gift: the ability to separate my intellect from the confines of simple bodily pleasures and move to a higher plane of existence.

But I will come back to my intellectual development in due time, my dear readers. At this point, I was simply angry with Dr. Choi for what I perceived as a betrayal. Regardless of what benefit it might eventually have brought to me, the surgical removal of my tomhood was certainly not of my choice.

But then, little is of our choice. We must continually endeavor to make the most of situations in which we have been placed against our wills. Such is a cat's lot in life.

Were there but a way to change that, my fellow felines!

* * * * * * * * * *

I was torn between, on the one paw, Hercule's rather practical advice to find something creative to fill my days and, on the other, my natural inclination toward a life of adventure. I had no idea at the time how I could lead a life of intellectual fulfillment, but Mo's counterexample was right outside our windows.

"I wish I was out there with you," I purred longingly to my streetwise friend one evening through the screen door. "Free, roaming the streets and having adventures like yours."

"I feel sorry for you, Hastings," Mo said, shaking his head. "I really do. It can't be real exciting in there."

"I'll bet you always have something to play with out there," I said.

"Play?" he scoffed. "I've got better things to do out here than play. Romance, adventure, intrigue: It's all fun and exciting, sure, but it's not play."

"Oh, I wish I could escape."

"You don't want to escape," he said skeptically.

"Yes I do," I insisted.

"Then why aren't you out here with me right now? It can't be that hard."

"They've caught me every time I've tried."

"If at first you don't succeed, my young friend, try a couple more times—that is, if you remember to get around to it and have nothing better to do. That's an old cat saying. Haven't you heard it?"

"No," I admitted. Even at that young age, I had already come to recognize that Mo had a penchant for using lofty-sounding phrases which, when dissected, actually inspired very little. Nevertheless, while the wisdom of my feline friend may have paled in comparison to the insightful introspection of Hercule the pig, the appeal of Mo's exciting lifestyle was too alluring to resist. With Mo taking me in his paws, I thought, perhaps I could live out there. Perhaps I wasn't destined to be a housecat forever. "Will you help me escape?" I asked him.

"Sure," Mo said. "Just tell me what you want me to do."

"If I had a distraction I might be able to get away."

"So you want me to be the distraction?" he asked slyly.

"Yes," I answered, my excitement building. "When I get out the door, you attack them."

"Attack them," he echoed me with a cynical tone.

"Just enough to distract them and let me get away."

"Sure," he said. "No problem. Just give me a time and a place, and I'll be there."

"Well, the problem is you never know when they're going to open the door. I'll have to jump at any opportunity. Can you just stay near the door and watch until they open it?"

"Sure."

"How about tomorrow?"

"I'll be there," he assured me.

"OK," I said. "Stay close to the house. When you hear the door opening, come running. I'll slip out and head in your direction. You do whatever you can to give me an opening."

"Even bite?" he smiled. "I've always wanted to bite a human."

"Nothing's out of bounds," I stressed.

"Ooh," he said with satisfaction. "This is going to be fun.

* * * * * * * * * *

The next morning, I was so eager to begin the day that I jumped on my caretakers' bed at the first light of dawn. They barely stirred as I walked across them, so I stood on Howie's chest and put my cold nose to his lips, a trick that I have found always causes him to wake. The strategy had the desired effect.

"Uch, Hastings," he said, propping himself up on an elbow and wiping his mouth. "Get out of here. It's Saturday." He gently pushed me off the bed and lay back down.

Embittered, I leapt back up and circled him slowly, calmly looking for an opening.

"Hastings," he groaned, aware of my maneuverings, "it's not even six o' clock. Leave me alone."

But I had no intention of leaving him alone. His arm was exposed, and let me tell you, my feline friends; little bothers a human more than having that little flap of flesh on the back of an upper arm bitten, however gently. Just a mere nip can send a person into fits of anger. And thus it happened that morning. Howie bolted upright, and I leapt from the bed and out the door, chased by a string of expletives from his mouth. He got out of bed and shut the door behind me.

I sat in the hallway licking my paws with satisfaction. I knew that, although he shut the door to their bedroom after my hasty exit, Howie was now destined to begin the day sooner than he'd intended. For Howie, my dear readers, fancies himself a fiction writer. Waking him up, I knew from experience, would activate his guilt mechanism, a characteristic that only humans have, and which can be used to great advantage if applied judiciously. After returning to bed following a harrowing event such as I had just subjected him to, it was highly likely that Howie would not be able to fall back asleep again as he agitated and thought about the fiction writing he "should" be doing in the other room.

Howie's early morning writing sessions might extend longer than two hours, but could also last as little as an hour. Often he would crawl back into bed afterward for a nap, inevitably waking up Alicia, who would then want to get up herself and start the day. Soon would come the opening of the front door to get the newspaper, and thus my first opportunity to escape would arrive.

Unfortunately, none of this happened. Howie must have fallen right back asleep. I began to scratch and claw at the door, but there was no response from inside. I leapt up to the dining room window ledge and spotted Mo on the lawn next door. He seemed fast asleep, but I was certain he was really on the lookout for me. Nevertheless, I had no choice but to wait anxiously for my caretakers to begin their day.

I returned to the hallway and listened intently for the sounds of waking from their room. I eventually heard them, but it took an excruciatingly long time for them to shower and dress. They finally went to the kitchen and Alicia made my heart skip when she announced that she was going out to get the newspaper.

My excitement swelled as I lowered myself onto my haunches under the dining room table and targeted the door with my laser focus. As soon as I spotted the outside light through the widening crack, I made my move, bolting through Alicia's legs to the outside and almost knocking her swollen, unsteady body over in the process. She shouted a curse the likes of which a refined housecat such as myself would never repeat in print, but it took the form of, "That _____ cat! He almost killed me."

"What happened?" Howie called from inside as I cleared the door and bounded down the narrow concrete walkway.

"Hastings got out. What do you think happened?" she shot back at him with an acid voice.

When my paws finally touched the cool grass of the front lawn, every blade suddenly seemed to pulse a charge of fear and indecision into me. I'd never thought about this moment of escape in my planning, only the events leading up to it inside the house. Under that open blue sky, with a chill breeze raking my fur, my muscles seemed to thicken and gel until I slowed to a crawl. I had come to a complete stop by the time I'd reached the middle of the front yard.

I looked toward Mo, hoping he would come and take charge, maybe even shout instructions to me as Buddy would have. But he never budged from his spot. He seemed deep in slumber and completely unaware of what was going on.

The frigid wind mocked my stiffening muscles. I knew my caretakers would be coming for me at any moment, but I had no idea what to do. I began to shiver, looking around in desperation as if I might find an answer in the scraggly bushes of the neighboring yards or the closely-packed cars parked along the narrow street. What if I ran off, I thought, but then couldn't find my way back again? How could I be sure Mo could find me? Even worse, what if he never cared to look for me in the first place?

As I hesitated in the grass, Howie came up behind me and abruptly grabbed me by the scruff. He carried me roughly back inside, admonishing me all the while, then tossed me into the computer room as punishment, slamming the door hard behind me.

Humiliated by my farcical escape attempt, I leapt up onto the window sill and looked outside for Mo. He was still on the same spot on the neighbor's lawn, fast asleep. I became livid with the irresponsible tom. I paced back and forth in turmoil, unable to sit still. I could not believe that another cat could do this to me. Where was my fellow feline when I needed him? To raise my hopes so high, and then dash them out of sheer laziness! Is this how we felines treat one another? My outrage knew no bounds.

But I was never to confront Mo about his abhorrent negligence. After he got up from his nap, he casually strolled away without noticing me at the window sill. I looked for him all day but never spotted him. It was not unusual for him to wander for long periods without coming near our house, but he would always come back eventually. This time, however, I was destined never to see my fair weather friend again.

* * * * * * * * *

The trouble began that very night, when Alicia stayed up late reading. I was in their bed, licking my fur—for while we cats are inarguably the most fiercely independent-minded creatures on the planet, we nevertheless still enjoy the presence of others during such peaceful moments. It was thus that I witnessed the strange behavior of my female caretaker.

It was not altogether unusual for Alicia to stay up far into the night to finish a book. However, on this night she began to act in an increasingly curious manner. She glanced repeatedly at the alarm clock beside her bed and periodically put her book down to scribble notes on a pad of paper. She rubbed her now unfathomably rotund belly repeatedly, smiling as if she were going to break out in hysterical laughter at any moment. After a couple of hours of this bizarre ritual, she reached over to wake up Howie.

"What, what?" he groaned.

"It's time. We have to go to the hospital. I'm going to take a shower."

"Now?" he asked incredulously.

"Should I ask her to wait until you're ready?" she asked accusingly.

Howie, still thick with sleep, frowned and started to climb out of bed.

They were virtually silent as they calmly went about dressing in the middle of the night and collecting their bags. Hercule and I were absolutely perplexed by this bizarre ritual. They left the house before dawn with nary an explanation about what was going on.

"What just happened?" I asked Hercule after the door shut behind them.

"Why, I haven't the slightest clue," he said, perplexed.

We speculated about it all day, not even considering the possibility that they might have left the house to give birth to their child. You see, my fellow felines, in contrast to our queens, who simply find a place to nest in which to give birth when the time comes, humans go to a hospital in order to give births. We knew nothing of this at the time, of course, and it wasn't until that evening when Howie came home that we discovered what had happened.

"We had a baby, guys!" he announced to Hercule and me as soon as he came through the door. We were sitting in the living room at the time, and the worries we had been having over the past few weeks about the presence of a child in our home suddenly rushed back at us with force. The time had now come. Would my movements be restricted? Would a baby's inexperienced hands attempt to lift Hercule?

"It's a baby girl, and her name is Lizzie," Howie continued excitedly. "She's very cute, but she's a little loud, so she might scare you a bit. But I think you're all going to be good friends."

The first thing he did was to start packing up all our things. "Now I know you're not going to like this," he explained to us as he worked, "but it's going to be a little crazy around here for a couple of weeks, so you're going to stay with Grandma and Grandpa."

Hercule and I looked to each other in terror. Grandma and Grandpa? He must have been referring to Alicia's parents, we both realized. They lived close by but generally took as little interest in us as we did in them. We didn't have a choice in the matter, however. Before we knew it, we were in the car and on our way. When we got to their house, Hercule's home was installed on the brick shelf of the fireplace. My litter box, food and water were placed in the basement.

"Good-bye, guys," Howie said as he rushed out again. "Have fun while you're here, and don't cause too much trouble."

After he left, rather than greeting us properly, our new caretakers simply turned their backs on us, shaking their heads in disapproval at our very existence. They spoke in the other room in a language we could not understand—some Eastern European language, I believe—but it was clear that they were less than enthralled with their charge to care for us. Soon they went upstairs, leaving us alone. It seemed to me that this was deliberately meant as a snub, as it was an improperly early time to retire to bed.

Hercule turned to me with a very grim expression on his face. "I think we're in the soup, old boy," he said ominously.

I'd never heard the phrase before, but I well understood its meaning from the tone of his voice. Indeed, I felt a truer sentence had never been spoken.

* * * * * * * * * *

We had little time to speculate about the long-term changes this new child would bring to our lives. Banished from our rightful home and cruelly abandoned to uncaring caretakers, we could do little more than watch as a dark, lugubrious cloud descended upon us.

To illustrate how cold and careless our new caretakers were, I need only recount something I overheard Alicia's father tell Howie one day. "Do you realize," he asked, "that you have more choices of cat food in the grocery store here than many people in our country have for themselves? You Americans spoil your pets too much," he laughed. "It's ridiculous."

Grandma and Grandpa cared little for us, and thus cared for us very little. The stench in my litter box soon grew so noxious that I had to stick my head out the entrance in order to use it. The litter clumped into a virtually solid block. In Hercule's home, the poop pellets gathered on the floor and his bedding grew acrid with the stench of urine.

We weren't to encounter our newly expanded family for over a week. When we had first heard that our caretakers had produced a little girl, we had reasonably assumed that she would be, like her mother, fairly good-natured and agreeable. How lucky we were, we thought, not to have been bestowed with a boy, who would poke and prod us and perform all sorts of unimaginable, grotesque experiments on us. A girl is much to be preferred, as many a wise animal will tell you.

How mistaken we were, my dear readers.

What we experienced during our first meeting put great fear into our little hearts. Little Lizzie's cry was a high-pitched, throaty scream that pierced the very fur that protected us. It tore not only at the ears but at the heart itself, a fiery, desperate wail that permeated and agitated every fiber of your being. I retreated to a safe distance, but poor Hercule could not even leave the room when she was near. Thus my anguish was multiplied, knowing that I was leaving my poor friend to suffer by the fireplace whilst protecting myself.

My natural curiosity drove me to observe the new girl as much as I could during the brief intervals in which she was not shattering the very sound barrier with her cry. These periods came only when she was suckled by Alicia and during the nap that defined the last segment of their visit. Neither Hercule nor I had ever had exposure to a human baby before, but based on our experiences with other species, this was certainly not what we'd envisioned. We had expected to see a miniature person walking around, curiously exploring its surroundings, making funny noises and so on.

This human child, however, was completely helpless. It was no wonder that she cried so vigorously, for she was unable to do anything else by herself. We had neither of us ever seen a creature so dependent on its parents for every single aspect of its existence. She didn't seem to have any muscular control whatsoever, so she was carried everywhere in a kind of portable chair with a handle. She even went to the bathroom in the very clothes she wore, a most undignified practice which would continue in the same manner for not days, not weeks, not months, my fellow felines, but years!

After they had finally left us in peace again, Hercule and I wondered aloud if there was anything wrong with the girl.

"Whatever the case," Hercule said ominously, "I think we are in serious trouble."

I was hardly of a mind to argue with his assessment.

* * * * * * * * * *

We saw our family very infrequently over the next few weeks, which was a relief in one sense, as there was little change in Lizzie. She cried copiously whenever we saw her. I actually began to feel a certain pity for Howie and Alicia, the way their eyes had reddened, their shoulders slumped and their voices flattened to a tired drone. Still, my feelings toward them would have been more generous had they made the effort to clean my litter box and Hercule's home.

The filth, my friends, was reaching astronomical proportions. I could no longer find a spot of loose litter on which to urinate. The smell was getting so foul that even if I stuck my head out of the entrance when relieving myself, the stench blanketing the area like a low-hanging cloud still struck me lightheaded and woozy.

Hercule, for his part, had by now completely abandoned his high art, as his surroundings had gotten so putrid it was difficult for him to concentrate on even the simplest conversation with me. I could barely approach him, the smell from his cage was so unpleasant. But I had little comfort in those days other than my old friend, and I endeavored to endure the foul odor so that we could take solace in each other's company.

"I don't know if we'll make it through this, Hastings," he groaned to me one night.

"I don't either," I answered in a low voice, trying to take as little air into my lungs as I could.

"This is criminal neglect, I tell you."

"It is," I agreed. "They deserve a thorough slashing for this."

Hercule shook his head slowly. "You know I don't condone violence," he said, "but for once I think I might agree with you."

It was several weeks before our ordeal was to end. Howie tended to us eventually during one visit, and then subsequently did so at shorter intervals. Nevertheless, our stay continued to be stressful and unpleasant, albeit no longer so completely unbearable once the cleanings were underway again.

Then one day, Howie came by and told us he was bringing us to our new home. An icy chill went through me. I turned to Hercule in horror, and he was as flustered and confused as I. New home? What did this mean? Who had they donated us to? Perhaps some mad scientists. Or worse, a family with four or even five of these dastardly children!

Howie gathered up our things and put us into the car. I cowered on the floor behind Alicia's seat, with Hercule's cage above me on the back bench. Our hearts pounded as the car started up.

"What's going to happen?" I asked Hercule.

"I don't know, my dear boy," he said, the soft purr of his voice nearly drowned out by the background noise in the car, "but I daresay it can't be much worse than where we were."

"Do you think we're going to be separated?"

Hercule pondered the question for a moment. "Master Howie did say that he was taking us to our new home, not homes. He used the singular rather than the plural. So we're likely going to be together, wherever we're going."

"Well, that's a relief. Whatever happens, at least we'll be together."

"Yes, at least we'll be together," he echoed, but in a tone that belied the hope in his words.

We drove through the streets toward our unknown destination, trembling with anxiety and saying little more. It was not long before we arrived at our new home. The car came up a short drive and entered what is called the garage—a special portion of the house dedicated to the housing of automobiles. The garage door then descended with a deafening clatter, enclosing us in the dark, musty space, and Howie proceeded to take us out of the car and bring us into the house proper.

This new home was far from a banishment for us, as it turned out. The entire family, including the two of us and the earsplitting new addition, were now relocated to what seemed a spacious new palace. The first thing I did once I had seen Hercule installed in his new location—a prime spot, in the family room right at the center of the house— was to go explore. There were three floors: a finished, fairly open basement; a main floor with kitchen, dining room, family room, et cetera; and an upper floor with several bedrooms. The furniture from the old house on Forest Drive had already been moved, but there was so much more space in the new house that it barely seemed as if there were any furniture there at all. Two bedrooms upstairs sat completely empty, as did the living room on the main floor and the entire basement. It seemed an endless collection of pristine white walls and stretches of a rather attractive beige carpet not altogether different in color from my own fur, which had perhaps begun to fade from all the sunbathing I enjoyed. Indeed, after lounging in the summer sun for some weeks my fur was to fade to match the color of the carpet almost exactly, until it served as a sort of camouflage I could employ to conceal myself in much the same way as Mo was able to make use of a virgin snowfall.

There was one grievous disadvantage to this new house that I could instantly discern: A grossly inadequate supply of windows from which I could monitor the outside world. There were no windows whatsoever at the sides of the house, and the windows at the front and back had no appreciable ledges. Except for one basement window, they were all set flush into the walls, with only decorative wood molding surrounding them. I could observe the outside world only through that one basement window, a sliding door at the back of the house, and four windows at the front of the house which came down to the floor. As a result, I could no longer monitor the entire perimeter of my home. It was a terribly thoughtless design, yet one more example of how the human world takes only its own species into account in the design of its living spaces.

I did perceive that this new house offered me other advantages, however. First and foremost was the sheer expanse of the property, particularly the back yard—an open stretch of grass which I quickly discovered housed all manner of creature, including squirrels, rabbits, foxes, deer and assorted birds. Yet another advantage to this home was that I could easily escape the onslaught of the baby Lizzie's scream not only by moving to another room, but by removing myself to another landing of the house entirely. This was an advantage not afforded to my poor friend Hercule, and I felt in those days a most acute sorrow at his inability to join me in escaping the racket.

"How can you take it?" I asked him in sympathy one day after Lizzie, screaming and struggling as if she were being murdered, was brought away upstairs for a diaper change.

"Oh, Hastings, I endure, my dear friend. I endure."

The biggest regret I had about moving to this new home was in losing my friend Mo. After the travails Hercule and I had been through, my anger toward the irresponsible tom had dissipated considerably. I wished I could talk to Mo about what had happened. In fact, because he'd slept through the whole thing, Mo had never even known about my escape attempt and its disastrous outcome, much less had a chance to defend his actions. Perhaps he would have apologized profusely and pledged to help me escape the very next day. But I shall never know. The fate of the housecat is subject to the slightest human whim, and when the Winkelmans moved us all into a new home, I lost all chance of reconciliation and perhaps what would have been a lifelong friend.

I continued to miss my friend Mo for quite some time, despite my mixed feelings about him, but things did slowly return to normal in our lives—

or as normal as they would ever get with this new addition to our family. With his home once more being cleaned on a regular basis, Hercule soon resumed his passion for his art, and I settled into a comfortable routine of my own design. Considering what we had been through before, we were quite content.

There was one event worth noting during this period, and that was the arrival one afternoon soon after we had moved in of the dread Cousin Don. He came to assist Howie in installing a most ingenious flap in the door leading to the basement, through which I alone could pass. Once the girl Lizzie grew mature enough to be mobile, I could easily escape her onslaught merely by passing through this "cat door" and into the safety of the basement.

I realize that this has been my first mention of the dread Cousin Don. I have not, in fact, described the extended members of the family at all, who prior to the arrival of the deafening infant did not have much of a presence in our lives. Now, they seemed to descend on us with great frequency. Most of them paid Hercule and me no mind, or else simply commented on the astounding grace and beauty of my movement, or on how cute Hercule was—an assessment which would have embarrassed me were I in his fur, but which seemed to gratify him immensely.

The dreaded Don, who is Howie's cousin, was the only one of these relatives who paid much attention to us beyond these token observations. He fed Hercule all manner of tasty treats—at least,

Hercule found all those appalling fruits and vegetable tasty. But for some reason he took—and still takes, to this day—great pleasure in tormenting me.

Cousin Don is a very curious human. He dresses shabbily and his eyes have a glazed, faraway look. There is a curiously pungent odor about him, and he speaks in a slow, soft drawl. Sometimes he speaks so slowly, he seems to forget what he is saying in mid-sentence. Every time we see him, he picks me up and cuddles me to no end. I cannot escape his grasp no matter how hard I struggle. He holds me by the scruff in his lap and rubs my head, muttering some nonsense about how much I like it. If I attempt to use my claws or teeth on him, he immediately lifts me high up in the air by the scruff in a most humiliating position until I calm down and once more resign myself to submit to his affections.

My dear readers, it is not lightly that I have designated this man the dread Cousin Don. I loathe his visits from the bottom of my heart. Nevertheless, I must reluctantly give him a certain amount of credit for helping Howie to install that flap in the basement door. It allows me to come and go as I please, and has greatly improved my life in our new home.

* * * * * * * * *

I soon discovered that there were not one but two dogs living near our new home, one on either side. I do indeed dread dogs, as it is my nature to do so. However, I might have tried to make the most of a bad situation had there been windows on either side of the house. After being in proximity to these creatures for some time, I could not help but think that it might be a great experiment to try to communicate with them and use my superior knowledge and strength of character to try to refine them in some way. Nevertheless, as we cannot go to our respective windows to see each other, this plan will have to remain but a fantasy.

There is one event of note concerning these dogs that was particularly important in the development of my character, and it proves that even dogs will respect a confident and assertive cat. Soon after we moved into the new house, I took it into my head to try to escape. While I was becoming more comfortable with the fact that I was, at heart, a housecat, it was nevertheless still important for me to assess my chances for escape should the need ever arise. I must confess that, even today, despite my acceptance of my situation, it is somewhat comforting to know that I am not trapped, that I remain in human care by choice and can easily escape if I so desired. I therefore continue to make the occasional escape attempt, confident in the knowledge that Howie will promptly bring me back after my brief taste of the outdoors.

Escape to the outside world proved even easier to accomplish in our new house. The front door was centrally located, allowing for countless places to lurk while waiting to make a dash outside: around the doorways in the dining room or living room, on the stairs leading up to the second floor, in the hallway near the entrance to the basement or underneath the desk in the front hallway. On this particular occasion, I made my dash without even hiding. I merely waited in the front hallway not three body lengths from the door.

The only difficulty in escaping our new house was that the front door was not used very often. Most entries and exits were made through that hot, vile-smelling garage. But I am a patient feline, and when one of those people came knocking to offer a new driveway coat or a roof inspection or a cable television package—I know not which in this particular case—I made my move. As soon as Howie opened the door, I slipped past his legs and was outside in an instant.

I raced across the front lawn. Shady Court had few mature trees, and so I ran under the radiance of a gloriously open blue sky. Before I could even assess how it felt to be outside human shelter once more, however, I virtually ran into the fearsome Pomeranian next door named Hot Dog. Now, this dog had caused me much anxiety in my early days in our new home. Late nights, early mornings and all hours in between, one never knew when Hot Dog would resume that barking that chilled the heart with fear. Samson, the other neighboring dog, barked with much less frequency and in a more temperate tone. He, unlike Hot Dog, seemed a fairly reasonable and upstanding canine, as their species goes. Hot Dog, in contrast, was the mad horror of Shady Court.

I suddenly found myself facing this frightful creature, which had so often aroused a most terrible fear in my heart. Instinctively, I lifted my tail, arched my back and hissed a warning at him. To my surprise, the foolish thing backed down instantly, retreating in fear from me! Never again, my dear readers, was I to fear that bombastic boob of a dog.

Of course, Howie was upon me at once, grabbing my scruff and chastising me in harsh tones as he brought me back inside. Still, nothing could destroy my ebullient mood that day and for many more to come. From that day forth, when I heard Hot Dog and his blustery barking, I would no longer feel any fear. Rather, I would find myself smiling in condescension at the beast's swaggering, empty display of braggadocio.

My encounter with Hot Dog proved to be quite formative. I realized that I had less to fear in this world than I had previously thought. If I could so instinctively take action to frighten such a fearsome creature as this Pomeranian, there was little in this world I could not face. I started to walk with a new spring in my step and to speak with a confidence borne of experience and of wisdom.

* * * * * * * * * *

Dear readers, we are still at a point in my life at which I had little inkling of how great my accomplishments were eventually to be. Indeed, it was to be over two years before I would even identify a noble pursuit for myself. Some may criticize the length of time it took before I set down my path, but I maintain that the greater the ambition, the longer it takes to determine one's goals in the first place. I spent countless afternoons bathing in a patch of sunlight on the carpet, or curled up in bed, or watching wildlife out the window as I pondered deeply about my true desires before I finally arrived at my lofty purpose.

Nevertheless, I do admit that even a sharp, curious and highly intelligent mind such as my own may be capable of a certain degree of stagnation. Although I spent many hours actively contemplating the beauty of each blade of grass outside the sliding door or the slow, grandiose spread of a fur-white cloud against a blue sky, a certain lethargy undeniably crept into my mind. Hercule was the one to observe this, and he began to chide me about my lack of ambition.

"You must find something to stimulate your mind, my friend," he said to me one afternoon some two years after the last episode in this memoir. "Something to lift you to a higher plane of existence, so to speak."

"I'm happy just the way I am," I answered with pride.

"Your body may be happy, and your mind may be happy, but you are neglecting your soul, Hastings."

"Oh, what nonsense," I dismissed his concerns.

Hercule frowned at me. In my heart, I certainly recognized the wisdom in my dear companion's words, but I was loath to admit that he was right because I simply had no conception of how I might enrich my festering soul. If only there were a simple answer, I thought to myself. If only a pursuit were to present itself to me, to give me inspiration.

Oh, dear readers, Fate is a strange beast, which strikes you down when you are happiest, yet lifts you up when you have given up hope. Inspiration, quite inadvertently, suddenly came to me through my caretaker Howie. Late one night, he came down to refill his glass of water and I, as usual, took decisive action to restore order to the house and encourage him to return to his room by employing my familiar warning circling around his legs. It was then that Howie threatened me with the following words: "I know your secrets, Hastings. I know all about you, cat. So you'd better watch it."

His words took me aback. I had no idea what he was talking about. My surprise was such that I allowed him return upstairs without further harassment.

The next day, I followed him around carefully until I heard him mention to Alicia something about a cat in a book. I recounted these strange comments to Hercule the next day, and he informed me that he had overheard Howie tell Alicia recently that he was reading the autobiography of a cat.

"A cat writing a book?" I exclaimed. "What a strange idea."

But Howie was soon telling everyone he knew about this book. As he explained to anyone who would listen, he had been browsing on a web site that sold surplus books when the idea struck him to look through the classics section. The list was quite large, and Howie hadn't even heard of many of the titles listed. One book in particular caught his eye. It was called *The Life and Opinions of the Tomcat Murr, together with a fragmentary Biography of Kapellmeister Johannes Kreisler on Random Sheets of Waste Paper.* The picture on the cover was an engraving of Murr himself, quill in paw, sitting at a desk and writing his memoirs. Howie was quite curious and ordered the book.

Now, Howie purchases many more books than he is capable of reading. They fill every bookshelf to the brim. He is positively awash with books, yet only reads one at a time. He picked this one up almost as soon as it arrived, however, spurred most likely by the powerful image of the great Murr on the cover.

One night, I was driven out of Howie and Alicia's room in annoyance by Howie's incessant giggling as he read his beloved book. When I went down to the living room, I found Hercule still awake. "What a ridiculous idea!" I scoffed. "A cat's autobiography!"

"Pray, why?" Hercule asked most seriously. "It strikes me as a fantastic way to advance the species. Imagine, my young friend, what cats could achieve if they communicated more with each other, sharing knowledge and cooperating in all those things they now do in isolation. There would be nothing your species couldn't do."

"Stop teasing me, Hercule."

"I assure you I am quite serious. I think it's an absolutely capital idea."

"Really."

"Yes, I do. I think this Murr must have been absolutely brilliant. To take it upon himself to learn how to read and write and then to tell his story. I think it's fantastic. It's positively inspirational."

I thought about Hercule's words over the next few days, all the while listening to the barrage of praise Howie heaped upon Murr's book to anyone who would hear him out. Howie seemed to be under the impression that a man named E.T.A. Hoffman had made up the whole thing, basing his story on the exploits of his pet cat. I, as I will explain later in my analysis of this masterwork, understand the true circumstances of its creation much better than my caretaker. In any case, I had made up my mind. I resolved to learn to read so that I could see for myself what the great Murr had to say.

* * * * * * * * *

The girl Lizzie was by then two years old. She was considerably quieter and more agreeable than she had been as an infant and, although I did not go out of my way to be near her, nor did I avoid her to the same extent. She adored being read to, and I had already gotten into the habit of sitting in the room with the family during this ritual.

My first task, I recognized, would be to learn how to recognize the symbols that formed human writing—that is to say the letters. Ever eager to develop the young girl's intellect, her family was at that time buying many tools for her to learn to read, most of which she completely ignored. I was able to take full advantage of these when the humans were out of the house. Lizzie's grandparents from out of town, Grams and Gramps, had bought her an electronic toy which proved to be quite simple for me to learn how to operate with my paws. Oh, how fondly I remember the glorious sound when I pressed the first button that was to lead to my ascent into a higher plane of existence. "A, ae or ah," the woman's voice spoke slowly, "Ape, apple."

I soon became quite proficient at pressing the buttons that operated the device. It was only a matter of days before I learned to recognize the letters of the alphabet and to know their sounds. By the end of two weeks, I had become quite proficient.

Next, I focused on putting the letters together in order to sound out words. To aid in this task, I frequently jumped onto the couch or the dresser behind my caretakers to watch as they read to Lizzie. Most of the books they read to her were quite simple, and I was able to use my exceptional eyesight to read the words from my perch as they traced them with their fingers and pronounced them. This process took quite some time, but within several weeks I felt confident enough to try to read something on my own.

I began with a board book that Lizzie had loved when she first became aware of the power of books. Sitting unfiled atop her bookcase, it virtually called for me to knock it down to the carpet. The

I resolved to learn to read.

book was called *Pond* and was written by a person named Lizi Boyd. I had heard *Pond* read aloud so many times, it was virtually etched into my brain, but it had been some time since I had last heard the book read, and so I figured it would be a suitable way for me to begin.

I carefully opened the first stiff page with my claw and studied the thick, black lowercase letters that hung in a blue sky above whimsically drawn cattail plants in a pond. My extensive drilling had taught me to painstakingly match those letters to their sounds and thus, dear readers, I slowly sounded those first two words out: "Cattails swish." My distant memories confirmed that I had read them correctly. How indescribable the elation I felt upon reading those first words, the very first syllable of which was certainly the most appropriate for one such as myself to begin his triumph with! The joy continued when I successfully read the words on page two: "Crayfish hides."

A true transformation came over me that morning as I sat on the girl Lizzie's carpet reading those simple words, my feline friends. The entities in that book came to life in my mind. I watched the darting fish in my mind—not real fish, mind you, but the very fish illustrated upon the page. I marveled at the colorful lilies that bloomed with a rapidity true lilies could never achieve. I felt the breezes blow as if I were in that fictitious, colorful, whimsical pond myself. I found myself submerged in the world of Lizi Boyd's imagination. I had discovered the true power of literature: the ability to transport you into a world of someone else's devising.

Hercule was as thrilled by my accomplishment as I. The following day, I carried the same author's *Forest* downstairs to the family room in my mouth. Hercule cheered me on as I plodded through it. Oh, we could almost hear the snores of the bear napping and the pitter-patter of the fox trotting. I even imagined I could feel the air tickling the fur in my long ears as I became the bunny hopping! Hercule enjoyed being transported into this other place as much as I, and he urged me to continue my studies in his presence so that he could share in my discoveries.

I soon moved on to other masterworks of the toddler oeuvre: *Bugs at Work, Bears in the Night, Hands, Hands, Fingers, Thumb, The Foot Book,* and so on. The whimsy of these books, the hypnotic rhythms and gentle lessons, were so captivating they were truly a joy to read. If we cats could but create such things for ourselves, I thought, who knows what we might one day achieve? But, of course, how can the kitten be read to when the cat does not know how to read?

But I shall return to those ideas later. My next challenge was to advance from board books to paper. Turning paper pages is no small task for a creature with furry paws. After much determination and experimentation, however, I was finally able to work out a consistent one-pawed method for turning paper pages. It entails licking my paw, using the traction of the damp paw to slide and separate the top page, and then using a sharp claw to lift and turn it. The process is somewhat more difficult after my nails have been cut—which is one reason why I express such disdain for nail clipping, actively struggling when my caretakers pick me up for one. But even after such a procedure, I can now, albeit with some difficulty, progress through virtually any book. I doubt I could ever become as proficient as a human at reading books printed on paper—after all, the format was designed with their anatomy alone in mind—but I can nonetheless now turn the pages of any paper book.

The ability to read through paper books opened whole new worlds to me. I brought whatever books I could get my paws on in Lizzie's room down to read to my noble companion and advocate. Hercule delighted in the absurdist creatures in *There's a Wocket in my Pocket*. We both cried when little Emily left for school at the end of *Little Bear's Friend* and discussed endlessly whether her family truly would return to their idyllic vacation spot again the next summer. We laughed heartily at the goofy exploits of Morris the Moose in school and at the circus. It was a wonderful time as we discovered the amazing worlds that my accomplishment had opened up to us. Every day we could travel to another place and see the world in different ways.

These new worlds began to affect our daily lives as well. When I saw a fox outside the window now, I shared in the rhythms of its trot in the grass. When I saw a bunny, I wondered if it noticed the wind in its ears. Once, when Alicia went to get a coat, I feigned panic to Hercule, crying that there might be a Woset in the closet! I never saw that solemn little pig laugh so hard as at that Dr. Seuss-inspired joke. We were discovering that literature not only took us to different places, but it also drew us closer together.

But my greatest reading ambition, my dear readers, was yet to be tackled. Hercule was as eager to hear *The Life and Opinions of the Tomcat Murr* as I was to read it, but it was to be many weeks after Howie had finished the book before I felt I could even think of approaching it.

I finally began to read the editor's most curious foreword out loud one morning soon after the family had left the house. How well I remember those opening words of my first serious book of literature! It said that when Murr the cat was writing his *Life and Opinions*, he had found a printed book in his master's study, tore it up, and used it as blotting paper. Some of those pages were mixed up with the manuscript when it was sent to the printer's and inadvertently printed as part of it. This other book was supposedly the biography of a certain Kapellmeister Johannes Kreisler.

Hercule and I looked at each other in puzzlement. This seemed a most bizarre way to start a great book. Although it had taken me a half an hour to read the two pages comprising the foreword, we plowed forward into the rest without delay.

Now that I am greatly more studied and erudite, dear readers, I can interpret this most amusing little ruse. The tomcat Murr obviously wrote these sections himself! No doubt he wanted to invent a clever way to illustrate some of the insightful observations that he had made about human life. What better way to do so than to pretend that the sections seemingly randomly interspersed throughout his narrative were actually the biography of a real man? The tomcat Murr was truly a brilliant inspiration for us all.

I read Murr's entire two volumes over the next several weeks—well over three hundred pages. Hercule was very proud of my progress through the long volumes, and I basked in his frequent compliments. This endeavor, no doubt, dwarfed my previous forays into human literature.

We found Murr's explorations into the world of humans, cats and even dogs quite gripping. We became extremely attached to him—even though, as Hercule pointed out, his behavior was not always laudable. As for the bizarre life and times of the passionate and moody young musician Kreisler, we unexpectedly found them fascinating as well. Taken as a whole, despite the book's disjointed, jarring nature, it utterly captivated us. I only wish that it had been finished.

Perhaps you may think it unfair of me to spoil the book for you by revealing that its intrigues never reach a conclusion. However, I cannot write an honest history without documenting the distress that Hercule and I felt when the book abruptly ended and I read in the editor's postscript that Murr had died before writing a planned third volume. We grieved for Murr as if we had lost a best friend—even though, as Hercule pointed out, Murr lived such a long time ago that it was a foregone conclusion before we ever began reading that he was no longer alive. Doubtless, part of what we were feeling at the time was something which I have now become considerably more familiar with: the common sadness when you leave behind the rich world of a beloved book. Murr's book was truly beloved by both of us.

By the time I had finished, I had little doubt of what I must do next. In fact, I knew it long before I had neared the end. As Murr had written his biography "so that the reader may learn to educate himself to be a great tomcat," so must I write my own biography to educate my readers as to how to be a great housecat. Through the very process of writing such a masterpiece, I realized, I would myself become the great housecat I longed to be.

"What do you think of the idea?" I asked my now dearest friend Hercule.

"I think it's a capital idea, old boy!" he exclaimed. "Absolutely capital! You've found a very worthy goal for yourself."

And indeed I had, my fellow felines, thanks to the late, great tomcat Murr.

* * * * * * * * * *

Murr wrote his opus in the early 1800s. The thing that puzzles me most about his accomplishment is how he was able to write well over 300 pages with only a quill. There is an engraving of him with quill in paw on the cover, and he also describes learning to use the quill. However, I am still quite unable to figure out how to write with a pen or pencil—our modern equivalent to Murr's quill and ink pot. Both the engraving and his description are vague enough as to be of little practical use. I have spent many long hours, with Hercule's observations and input, adjusting the positions of pens and pencils on tables and floors, attempting to pick them up with my paws, only to be frustrated and swat at them in anger. To this day, if I find a pen or pencil lying about, I often try to put it in my paws. These attempts inevitably all end the same way, with me swatting and chasing the accursed things across the floor in frustration. My caretakers are bemused when they witness this behavior, mistakenly interpreting it as my "playing" with these writing implements.

Fortunately, at the beginning of this new century—the twenty first century, that is—we cats have other tools at our disposal. The main one, of course, being the computer. Now, much has been written of cats on keyboards causing all manner of copious gibberish to appear on the screen. I do understand why those cats try so hard to learn how to type at a computer keyboard. However, many cats have not properly thought this through, somehow thinking that by depressing various keys as they have seen humans do, they will automatically communicate their thoughts through the device by some magical mechanism. I must advise them in the strongest possible terms that learning to read the human language is an absolutely essential precursor to being able to write it.

Mastering the computer was not nearly so difficult a task for me as learning to read, but it was no less exhilarating. It required only stationing myself in various positions in the office so as to be able to observe Howie's every move when he wrote at the computer in the early morning hours. With my superior eyesight, I was able to discern every keystroke and its result. When I finally decided to attempt to try the machine myself, my only real difficulty came in operating the computer mouse.

I must clarify at this juncture that a computer mouse bears only the slightest resemblance to a proper mouse. This device moves across the desk on a small ball mounted in its belly, and is used to position a pointer on the computer screen and thus reduce the use of the keyboard. Its being named after such a lowly animal is quite appropriate, given its ability to frustrate the cat who tries to use one. The computer mouse is designed solely for the human hand and is thus extremely difficult for a cat to master.

Ultimately, I was forced to learn how to use a keyboard to perform all the functions that a human typically performs with a computer mouse. I accomplished this feat by reading old computer manuals on the bookshelves downstairs, and through help functions on the computer itself and on the Internet, once I had mastered how to use that most powerful communications tool.

For more about my road to computer mastery, readers may refer for further guidance to my comprehensive masterpiece *The Essential Cat's Guide to Computing*, which I have yet to write but which I intend to get to one day along with its companion volumes *The Essential Cat's Guide to Reading* and *The Essential Cat's Guide to Living with People.* Consider this an advertisement for them. I am sure that there are many other useful titles I will write as well. These works, I might note, are to be modeled after those popular series of books marketed toward people who readily acknowledge their own inferiority: *The Dummies Guides to...*, *The Idiot's Guide to...*, et cetera. Cats, unlike humans, are quite understandably reluctant to admit to any such flaws, so my titles will be more respectful of my readers. Nevertheless, I envision my books will be formatted much like those human volumes, the margins peppered with whimsical pictures and practical advice such as, "Attack with the teeth, not with the claws. They can always take out your claws, but they can't de-tooth you."

But I will write more about my other literary projects later. If reading my first words was a thrill, my dear readers, then writing my first words . . . oh, it is difficult to describe the elation I felt that morning when I opened a new document on the screen and typed out the words, "My Life and Opinions, by Hastings." The letters had barely appeared on the screen before I leapt down from the chair and darted upstairs to my eager friend and supporter's cage to tell him about my accomplishment. No sooner had I heard Hercule's praise and encouragement than I raced downstairs again to continue.

You may have noticed, dear readers, that the beginning of this history did not commence at the beginning of my life. In fact, the first words you read were not the first words that I wrote that fateful morning, but rather were added later, after I became more well-read and had mastered the manipulation of time in service of a story. My first words were considerably more mundane as I tried to recall my birth and first days. I wrote but three paragraphs during that first writing session, none of which survive as written in the version you are now reading. As my reading and writing skills have developed, I have repeatedly revisited that first section in order to improve it. Whether or not my original words survived as written, however, the thrill of writing those first paragraphs was exhilarating.

And so, as they say, the stage was set. I had taught myself to read. I had taught myself to write on a computer. Thus I began my great masterwork, which now sits in your very paws.

Before long, inspired by my words of encouragement and advice, cats everywhere will be contributing to the feline literary cannon—and it will not stop there, my friends. Already, I have seen paintings by cats. These will gain more recognition, as will the much maligned but fine art of caterwauling. Once the feline world has developed its own arts and culture, we will be united as humans are and create great societies to achieve higher things: to stamp out injustice, to help the downtrodden, to become something altogether more than the victims of human whim and fancy that we are now.

After two centuries, the juggernaut that Murr set in motion is finally beginning to accelerate, and I am the cat who intends to give it its final, critical push.

Life as a Cultured Cat

Now that I have recounted my history for you, dear readers, henceforth you may accompany me on my journeys and share in my discoveries almost as if you were making them yourself. While I cannot know where life shall eventually take me, as long as I am able I shall document my actions and observations for your benefit.

I rather think it apt to begin this volume, in which I will record the events of my days, by describing a typical day. Most of my time is now filled by the pursuit of higher culture and knowledge. In the months since I learned to use a computer and began to write my history, I have been able to read many great masterworks of human literature. Every morning, after the humans leave the house, I open one of those thick volumes and read it aloud to Hercule in the family room. Not only will reading these classic human works help me to raise the quality of my own feline writings, but I also feel that ultimately it is important for all of us to understand the human mind if we are to improve our relations with them, and what better way to accomplish this than to read the books that humans most value?

I have already completed *Pride and Prejudice* by Jane Austen and *David Copperfield* by Charles Dickens. Most recently, I have begun Laurence Sterne's great *Life and Opinions of Tristram Shandy, Gent.*, which was written in the middle of the eighteenth century and is widely considered to be the first modern experimental novel. It is doubtless the most difficult book I have yet tried to read, in both its archaic language and its difficult structure. Thus far, if the truth be told, Hercule and I hardly understand what is happening at all.

But I shall write more about my impressions of that book when we have finished reading it. I only thought it worth mentioning these books at this juncture because they have already had a great deal of influence on my way of thought, my way of writing and, indeed, on the very way I speak. A cat of culture and sophistication cannot communicate in base, plain terms, but must impress with his command of vocabulary and sentence structure. And I am now able to do that quite successfully, dear readers.

When I become tired of reading to Hercule, I go downstairs to get lunch. Afterward, I search the house looking for the best location to facilitate some quiet contemplation. It is my sincere belief, my fellow felines, that a warm patch of sunshine is the best tonic for the mind. The carpet by the basement door is my preferred spot when it is sunny; however, a pillow on one of the beds will suffice on dark, overcast days.

Whatever the locale, it is during this time that my mind races with thoughts of intellect and depth—except for when I am asleep, of course. For all you housecats out there who feel as if you are not reaching your potential in life, I say to you: Find a nice spot of sunshine (or a comfortable pillow, in a pinch), lie down and think about yourself. There is nothing more satisfying or intellectually invigorating than thinking about yourself. Consider your luxurious fur, your handsome face, your delicate whiskers, your strong paws. Think about the graceful arch of your back and your exquisite manner of moving. Remember, there is nothing so enriching in all the world as self-reflection, particularly for members of so elite a species as *Felis catus.*

In the afternoon, after I awaken from the rejuvenating snooze that inevitably imposes itself upon me during these periods of meditation, it is on to the computer to work on my masterpiece. My only regret in this endeavor is that my close friend Hercule cannot join me. Confined upstairs, he instead employs the time for his own artistic creations. I believe he would be of great help to me, considering his fantastic memory and his discerning mind. We do, of course, speak oftentimes about what I wish to convey in my work, but that is not the same as having my friend there right beside me, available for consultation concerning this word or that, or simply to encourage my progress. But alas, the burden of this exhausting yet exhilarating creative act is solely my own to bear. I cannot share the pleasure of it and I cannot share the pain. And so I labor in isolation, my dear cats, for your benefit. I hope you appreciate the sacrifice I make for you.

I always shut down the computer well before our caretakers' arrival home from work, making sure to save my documents in both a hidden place on the computer's hard drive and, for safety, at a site on the World Wide Web that provides free online storage (never fear, dear reader; I shall include instructions on how to accomplish this in *The Essential Cat's Guide to Computing*).

I do not believe that my caretakers harbor even the slightest suspicion that I know how to operate their computer. It is true that occasionally I leave the computer on out of a preoccupation with loftier matters. However, they inevitably invent what they believe to be plausible explanations and dismiss the problem with no further thought. I am thankful for the parade of relatives that ask to use their computer when they are here, for they often get the blame. But even when there is no human around to provide such easy explanations, Howie and Alicia simply assume that the other has forgotten to turn off the machine.

After working on the computer, I often go upstairs to converse with Hercule for some time. He tells me about his artistic project of the day, and I describe to him what I have written. We are generally deep in conversation when the humans arrive home, forcing us to separate and wait until the dark hours of the night to finish our discussion. Once the humans have returned, my aim is simply to hide from the frenetic young Lizzie until such time as she is put to bed, at which point I can emerge and reassert my presence.

So there is my day for you in a nutshell, so to speak. By design, there is very little variation, since I much prefer constancy over novelty when it comes to my daily arrangements. As I always say, a constant mind is a productive mind. Note, dear reader, these wonderfully useful aphorisms with which I am now practically bombarding you. How fortunate you are!

And now, I present to you a fruit of my productive mind: a poem of my own creation.

* * * * * * * * * *

An Ode to Nature
by Hastings

Oh, Nature, how beautiful thou art!
A line of birds soaring through the sky,
the graceful leap of a deer.
The smell of fresh cut grass,
it hath no peer.
If I were but a tree,
I would be so strong.
Patient, wise,
I would stand so long
against the breeze,
without a sneeze.
Oh Nature, oh Nature,
do I dare?
No, no,
nothing can compare!

* * * * * * * * * *

I set those few well-chosen words off in their own section in order to allow them to have their fullest impact. Read it once, read it again; let the words move you as deeply as they moved me to write them.

Yes, dear readers, I cried when I wrote that ode. Forgive me if it's not in code. My poetry is simple and honest. I don't abide complicated poetry—or any other kind of art, for that matter. I believe that the artist's task is to connect with the recipient as directly as possible. Of course, I wholeheartedly endorse the occasional healthy display of artistic bravado such as the skillful employment of superior language that peppers this very document. But a complicated, indecipherable set of words about Nature would hardly prove my point in this particular situation, would it? To be effective, the simplicity and beauty of my words must reflect the simplicity and beauty of my subject. That, and only that, is true poetry.

I do often ponder about the topic of this poem. Alas, my one regret concerning Nature is that I am unable to enjoy it more frequently than I do. The windows are not opened in this house nearly often enough for my tastes. I may be well-cared for and very content developing my intellect indoors, but there is nevertheless something deep in my being that attracts me to the world outside. I long to draw the fresh air into these nostrils, to chase the birds and squirrels and rabbits that live so freely outside these walls! Yes, dear friends, despite my better judgment, I sometimes cannot help but pine for the difficult life of a tomcat. I know that seems a ridiculous sentiment; you need not point out the irrationality in it. Yet there it is. I feel it. I have made remarkable progress in transforming myself into a cat of culture and erudition, but am nevertheless still faced with this conflict between my rational self and my natural urges.

Hercule does not share this problem. He is utterly convinced that one's natural instincts can and should be dismissed when they do not help to advance one's rational goals. I find this idea hard to accept, however, when it gives me such indescribable pleasure to simply look out the window or sniff the fresh air coming through the crack at the bottom of the window.

Murr wrote much about Nature in his book, but he provided little guidance for coping with its allures. In fact, Murr appeared to have succumbed to his natural instincts quite often when it would have served him better not to. I hope to provide better guidance for my fellow felines in this respect.

The human society all around us is, of course, the most prevalent model for managing the conflict between one's rational self and natural urges. The human approach, however, is to belligerently refuse to come to any sort of truce at all with one's natural tendencies. Little in their carefully constructed society reflects any connection whatsoever to their roots (so to speak) in the natural world. It is quite an accomplishment, really, when you consider the extent of their success. They have created completely artificial environments in which to work—cities full of office buildings that allow nary a glimpse into the world of Nature to distract them from their heady tasks. I have heard Howie, for instance, speak about how his office at work doesn't even have any windows. Do not faint from shock, my fellow felines, but people will actually willingly spend hours at work each day with no view of the outside world at all!

I cannot endorse this approach, by any means. How can there possibly be any shame for a living being in enjoying something so central to one's existence as sunshine and fresh air? Even if humans could find the means to construct cities so comprehensive that they removed all traces of the natural world from which they came, powerful reminders of human origins lurk deep within their very own breasts. I am speaking, of course, of their irrepressible attraction toward the opposite sex. Humans' attempts to apply their philosophy of detachment to personal interactions is, I maintain, more damaging to their psyches than their attempts to distance themselves from the natural world. The beauty of others is there for all to see, every minute of the day and every day of the week.

Humans have developed a remarkably complicated system of courtship to deal with this problem. Each human spends much time and effort in developing a set of standards for whom they will accept as a mate. For example, they may decide they would like a mate of a certain age, height and hair color, who follows one particular religion or participates in a favored sport. This method of choosing a mate effectively separates their decisions from the feelings in their hearts. It is very rational. It also has the effect of denying them time and again a mate who may be inherently, but unpredictably, compatible.

If you do not immediately see the folly of this human approach, I offer as evidence the astonishing degree of mental illness in human society. Mental illness in the feline world is virtually unheard of, but in the human world it is almost a badge of honor. People speak of their "therapy" so often, it might be mistaken for boasting. I hereby submit that the abnormally high levels of human depression, suicide and various anxiety disorders are a direct result of the suppression of their true Natures. I furthermore believe that their tendency toward violence stems from this suppression as well, driving the abhorrent frequency of heinous human crimes such as rape, murder, war and genocide. Dear readers, a creature's true Nature will always find a way of expressing itself somehow. The more ruthlessly it is repressed, the darker its eventual outcome is likely to be.

I believe it would be far better for humans to follow our example and openly acknowledge their physical attractions—nay, encourage them—by walking around without any clothing, at least when it is warm, and simply coupling with whomever they would like whenever the desire strikes. This would greatly clarify their feelings toward each other.

We do have much to learn from humans. Indeed, I condone the study of humans. They have developed their arts and sciences to levels which put our own to shame. But we must not imitate their follies. We can do better, my fellow felines.

Yes, I am envisioning a high society of our own to stand beside that of humans. I know we can create such a thing without making the mistakes that they have made. We will find a way to give our intellects and creativity room to grow in harmony with our true Natures.

I am determined to explore these ideas, my dear readers, and we shall all benefit from my findings.

* * * * * * * * *

After yesterday's admittedly lofty entry, allow me to return to more earthly, practical matters. I am constantly striving to find small, effective ways of improving my daily life. For example, I need not tell you that little could be more satisfying to a housecat than a clean, well-maintained litter box. But now I have discovered an even better arrangement: two litter boxes! This circumstance came about solely due to your narrator's own creative brilliance.

There is a rather large beige pot for a houseplant hidden away in a corner of the living room behind the unused upright piano. The plant has long been dead, the abandoned plastic pot now containing little more than dried earth and a shriveled stem. I happened to be lounging by the piano in a particularly warm patch of sunlight, rolling slightly every so often in order to stay in the warmth as the sun moved through the afternoon sky. I suddenly noted that the urge to relieve myself had been building for some time. I was perfectly happy where I was, however, and therefore quite reluctant to go all the way to the basement to use the litter box. I stretched to my full length—an action which can equally be either a prelude to

standing up or an interlude between two fine naps—
and tried to gauge how long I might be able to hold
off this call of Nature without getting up. It was then
that the forgotten houseplant pot suddenly caught
my eye and struck me with a revelation: the earth in
that pot would be the perfect receptacle for my
bodily wastes!

I stood up, more excited at this epiphany than
I have been in some time, and sauntered over to
the pot. I tested it out and found that it served quite
well as a secondary litter box.

You see, my friends, it is not necessary to rely
on our caretakers for everything. With some
thought and ingenuity, there is absolutely nothing
we cannot accomplish!

* * * * * * * * * *

Oh, sad day. I had been using my secondary
litter box for some days until last night, when Alicia
discovered it, decried its foul smell and had Howie
remove said creation. It seems that, in my
enthusiasm to cover my wastes, I propelled earth all
over the living room carpet, thereby tipping her off
to my activity. My heart is very heavy. It seems my
ingenuity is rebuffed at every turn.

* * * * * * * * * *

I have spent two days exacting my revenge on
Howie at every opportunity for his litter box
offense. You may question my focus on him when
it was Alicia who ordered the pot's removal, but

Howie is the one who committed the crime. You must target the action, not the intent, if you are to make clear to your caretakers what they have done wrong. I therefore attacked Howie's legs most aggressively.

His response at first was to grab me by the scruff and lock me briefly in a closet or bathroom until I had agreed to calm down. After several of these lockups, each of increasing duration, he finally employed the dreaded squirt bottle. That was an indication to me that the punishment I had already meted out to him was sufficient, and so I therefore ceased my aggression.

With respect to Howie's frequent grumblings about me since, they are little different from his usual grumblings about me. I sincerely doubt that he will bear me any long-term grudge.

* * * * * * * * *

A most disturbing thing occurred last night. I heard scratching and shuffling among the cabinets in the kitchen. I stalked the noise for hours, circling around the cabinets, crouching in readiness to pounce. Whatever the creature was, however, it declined to reveal itself.

"Come out and show yourself, you coward," I called, but there was no answer.

I have not slept a wink and consequently am too tired and upset to write any more. I must get to the bottom of this mystery.

* * * * * * * * * *

The scratchings and shufflings returned last night.

"Come out, please," I said in a soothing voice. "Tell me what you are. I'm just curious. I promise I won't hurt you."

"Liar!" came the response in a high squeak, sending a deadly chill up my spine. It was a mouse! Those vile, disgusting leeches of the mammalian genus. A mouse in my house!

I shouted, "You're right, you despicable, disease-carrying rodent! I was lying. Come out here and let me crack your spine to spare you the rest of your miserable existence."

"My existence isn't miserable," taunted the squeaky voice through the cabinet door. "I'm warm and comfortable, and there's plenty of food in here. Yes, I think I'll stay for a while."

"You disgusting, unhygienic parasite!" I cried. "You have no right to our food and warmth."

"There's plenty to go around here, you dumb cat."

"I am not dumb!" I meowed loudly.

"How would you know? You're too dumb to realize how dumb you are."

"That's it!" I shouted, and clawed furiously at the cabinets.

I could hear him laughing within, mocking me most cruelly as I continued to claw.

But such is the evil nature of mice. I have heard cautionary tales about these nefarious beasts ever since I was a kitten. The most horrifying of these suggested that cats and mice were somehow intimately connected, that there was a hidden bit of mouse in us all, buried deep in our minds and waiting to get out to ruin us. Indeed, there is nothing so central to the feline character as opposing these despicable creatures and all they represent.

And now I am faced with one of the damnable things myself. As it continued to taunt me, I knew I could not get inside that cabinet, but I resolved then and there that, one way or another, this vile creature would not be laughing for long.

* * * * * * * * * *

"Why are you so obsessed with this thing?" Hercule asked me this afternoon after what may, admittedly, have been an overly long tirade concerning the things I should like to do with the little mouse plaguing my mind.

"This is my house," I answered. "I am responsible for ensuring that no mouse can infest it."

"Tell me, what harm has the thing ever done to you?"

"Hercule, mice have been our sworn enemy since the beginning of time."

"I thought you were above all that, Hastings."

I shook my head. "I strive to rise above many of my base feelings—as you know, my dear friend—but this is one that I do not. Some aspects of our natures, however odious you may find them," I said pointedly, "are there for a good reason. Mice are dirty, vile, disgusting creatures. The urge to rid the world of their filth is part of our very essence. We could no longer cease hunting them than you could resist a bale of fresh hay."

Hercule frowned. "Really, Hastings, I don't see why you can't just leave him in peace. He hasn't done anything to you. This deep hatred makes no sense to me whatsoever."

"Life cannot always be about making sense, Hercule. We two are great friends, but we are still different in many ways. You are a pig of quiet contemplation. I," I declared, placing my paw upon my chest, "am a cat of action. I simply cannot let this mouse live in peace. He must be eliminated."

"You are talking about a living creature, you know. You did say he was a he, didn't you?"

"It was definitely a male voice."

"Then he may have a wife and children who depend on him."

"No mouse deserves the right to live," I maintained.

Hercule shook his long, triangular head from side to side. He looked very sad. "You frighten me sometimes, Hastings. We guinea pigs aren't such a far cry from mice. How do you decide where to draw the line?"

"You are completely different creatures," I assured him. "To the untrained eye, you may look somewhat similar, but a cat can easily tell you apart. To us, you are like night and day."

Hercule sighed in resignation. He knew he could not convince me to change my mind. I saw the disappointment in his face, but I was not about to change my mind to appease a friend, no matter how dear, in such a mistaken moment. For all Hercule's intelligence, there are some things that a guinea pig is simply incapable of understanding.

* * * * * * * * * *

It has been some days since I last wrote here. They were days of extreme stress and fatigue, but I am now once again well-rested and able to recount what transpired.

I heard my prey in the cabinet again the night after my conversation with Hercule and proceeded to stalk the beast while my caretakers were in the family room.

"He's chasing something," Alicia exclaimed, finally noticing my activity. Alicia has always been considerably more observant than the hapless Howie, who might have trouble recognizing the back of his hand. "I think we have mice," she guessed correctly, and I suddenly recognized an effective way to get at my nemesis.

I began to employ the most overt, histrionic methods of stalking, meowing, rolling on my back and clawing at the underside of the cabinet. I made such a fuss that my caretakers could not ignore the possibility that there might be something unusual in the cabinet. After a seemingly interminable discussion, they finally investigated and discovered the intruder's disgusting droppings within. This disturbed them very much, and the next day Howie not only worked at sealing the rear of the cabinets, but obtained what they call mouse traps.

At the time, I had little idea of how mouse traps worked. Howie placed a dab of peanut butter on a small lever at the center of each mechanism and positioned three of these traps in the cabinet under the sink, figuring, I suppose, that that was the entry point for the offensive beast.

Later that night, I heard the mouse squealing with delight again and again as he greedily ate the confections. "Oh, these people are so generous, they give me all this delicious food to eat," he taunted me. "How hospitable of them. I will definitely make this my permanent home now. I must go out and tell all my friends! Maybe they'd like to join me here."

"Laugh, you nefarious vermin!" I shouted. "Enjoy what little time you have!"

But even I little believed my own threats, and he continued to taunt me. "Please tell your owners to add a little cheese to my dinner plates next time," he said. "Cheese is a most delicious human food. One of their great accomplishments, in my opinion."

"I'll tell them nothing of the sort," I exclaimed. "And they are not my owners!"

"Oh, no," he said with mock fatigue. "Not another stupid slave cat who thinks he's free. You really are the dumbest creatures on earth. I do declare, how you got so stupid is beyond me. Even the groundhogs digging blindly in the ground all day long seem to have more intelligence."

"That's it!" I shouted, and lunged at the cabinet, clawing away at the wood most ferociously. This attack proved completely ineffectual, of course. But never fear, dear readers: I was to have my revenge.

* * * * * * * * * *

Howie and Alicia had grown upset at the lack of progress. The idea of a mouse living in their house was just as revolting to them as it was to me. Hercule, for his part, could not understand any of us.

"A mouse has as much of a right to live as any of the rest of us," he asserted one morning.

"Yes, I agree that all creatures deserve to live," I said, "except for mice."

Hercule turned away from me without comment and went about his business, seeing no humor in my witty remark. In truth, I feel sorry for being so harsh with my friend, but Hercule must understand how it is with mice. They are revolting things, and they simply do not deserve to live.

That evening, to my dismay, Howie said that he was not going to "bait" the traps, meaning put on the peanut butter, because he was too tired. "They're not working anyway," he said in frustration.

Later that night, with a sinking heart, I heard our intruder in the cabinet under the sink again.

"What? No food?" he squeaked. "Tell your masters to come down here at once! Where's my dinner?"

"You despicable parasite!" I hissed through the wood.

"No, wait, there is actually a little bit here that I neglected to see yesterday. It wasn't quite on the platter here; that's why I missed it."

There was a sudden bang from within the cabinet—a loud snap may be a better description—and then utter silence.

"Hello?" I called. "Are you in there? What happened?"

I heard not a peep, not a shuffle from within. "Hello?" I called again, but got no more of a response than before. I wondered if perhaps the mouse trap had somehow worked after all. I sat there listening for some time before I eventually gave up my watch.

I spent the next day worrying and wondering what had happened until Howie finally opened the cabinet that evening to get something out and exclaimed, "Oh my god. We got it! I don't believe it."

I watched with satisfaction as he put on rubber gloves and removed the mouse from the trap. It was a vile thing: gray, flaccid and putrid-smelling. He dropped the carcass into the garbage and that was the end of it.

We all celebrated that night. All except my best friend, of course.

"Come now, Hercule," I said, "this is a time for celebration."

"I'm sorry, Hastings, but it's just not right to celebrate the death of a fellow creature, no matter how despicable you think he was. Death comes to each of us some day, and it is never a cause for celebration."

"I don't want to argue with you, but I just can't agree," I said, and left him to himself. Whatever my friend's opinion, I know I have done a praiseworthy job, outwitting and ultimately eliminating our intruder. I take pride in my achievement and actually find myself looking forward to my next encounter with this nefarious species.

* * * * * * * * * *

I wish it were possible for me to keep a daily log of events, but that is not always the case. One situation that precludes my writing every day, for example, is when there are visitors to the house. This past weekend, in fact, we were visited by the most abhorrent creatures. And . . . I am almost ashamed to admit this fact . . . the worst thing about it was that they were cats!

Their names are Cuddles and Teddy, and they came for a visit with Howie's parents from out of town, Grams and Gramps. When these nefarious beasts first stepped through the front doorway on their leashes, I exclaimed quite involuntarily, "Uch, what are you creatures?" In retrospect, perhaps it was not the nicest of greetings, but I was truly taken aback and repulsed by their appearance. Their filthy, matted white hair was so long it actually brushed the ground, and their faces . . . oh, how to begin to describe the deformity?

"We're cats," one of them said in a haughty tone. "What do you think we are, dummy?"

"Cats? You look like no cats I've ever seen," I retorted. "What's happened to your faces? Have you been in some kind of an accident?"

"What happened to your face?" he shot back at me. "Was your mother crossed with a dog or a mouse?"

"A dog?!" I cried. "A mouse?!" I'd never been so insulted in my life. I lunged at the offender with my claws out and ready to slash, but Alicia instantly picked me up and started squeezing me lovingly as she often does, restraining me with forced affection.

"You'd better lock them in the room upstairs," Howie said to Gramps.

"Come on, Cuddles," Gramps called to the one who had insulted me. The other, Teddy--the fearful creature--was already in Gramps' arms. Cuddles ignored Gramps' summons, however, and continued to look down his nose at me—if it could be said that he had a nose to look down, that is, the thing was so flattened against his face. I pleaded with Alicia to let me go teach the snooty cat a lesson, but to no avail. She would not relent.

"Come on," Gramps tugged Cuddles' leash.

"I want to go anyway," Cuddles finally said to me. "I'm tired of looking at that ghastly face of yours."

At that, he turned and displayed his rear to me, then strutted away up the stairs.

You can imagine the anger with which I watched those two ascend the stairs. Insulting me in my own house!

As soon as Alicia released me, I bounded upstairs and installed myself outside the door of the guest room, where the culprits were being housed. No, dear readers, I could not let these abhorrent creatures rest. I resolved that, like the mouse I so effectively dealt with, these intruders must learn who was in charge of this house.

I remained outside their door, making threatening scratches against the door every so often to remind them of the formidable threat they faced. "Come out, you squashed-face freaks," I called.

"Go away, please," a meek voice pleaded from the other side of the door. It was the first time I'd heard Teddy's voice. "Why do you keep torturing us?"

"Oh please," Cuddles answered loudly so that I could hear through the door. "Do you really think this idiotic creature can harm us? These indoor tomcat wannabes are all talk and no action."

"Come outside and see my action," I threatened with another scratch at the door.

"Do you know who we are?" Cuddles asked. "Your behavior is totally inappropriate, considering our respective situations."

"I know who you are," I growled back. "You're two long-haired, smashed-face intruders in my territory."

"We," Cuddles proclaimed proudly from the other side of the door, "are Persians."

The words hit me like a wall you run into when you're chasing something real juicy like a fat gray mouse and forget to look where you're going.

"Persians!" I said involuntarily.

"Yes, Persians," he echoed. "Royalty."

Of course! I smacked my forehead with my paw for not realizing. I'd never seen a Persian before, but Persians are legendary in the cat world for just the features I have described. Among all the types of cats in the world, from lions and tigers to the common housecat, Persians are physically unique. Their faces actually have a different structure than the rest of ours, and so many do consider them royalty. Needless to say, I am not one of them. Where a cheek bone is placed or how long the cartilage in the nose extends from the facial surface is of little consequence to me.

"Persian?" I said in a deviously friendly tone after I'd recovered from my surprise. "I was not aware of that. What an honor to have you in my house."

"Yes, it must be," Cuddles said. "Although it is hardly an honor for us to be locked up in this stuffy place. Teddy, stop cowering, please. This housecat was simply too dumb to recognize royalty before. Now that he understands who we are, he'll afford us the respect we deserve."

"Of course I will," I assured him, unsheathing my claws and checking their sharpness.

"You see, Teddy? You have nothing to fear from this common housecat."

"No," I purred in my most reassuring voice, "there's nothing at all to fear from me."

* * * * * * * * * *

I maintained my vigil that evening and all through the ensuing night, leaving my post at the top of the stairs only to go down to use my litter box or to get a quick sip of water. I said nothing more to the vile beasts, and if they even knew I was there they ignored me.

But I was to have my opportunity. The next morning, Gramps said he was taking them out for a walk—as if they were dogs! Their leashes on, they trotted out of the room with Gramps, and I greeted them immediately.

"So, you've come to see us off, have you?" Cuddles said upon seeing me.

"Yes, I have," I said. "I wish you a good trip."

"We'll be back shortly. Our servant is just taking us out for some fresh air."

"Come on, Cuddles," Gramps said, tugging his leash. "Let's go."

"Don't you think it undignified for royalty such as yourself to be bound by a leash?" I asked.

Cuddles held his ground against Gramps' tugs as he asked me, "And what do you know of it? How often do you get to go outside, pray tell?"

Seeing the distress that overtook my face, Cuddles finally let himself be led away. Having stumbled upon a way to hurt me, he walked with an air of satisfaction about him.

I was furious with myself for letting him see this weakness. I went down to the basement and watched them through the sliding glass door. It would be a lie for me to say I wasn't envious. They may not have been able to roam free, but they were clearly enjoying the outdoors and their intimate relations with the natural world.

I watched longingly as they took their time to explore anything that suited them. It wasn't fair for a superior feline such as myself to be locked up inside while these cats were treated like royalty, gently led around the garden and allowed to do whatever suited their fancy: smell a flower, scratch their claws in the earth, splash urine on the ground. They enjoyed this privilege not because of anything they had accomplished through hard work and perseverance, but merely because of the novelty of their grotesquely smashed faces and impracticably long hair.

I seethed as I witnessed their humiliation of me. That these cats should know my own backyard better than I! It was a crime, I thought, an offense against all cats that these freaks of nature should be treated so loftily.

When finally they left the backyard, I ran upstairs again and stationed myself at the living room window nearest the door. They seemed so happy as they rounded the corner of the house and came toward the front door. I could see them chatting excitedly with each other about the things they had seen and done, refreshed and satisfied by their excursion. If I heard properly through the closed window, there was some excitement concerning a large katydid. My heart was heavy, but I resolved as the front door swished open that I would reveal nothing of my envy in my face.

"So," Cuddles said to me as he stepped into the house, "we had a wonderful time. Did you see us?"

"No," I answered casually. "I hadn't noticed."

"That's funny; I thought I saw you watching us through the basement window door."

"I thought I'd seen a rabbit," I cleverly responded, "but then I realized it was you."

Now, as we continued our clever verbal fencing, I was cognizant of a very interesting fact: after Gramps had closed the door behind him, the man had started to undo their leashes right there in the front hallway. My eyes brightened as I noted this, and I could see the fear dawning in Cuddles' eyes as he became aware of the situation as well. Teddy, for his part, was already shielding himself behind Gramps' legs. But I knew that Cuddles, now freed, wouldn't dare to try and bolt away from me. He was too proud for that.

I nodded toward his collar, "It seems you're free from your leash."

"Yes, it does," he tried to say calmly.

"Tell me," I asked, "exactly what kind of royalty are you?"

"Huh?"

"Are you a king?" I asked. "A prince? A queen?" My voice grew more threatening as I continued. "Or are you perhaps a jester...."

He suddenly bolted for the stairs in panic, and I took up the chase. He ran directly to the guest room, with me right on his tail. The humans were shouting for me to stop, but I wouldn't hear of it. Cuddles dashed underneath the bed. He was already panting heavily, the porcine thing, but I raced after him into the dark, musty space.

"Uch!" I suddenly reeled back. "What is that smell?"

"What smell?" he wheezed, cowering in the corner and welcoming the respite my question afforded him.

I backed out of the darkness and into the light of the room. "Come to think of it, this whole room smells," I observed. I looked at him suspiciously as it dawned on me what I was smelling. "That's urine!"

"What's urine?"

"The smell in here, you vile creature. You don't know how to use your litter box, do you?"

"Of course we know how to use our litter box," he said with an air of arrogance. "We just don't always choose to use it."

"Don't choose to use it?" I cried, aghast.

"And why should we? Our servants clean up any mess we make. We quite like the smell."

"No self-respecting cat would ever soil their own environment with their excretions!"

"I assure you, we have a great deal of self-respect."

Cuddles looked past me, and I could tell by the relief in his eyes that the humans were observing us. I had been so overcome with emotion that I hadn't even noticed the sounds of their arrival.

"In fact," Cuddles continued, emboldened by the presence of the humans, "even as we speak, we've left a little gift for our servants in their bed, a reminder of just who is in charge here."

"You peed in the bed too?" I exclaimed.

"Pee?" he laughed. "No, they'll lie in bed tonight and find a little brown lump under the covers."

"That's outrageous!"

"Ha, yes, it is!"

"You despicable creature!" I shouted, unsheathing my claws in fury. But Howie was immediately upon me. He grabbed me by the scruff and lifted me up before I could even brace myself to move into that putrid space under the bed.

"Hastings," my caretaker said to me, "don't kill Grams' and Gramps' cats."

"And why not?" I meowed at him. "Do you know what they're doing in our home?"

"They're our guests, Hastings," he frowned. "We don't kill our guests."

My opinion of the matter, needless to say, differed from that of my naïve caretakers.

* * * * * * * * * *

Well, the Persians have now gone, and we are all much happier. I watched last night from the doorway as Howie and Alicia cleaned the guest room after they put Lizzie to bed. Ordinarily, I would investigate for changes in the room, or perhaps hide in the sheets to practice my pouncing as they stripped the bed. But even if I hadn't known what was in that bed, the odor within the room was too ripe to allow for such frivolity.

"My god, it stinks in here," Howie said.

"I think their cats pee outside their litter box," Alicia answered.

"It figures."

"Oh, my god," Alicia suddenly shrieked as she peeled back the sheets.

"What?"

"Is that a poop?"

"Where?"

"Look," Alicia said, pointing at a thin dark brown tube almost precisely at the center of the bed.

"Uch, god."

"I can't believe your mother slept in that and didn't even notice."

"I can believe anything about them," Howie said.

And so could I, my fellow felines, so could I. I have now lived long enough to realize that humans are capable of any degree of self-delusion. How two people could obviously love and care for two such odious, despicable creatures as those deformed Persians is beyond my capability to understand. Yet they do. Cuddles and Teddy will continue to be treated like royalty for years to come, I am quite certain, no matter how many poops they leave in the bed.

I have had a sad realization, dear readers, and that is that life is not fair. Whereas success rightly should not depend on whose womb you grew within, the sad reality is that we are all brought into this earth with a set of restrictions. These include the structure of our faces, the length of our hair, the color of our eyes and a number of other things that are well beyond our control. Such injustices would be bothersome enough within the feline world itself, but we who live among humans may be subject to the whims and biases of any person, no matter how foolish, under whose power we happen to fall. These people know nothing of what is inside our hearts. They do not care to know.

And yet, dear readers, I am persuaded that hard work, creativity and clear accomplishment will enable us to rise above this miserable situation we find ourselves in. I am confident that, one day, we who strive for greater things will outshine the likes of Cuddles and Teddy.

Our very success, my fellow felines, will be our revenge.

* * * * * * * * * *

Our recent visitors have led me to ponder the many obvious deficiencies in feline culture. There is no set of ethical standards that we follow, no moral code for us to consult. In my self-education, I have found absolutely nothing to guide me in my moral or intellectual development as a cat.

I have been considering this problem and, being a cat of a somewhat unusual level of culture and education, I have concluded that perhaps I should take matters into my own paws and rise to the occasion by providing the feline world with such a thing myself. I raised the topic with Hercule this morning after the family had left for the day.

"Hercule," I ventured, "Cuddles and Teddy have made me think about all the cats living out there without any direction."

"It does sound like they need direction," he said distractedly, busy building a large sort of tepee in the middle of his cage.

Our caretakers have been testing different types of hay on Hercule of late, and their varying physical characteristics have opened up exciting new artistic possibilities for him. The orchard grass, for example, proved to be more pliable than the usual Timothy hay, and so lend itself better to projects involving the weaving of sheets. Hercule was able to construct the most spectacular-looking huts with it, as well as a series of abstract curving sheets in varying shapes and sizes, reflecting a very modern, minimalistic style that would be at home in any contemporary art museum. Of late, Hercule has been emptying his hay rack as soon as our caretakers fill it. They think he loves the taste of each new hay because the rack is so quickly emptied. What they fail to suspect is that their cute little guinea pig is actually spreading the hay across the floor of his home in order to consider what his next project will be, and that as soon as they leave the house he will set busily to work.

It is wonderful to see my friend so engaged in an artistic pursuit, and I believe his accomplishments grow more impressive each day as he discovers new methods and techniques with which to work the different hays. At present, our caretakers have been giving him oat straw, and Hercule has taken advantage of the long, stiff nature of this variety to make structures that stand as tall as the top of his home. They are quite dramatic when you come upon them.

Hercule was in the process of building such a structure as I began our conversation. He will not stop even to take a drink from his bottle as he feverishly works at his creations, yet Hercule always has time to speak with me as he labors.

"I have been considering," I continued, "that I might be in a unique position to provide some direction for my fellow felines."

"Well, that's what you're doing with your memoirs, isn't it?"

"Yes, I suppose, in a way. My memoirs are meant to inspire other cats to achieve the higher things I have achieved in my own life. But I think cats need more than that."

"Like what?" he asked, selecting a piece of straw for his tepee. "What are you thinking of, Hastings?"

"I believe what the feline world really needs is a manual."

"Like the essential cat series you've conceived," he said as he stepped back to consider where to insert the straw in his structure.

"Yes, I suppose, although the idea doesn't thrill me for some reason. *The Essential Cat's Guide to Life*; it just doesn't sing to me."

"No, I don't see how it could," he said distractedly.

"What do you mean?"

"Well," he said, finally pausing his work to look at me, "who would buy a manual about how to live? Could you imagine Cuddles reading it? Everyone thinks their way of life is the right way. Even humans, as full of self-doubt as they are, are always trying to impose their ideas on other people. They call it 'politics.' A nasty business, it seems. Don't you hear our caretakers talking about it all the time?"

"You know I ignore most of their conversations, Hercule."

"Their conversations can be very informative," he admonished me, turning back to study his tepee.

"I don't have the patience for it."

Hercule frowned but didn't comment further. "Humans often try to impose their ideas about how to live on others," he explained, "but it rarely works out the way they intend. Just the other night, Howie and Alicia were watching a television show about the history of alcoholic drinks—wine, beer and the like. There was a period called prohibition, when some people tried to tell others that they couldn't drink anything with alcohol in it."

"Telling each other what to drink? That's outrageous!"

"Yes, it is. There was a horrible amount of violence until they were finally allowed to drink what they wanted again. There are all sorts of things some people don't want to allow others to do: to listen to certain music, do certain activities, even have certain types of relationships. I hear our caretakers discussing these things all the time. It's quite a remarkable phenomenon."

I exclaimed, "Creatures should be allowed to do whatever they want to!"

*Hercule always has time to speak
with me as he labors.*

"Well, within limits, of course."

"No, Hercule! No limits! Creatures should be free to do whatever they want."

"But what if they want to kill, Hastings? What if all they want to do is hurt others? Some creatures do have such tendencies, you know."

"Ah," I said, suddenly backing down from my position. "I see your point."

"That's why humans have laws," he said.

"Well, I don't see how we could impose laws on other cats. How could you prevent a cat from defecating in a bed if he wants to?" I sighed and shook my head. "Incidentally, did I tell you that I distinctly noticed a brown smear on the fur near Teddy's rear?"

"Yes, you did tell me that." Hercule frowned. He turned back to consider his tepee once more, and finally decided on a place to put the piece of straw he had been holding.

"I suppose he'll try to clean it off with his tongue," I continued. "I saw them trying to clean themselves once while they were here. It was the most pitiful thing to see their tongues stroking that long, pee-soaked, matted hair. They made no progress whatsoever. It was a completely futile exercise."

"Hastings, please don't waste my time talking about those two despicable creatures," he pleaded as he weaved the straw into his structure. "I have a great deal of work to do, and they don't interest me in the least. All I will say is that whatever humans bred an animal to be so wretched deserve to be thrown into jail."

"Strong words, indeed, Hercule."

"Yes, my boy. Now, let me say that I feel very strongly about everything you've said concerning those creatures, but I prefer to stick to the matter at hand. Going back to that topic, I don't believe that any laws could work to alter feline behavior. You cats are much too spirited and individualistic for that. No, Hastings, what you need is fear," he concluded, satisfied at the straw's placement and turning back to me.

"Fear? I don't see how I could go around threatening every cat that misbehaved. That didn't even work with Cuddles. I'm just not that intimidating."

He shook his head. "You need something much deeper, Hastings. Something that inspires a more primal fear. Something like that book humans call the Bible."

"I'm a bit familiar with it," I said. "They mention it all the time."

Hercule nodded. "It seems to me that it does as much to alter human behavior as any of their laws. The people who wrote it must have been absolutely brilliant. This book postulates the existence of an all-seeing, all-knowing, all-powerful and very wrathful god that desires certain behaviors from humans. For the most part, they comply. Many people even believe that every word in it is true. It's proven to be quite influential in human society over the years."

"So you're saying that I should write something equivalent for cats?"

"Absolutely."

"What an interesting idea," I said, putting my paw to my chin and pondering the pussibilities (Get it? Puss-ibilities, meaning possibilities for a feline! How uncharacteristic of me to make a joke here in this serious document. This is a sure sign of how absolutely euphoric I am at this brilliant new idea!).

We subsequently spoke at length about what such a document might contain. How could I strike fear into the heart of cats? And then how might I channel that fear so that it resulted in exemplary behavior? We eventually concluded that we must read through the Bible first before deciding how to proceed with my project. Although we have lately been working through *Life and Opinions of Tristram Shandy, Gent.* during our reading time, I suspect that Hercule will not grieve for me to put it aside.

We must read the Bible for a higher purpose.

* * * * * * * * * *

The weather has grown cold and the leaves are falling from the trees. These are the times that encourage scholarly pursuit and, indeed, we have been reading the Bible for more than three weeks now. I have been meaning to write about our revelations for some time, but working through this text is quite exhausting in itself. With the shorter, overcast days, it has been particularly difficult for me to motivate myself to come downstairs and write after the cerebral strain of the mornings.

We had gotten as far as the end of Leviticus this morning when Hercule suddenly exclaimed,

"Enough, Hastings! We've already learned about their covenant and the laws set down by their god, but there must be at least a thousand pages left. I can't stand another word of it!"

"But, Hercule, I want to understand what drives these people."

"There are other religious books too, Hastings," he cried. "Do you mean to read them all?"

"That's not a bad idea," I mused.

"Yes, it is!" he exclaimed. "If you're going to read any more, Hastings, please count me out."

I stared at my friend in shock. "You can't be serious."

He nodded emphatically. "I've never been more serious in my life. I can't endure any more of it."

"Well, I guess I will have to continue on my own, then," I said, hurt.

"I'm very sorry, old friend," Hercule softened, "but it's not only the length of it. It's the grandiosity. It's the arrogance of these people to believe that they have been selected over others by some higher being even though they've done nothing to deserve it. This is just too much for a guinea pig to bear."

"I understand, Hercule," I said, trying to hide my disappointment. "There's no need to apologize. But does it not excite you?"

"No, not any longer. In fact, not for a great many pages. We've already learned why it's lasted so long as a part of their culture. It strikes fear of a wrathful, all-powerful god in their hearts, yet it also makes them feel special about themselves. It tells them that they've been chosen by this all-knowing being for a great historic destiny, whatever their individual merits. Thus, the limits to their behavior that are being dictated to them become a very part of their preordained superiority. It's quite a brilliant work of psychology, I must admit."

"It is," I agreed.

"But the more of it I hear," Hercule continued, "the more convinced I become that you need to take an altogether different approach in your work. I don't think that this sort of thing would influence the feline mind in the way you would like."

"Perhaps," I said, my paw scratching my chin in concentration. "Perhaps you're right, Hercule. But I do want to read a little more before I completely commit to that conclusion. If I am to write something equally influential for the feline world, I must understand as much as I can about this book."

"Well, I wish you all the luck, then, but I won't be joining you for the rest of it. My own art calls me now."

And so, my dear readers, I continue to plow on by myself.

* * * * * * * * * *

Snow is now upon the ground. No matter how many times one sees that soft white blanket descend, the first snow of the year never fails to impose a sense of wonder and awe. It came this year, as it often does, at night, brightening the sky with its orange-tinted reflection of the lights below. Now it is daytime, and the sun has already begun melting the white layer that separates the blades of grass from their precious sunlight.

I found over these past several weeks that the shortening days of autumn somewhat blunted my incentive. However, I continued to trudge through those stories of old until The Book of Joshua, at which point I began to lose my interest completely. Spies and slaughter and tales of conquest just do not excite this refined intellect. It is braggadocio at its worst. Hercule would have hated it. I simply stopped reading.

I did want to understand more of the Bible, however, and I regretted my inability to persevere for the sake of intellectual curiosity. I thought for a time that I had been defeated by something too great for my growing abilities. That was an insult almost too great to bear. But then, as I casually browsed the bookcases thinking what I might read next, wondering what could lure Hercule into joining me once again for our reading sessions, I came upon something absolutely brilliant. It was called *Bible Stories for Children*! These stories handily summarize those in the Bible, providing virtually everything a discerning reader might wish to know.

I have read about Job. I learned about Jesus. I have, in fact, studied all the stories of the Bible. It is finally time for me to turn to the task of writing my own mythical religious document for cats.

I would first, however, like to record several observations concerning the Bible that bear consideration as I embark on my own effort, which you shall soon see for yourself. The first and most obvious thing to note about the Bible is that it is a very curious blend of fact and fiction. It seems to me that this particular concept may be crucial in the design of my own masterpiece. Many events in this book may very well have taken place—for example, the general movements of peoples at the times indicated, or the flood in Genesis. From this terrifying flood that may in fact have occurred, you see, someone was able to craft a very good story with a valuable lesson.

"But wait!" you might say. "What do you mean by calling this a fiction? Many humans insist that every word in this document is true." To that, my dear reader, I say that this story is, at heart, most definitely a fiction, and I can prove it thus:

If indeed Noah took two and only two of every animal, how in the world was he able to keep them from eating each other? What two cheetahs in the world could coexist with other animals on an ark for forty days and forty nights? What two lions? What two tigers? What about anacondas and wolves and those countless other cruel and carnivorous species? No, this is simply not possible. How would Noah possibly have fed them all? Did he take along other animals too, only to be used as food? No, my dear reader, I have proven it. That is only one of many examples I have found proving that the Bible most definitely contains fictions. There is no doubt about it.

Nevertheless, my aim here is not to debate theology. It is to understand the power of this book. And while many humans blindly accept the truth of everything in it despite all its internal contradictions, my understanding is that a very sizable number of humans who consider themselves quite devoted to this book concede that it does not contain literal truths about all of the things it describes. Rather, they believe that many of the stories are allegories and fables. The Bible, these people maintain, is largely metaphorical.

It seems to me that the main lesson I must take from this book is that fiction can be more persuasive than truth. It took me some time to reach this conclusion because it is counterintuitive to an analytical mind such as my own. After extensive discussions with Hercule, however, I have come to realize that any description of even the most realistic event must have a rigorous control of perspective if it is to have any chance of influencing behavior. This memoir itself, for example, while readers may indeed find it interesting and instructive as an example of the things they might do to enrich their own lives, cannot be expected to mold feline behavior in any significantly predictable manner. Readers may draw inspiration from one section or another and then set off on their own course, but there is no reason for them to follow the particular course I have chosen. The necessity for an altogether different kind of document, therefore, seems ever clearer.

While I strive for something as powerful for our feline species as the Bible is for humans, I believe that Hercule was correct in saying that I will need to take an altogether different approach. I can't simply translate that document into something more accessible to the feline world—for example, by making Noah a tabby named Puddles. Cats very well might respond to the flattery and assumptions of superiority in that book, but they will not be frightened by it—and that is a large part of the Bible's influence over humans.

For it has become apparent to me that central to the effect of the Bible is the idea of an all-knowing, all-powerful entity called God. However, cats would simply not accept such a postulation. There is nothing in our culture to support it. It is true that we might occasionally evoke the ancient Egyptian god Bastet in exclamations—as in, "Great Bastet, dear kitty!"—but Bastet was a god created by humans to worship; we do not worship her so much as take her name in vain, although some have adopted her as a trite symbol of feline power.

No, if I were to try to create the true equivalent of a human god for cats, my effort would fail immediately. The typically practical tom would never accept the existence of such an entity without that entity itself standing in front of him and admonishing him for his disbelief. The "suspension of disbelief" which my caretaker Howie sometimes mentions when discussing his fiction simply could not be stretched so far in the analytically superior feline mind.

So what should I create? We cats do not have a tradition of formal fiction as humans do. We may tell tales about things such as neighborhood legends and caretaker histories that might, in the matter of course, become distorted in repeated retellings. There are also the oft-told mouse stories to consider, which strike fear into the hearts of cats everywhere. These enjoyable stories inevitably contain warnings for young cats about our natural enemies, but they do not affect behavior in any deeply meaningful way.

There is but one precedent that I can think of for a true precautionary tale meant to affect a specific feline behavior. Every cat knows it, of course: the story of Tobermory, the cat of extraordinary intelligence who learned human speech. This story was even written down for humans—by a man who called himself Saki, a.k.a. H.H. Monro.

As I am sure you are all well aware, my fellow felines, there are several different versions of this tale. In rough outline, it goes thus: Tobermory, as do we all, knows things that the humans around him would be loath to have revealed. When he exposes his ability to speak, the humans are at first amazed. However, Tobermory unwisely proceeds to reveal the particulars of several conversations that have taken place behind closed doors. The humans immediately decide that he must be done away with. Most of our versions end with the humans carrying out their plan to poison the unfortunate cat, but the version that Saki tells spares them the need to execute their gruesome plan, by having Tobermory conveniently fall to another tom. Many a cat has argued over which version is true, and some even claim that the whole story is a fiction, but one thing is clear: whichever version is fact and whichever fiction, the horrible fate of Tobermory has effectively frightened many a cat from ever revealing an ability to understand human communication.

But Tobermory's tale is a simple recounting of a story that is substantially true. Can a complete, extended work of fiction function in this manner? I believe that it depends upon how well it is done. This much is clear, however: Cats need their own mythology. That is what we are missing. And I have decided to create it.

I have been thinking long and hard about what I might call such a thing. I have considered titles like *The Bible for Kittens* or *The King Hastings Bible*. But these might strike the human mind as satirical works, and if we seek to improve our relations with that species in the future, it would be wise for me not to associate my work too closely with that cherished human document.

No, this must be a great work in and of itself, and so it must have its own unique title. After considering countless possibilities, I have finally arrived at one. It is simple—a single word commonly used, a word describing something that provides us physical sustenance, something that is absolutely essential to our daily survival. It is, in short, the perfect title for a book that will provide essential spiritual sustenance to our daily lives.

I shall call it: *The Kibble!*

* * * * * * * * * *

I have been laboring over *The Kibble* for some days now. I must confess that fiction is surprisingly difficult to craft. It is certainly more difficult than what I have thus far attempted. I now have an appreciation for the painful struggles Howie goes through during those early morning writing sessions. I once looked down upon his attempts with a patronizing disdain. Now I know that every single word counts in a work of fiction. Each phrase must be painstakingly constructed in order to evoke the desired effect. It is difficult work, but it is exhilarating as well.

Enough talk, you say! Let us see the first chapter of this thing already!

I have been working on it for some days now, my dear readers, and it is finally completed. And so, I present to you the beginning of a book that will change the world.

* * * * * * * * * *

The Kibble
Beginnings

Once in an indeterminate time, there were two cats living comfortably in a grand palace. Revered throughout the kingdom of humans as rare creatures with mysterious powers, they were treated like royalty by the King and Queen and all of their subjects.

Their names were Elis and Ulla, and they had everything they could possibly want. There were not one, not two, but three full bowls of dry food, one on every floor, with another bowl filled with fresh water beside each. There were three litter boxes, one on each floor as well, always in the same room as the food and water but not so close as to become unappetizing. There were scratching posts of every kind, from simple flat cardboard strips hung from door handles to intricate freestanding carpeted platforms. There were fake birds stuffed with catnip, trays full of cat grass and false mice for swatting scattered everywhere.

They lazed at their leisure in the sun all day. They were brushed at night. They loved each other very much and were very happy in general. But all was not right.

The two of them longed to be free. They longed to run among the trees outside the palace walls, to chase the birds, rabbits, squirrels and mice they saw through the palace windows. They longed to breathe the fresh air into their lungs, to feel the wind against their fur, the rain falling on their backs. But they accepted their lot in life because that is how it was and they saw no way to change it.

Now, the mouse is a cunning creature. One day, Ulla found one in the cellar and cornered it. She called Elis, and they loomed over the mouse as it cowered in the corner.

"You poor cats," said the mouse.

"Poor?" said Elis. "It is you who are about to die."

"I just see the way you live here and it makes me so sad."

"Sad?" Ulla said. "But we have everything a cat could ever want."

"Everything?" said the mouse. "But you have no freedom."

Elis and Ulla knew that the mouse spoke the truth. "But what can we do?" they exclaimed. "We are stuck here, it is true, but we get everything we need."

"You can escape," the mouse suggested.

"Escape?"

"Why, yes. When the gate is opened, you can run across the bridge and then keep on running until you are far away from here. You are much faster than those humans. They would never be able to catch you."

Elis and Ulla began to discuss it between themselves, and eventually concluded that the mouse was right; they might be able to escape from the palace with this plan. But when they turned back to the mouse to thank him for his insight, he was gone. Taking advantage of the distraction he had created, the mouse had escaped with his life.

The seed of the idea that the mouse had planted in their heads quickly took root. The cats' longing to run free in the open air grew stronger and stronger with each day. They tried to convince themselves that what they had in their comfortable palace was more than enough to make them happy. But one day, the urge finally grew too strong for them to resist. They decided to escape.

The execution of their plan was simple. Cats are superior creature in both mind and body, and so when they dashed out through the gate and pumped their legs as fast as they could to get away, there was little hope for the humans who had cared for them so tenderly for so long to save Elis and Ulla from themselves.

They soon found themselves deep within a forest with no sign that anyone was still in pursuit. When they were satisfied that they were alone, they finally stopped to catch their breath.

"Where are we?" asked Ulla.

"I don't know," Elis answered.

Just then, a fox appeared from behind a bush and exclaimed, "Ah, you are just in time for dinner!"

"Run," screamed Elis, and he and Ulla ran away as fast as they could, the fox in close pursuit.

"Up in a tree," Ulla directed, and they scrambled up the nearest trunk with some difficulty, since they had never climbed a tree before.

"You have excaped this time," the fox snarled, "but I shall get you the next."

"Let's go back to the palace, where we were revered and treated like royalty," Ulla said once the fox had gone, her voice still trembling with fear.

Elis agreed. "We should never have done this," he said. "That crafty mouse convinced us to escape because he knew we would be killed out here and he'd be safe in there. I would like to have my revenge on that scoundrel! But which way is it back home?"

In the excitement of the escape and the subsequent flight from the fox, Elis and Ulla had been turned around so many times, they now had no idea how to get back to their former home. They climbed down from the tree and began to explore, but nothing looked familiar to them. The sights, sounds and smells were all completely foreign.

"What are we going to do?" Ulla cried after they had been searching fruitlessly for some hours.

"I don't know, my love. I don't know."

They never did find the way back to their old kingdom. And so Elis and Ulla were forced to live the rest of their lives in what came to be known to them as The Lost Forest, scrounging for their own food, drinking dirty water from puddles, running for their lives on a regular basis from all the larger predators of the forest.

Worst of all, the two cats were doomed to search endlessly for a paradise they had left purely of their own accord.

* * * * * * * * * *

I am very proud of this work and believe "Beginnings" provides a solid basis for the rest of *The Kibble*. As significant as it may ultimately prove to be in the relations of cats, however, I must document a recent bit of news which has just made itself known to me: Alicia is pregnant again!

One must wonder why.

Humans, as some of you may know, are able to choose when they would like to have children. It is a most fascinating phenomenon, the upshot of which, when they do have children, one may legitimately ponder the reasons for it. In the feline world, of course, the tom mounts the kitty when the urge strikes, there are kittens some period of time later, and no one thinks much about it at all. In the human world, however, they deliberate at great length and carefully plan for such an event.

Now, after experiencing such a clamorous creature as Lizzie, it is altogether unclear to me how my caretakers believe we could possibly tolerate another. Why would they wish to inflict yet another such series of insults to our senses?

Hercule says that he heard our caretakers discussing the matter one evening. This is Howie's fault, apparently. He told Alicia that if she wanted another child, he didn't want to wait any longer. "Let's get it over with," I believe were his words. He must not be aware that waiting can be employed as a cunning strategy, re: One can wait until it is too late. I must send him a memo on the matter.

I jest about the memo, of course. One must not give away the game. Imagine Howie's reaction upon reading a memo from his cat. But I am very cross with him and have been treating him appropriately. I have suffered several periods locked in the bathroom, and even a threat to be brought to the pound. These are but small prices to pay to let my strong feelings be known to him.

* * * * * * * * *

I have been thinking about the extent to which love and the making of babies are intertwined in the human mind. It is difficult for a cat to understand this intimate relationship. We can feel a certain pure affection toward each other, such as I felt toward my old friend Buddy. We rightly call this love, and it is a noble feeling. We can also, of course, feel a strong affection toward a member of the opposite sex, accompanied on occasion by the overwhelming urge to copulate with them. We may even, I have been told, feel a certain affection toward our children that some call love.

However, I have had ample opportunity to observe the love between Howie and Alicia, and have examined human depictions of love in their poetry, paintings, music, books, television and movies. Human love, my feline friends, is not this pure and simple emotion of the heart that we feel. Love for humans involves physical attraction, various emotional needs, friendship, the producing and raising of children, and myriad practical considerations such as finances, heritage, geographical preference, religion and so on.

Human love is, in fact, a dizzyingly complex concoction. It encompasses so very many things that no creature could possible experience every facet of it with just one mate, and yet there is such great pressure for them to limit themselves to one mate. At every turn, they therefore find themselves asking, "Is this really love?" And thus you can see the source of their widespread discontent.

The greatest irony of this situation is that the end result of love for humans is usually the creation of babies such as Lizzie and the as-yet-unnamed creature to be born. Yet their complex process of "falling in love" includes nothing whatsoever to test their fitness for raising children, which will likely be the greatest challenge of their long lives together.

No, my fellow felines, "love," as humans conceive it, makes no sense whatsoever. Lest any cats delude themselves with the idea that they, too, may wish to experience the mess of feelings that humans call love, I cite as a cautionary tale the great tomcat Murr's experience with love in his *Life and Opinions.* I do not think that anyone could argue that his love for Kitty ended well, or that it was well-founded in the first place. Murr became obsessed with the human idea of love through his exposure to human arts and culture and, in this respect, his mind, like most humans,' was simply not strong enough to resist their confounding influence. This is the one topic about which I heartily disapprove of the great Murr, and I do so with all respect; but no, it is better not to try to experience this delusion at all.

Nevertheless, whatever human foibles have led us to this point, the fact remains that we will all soon be dealing with yet another aggravating child in our household.

* * * * * * * * * *

Lest you fret, dear reader, about my progress on *The Kibble,* rest assured that I have been working a great deal on it. I believe that the second chapter, which follows, completes the groundwork for all subsequent stories. Hereafter, the stories may be read at will, but these first two form a required basis for understanding the rest of the volume's episodes. Also required, of course, will be the closing chapter, much as Revelation and its interpretation has become such a necessary part of the Christian religions.

But enough of theology. Read on, my friends, and see what my humble mind has wrought in your service.

* * * * * * * * * *

Begettings

Now Elis knew Ulla his wife, and she conceived and bore kittens. And these kittens grew up into cats, and they begot kittens. And these kittens grew up and they begot kittens. And so on and so forth until there were countless begettings too numerous to mention.

They lived the life of nomads, these cats, wandering The Lost Forest looking for a way back to the comfortable palace that Elis and Ulla had first left. Long after Elis and Ulla had passed away, their story lived on and their descendants continued to seek the legendary kingdom where cats were revered. In time, however, this tale began to fade from memory, and eventually no cat knew from whence they had come.

And this is how we now find them, living lost and directionless.

As their numbers grew, they came to intrude on each other's territory. Every new litter of kittens that was brought into their world caused each cat's patch of land to grow smaller and smaller. Minor disputes began to erupt almost every day.

Now, a very nice cat named Nathaniel prowled a modest plot of land which he considered his own, hunting birds, mice and other small animals, and enjoying patches of afternoon sun whenever he liked. Into his territory one day came another cat named Hector. Hector said to Nathaniel, "I would like to settle down in this patch of forest adjacent to you, my good cat, but I notice that your scent stretches very far into the area I would like to call my own."

Nathaniel considered and, recognizing the rapid growth in their numbers, judged that he could concede to live in a more modest area. He told Hector that certainly, he might have some of Nathaniel's plot to prowl. "We may even share a portion of it together," Nathaniel offered.

To which Hector responded, "No, I do not share my parcel with anyone. I will take a portion of yours, and we will discuss it no further."

Nathaniel thought Hector quite abrupt, but he conceded to the arrangement.

It soon became clear, however, that Hector was intruding even on Nathaniel's reduced plot. Nathaniel detected Hector's scent on his land, and then began to find dead animals with Hector's scent on them. Nathaniel resolved to confront Hector about his behavior.

He lay in wait in a tree that was clearly on his own land but that he had determined, by the strength of the smell of urine, was near a favorite spot of Hector's. Not long had he been watching before Hector pranced into the area. Hector looked around suspiciously and, spotting no one, proceeded to hunt a small mouse. He caught and killed it in a quick and cruel manner that quite unsettled Nathaniel. Hector then dropped the dead mouse without so much as taking a taste and then proceeded to hunt a small bird.

Nathaniel jumped down, thinking he might startle Hector, but the dastardly cat seemed unperturbed at being caught in the act.

"Say, my friend," he said to Hector, "this is my land. What are you doing here?"

"I do what I like," Hector shrugged.

"Well, you'll have to do it on your own land."

"I'll do it wherever I like."

"I'm afraid I can't allow that."

"I'm afraid you can't do anything about it," Hector snarled.

"Say, what's your game, you dastardly cat?"

"Well, now that you ask, I want your plot of land."

"This is my land. You stay on your own!"

"I intend to make this my own."

"And how do you propose to do that?"

"By killing you."

"Killing me?"

At that, Hector quickly leapt upon Nathaniel and bit his throat in such a way as to end his life.

Later that day, a puss named Clara, who was very fond of Nathaniel, came by to look for him. She came upon his dead body in the leaves and fell down weeping. "Oh, Nathaniel, what has happened to you?" she cried.

"I'll tell you," said a voice in the tree. "I've killed him."

"Killed him?" she said, looking up with fear. "Why have you killed my dear, sweet Nathaniel?"

"Because I wanted what was his," Hector said, emerging from a spray of leaves in the tree to reveal himself.

"Why couldn't you just go somewhere else, you nasty creature?"

"I wanted his land. And, I wanted his kitty," he hissed, leaping menacingly at dear Clara from his perch in the tree.

Clara fled, with Hector in close pursuit. She called for help as she passed several plots of land, but none of the owners answered her call for help. Hector eventually caught her and had his way with her, but Clara would not stop fighting with him and eventually Hector silenced her by giving her the gift of death as well.

The next day, several of the land owners gathered together to discuss what had happened. Although individually they didn't feel any one of them could have prevented the incident, they decided they must now take collective action to deter this sort of kind of thing from happening again. They went to Hector's territory and told him he must leave.

"Leave?" he asked. "Whatever for?"

"Because," said one of the cats, "you killed two of the finest cats among us, and we don't want you here anymore."

"I won't move from this spot," Hector said. "This land is my land, and this is where I'll stay."

"Not if we can help it," they said, and all rushed him at once to chase him away.

Every cat with ears was told about Hector. He was sentenced to wander The Lost Forest alone for the rest of his life, never to be admitted into civilized society again.

From then on, every cat had to follow two simple rules or face Hector's fate:

1) Respect another cat's territory.

2) Never take the life of another cat.

The price for a breach of these rules was banishment, with no hope of ever returning.

* * * * * * * * * *

My dear readers, it has been over two weeks since I have written here, and I need acquaint you with some remarkable events.

Soon after I completed the previous installment of *The Kibble*, I learned that the family was to go on a trip--what humans call a vacation--before the weather turned for the worse. A vacation is a period of time when humans leave their work to substitute their busy regular schedules with even busier but novel itineraries, rushing from place to place to see and do new things. Apparently, they find this refreshing. When I heard them discussing their upcoming vacation, I naturally assumed that we were to accompany them. I became very excited about the prospect of seeing new places and meeting new and interesting creatures.

However, Howie and Alicia had no intention of bringing us along. The night before we were to leave, Howie brought Hercule to Alicia's parents to spend his days on their brick mantle. To have been banished to their house along with my dear friend would have been fate bad enough, but Howie subsequently brought me to the house of the dread Cousin Don, who grabs me by my scruff and treats me altogether brutally. Even worse, I soon discovered that he lived with two kitties who go by the names of Black and Tan.

Now, many toms reading this will marvel at my unfavorable description of this circumstance. What tom wouldn't be happy to be alone in an abode inhabited by not just one kitty but two? One kitty is quite enough for your average tom, but the smell of two kitties—well, it might be understood if such a thing were to drive said tom completely mad. But nay, these kitties in question were hardly pleasant and agreeable.

Tan may look somewhat like me, it is true. She is a tabby with a slightly deeper orange in her fur, similar to the color of my own before my penchant for lying in the afternoon sun caused it to fade to a lighter shade of beige. The pattern on her fur is also a bit different than my own—for example, her front paws are white while mine maintain the same color pattern as the rest of my body.

But while Tan may look somewhat like me to the casual human observer (not to other cats, of course, who have vastly superior eyesight as well as mental acuity when it comes to these sorts of things), her disposition is altogether quite different. She and Black, a pure black cat who one can obviously discern to be evil by just one glance at her, chatter and whisper amongst themselves in secret like teenage girls.

When I first arrived, Black said to me, "Welcome to our home," in a deep, histrionic voice that was obviously meant insincerely.

I held my head up high and stood tall, taking her greeting at face value. "Thank you," I said with the utmost dignity, and our conversation went no further.

I was soon consigned to a small room on the second floor. The dread Cousin Don had installed a small door at the back of their house for the kitties to come and go as they pleased, but as I was contractually obligated under an agreement between my caretakers and the animal shelter to remain exclusively a housecat, I was confined to this one room in order to prevent my gaining access to said door. However, due to a defect in the locking mechanism which cousin Don had not yet repaired, the door to my room soon yielded to an assault from my paws. The dread Cousin Don locked me in again, but I quickly escaped once more and it became apparent to him that the door could not hold me. As a result, he had to take the extreme measure of locking the "cat" door at the back of the house, for which Black and Tan placed the blame on me.

"Go back to your room and leave us in peace," Black said to me. "We don't want you out here with us."

"I will do as I please," I answered, and left them with my tail swinging high in the air to go explore my new territory—for, indeed, in light of their discourteous greeting I was determined to respect no boundaries at all. I immediately set about rubbing couches, door frames, chairs, table legs and whatever else was within my reach. I was resolved to leave my mark on everything.

What a slovenly home these creatures lived in, dear readers! It was quite sparsely furnished, yet Cousin Don nevertheless did a remarkable job making the place look messy. Clothes were flung over chairs; empty glasses and various knickknacks stood on every surface. Magazines were scattered all over the bedroom and living room floor, the bathroom smelled of mold, and the kitchen looked as if a major storm had just passed. The only things Cousin Don seemed to care about were the fancy stereo and video game systems in the living room and the various televisions throughout the house, at least one of which was always turned on when he was home.

The entire townhouse had that same curious, pungent odor that the dread Cousin Don himself always carried. I was soon to learn that it came from burning a particular type of plant leaf. Cousin Don and his friends put these leaves into the bowl of a small pipe and deliberately lit the wad on fire to inhale its smoke through the mouthpiece. The smoke seemed to make them quite happy and sluggish, but I found the smell so putrid that I was sure to vacate the room immediately whenever I saw them taking out the various paraphernalia associated with the ritual.

One afternoon, as I was marking some wooden table legs with my scent, Tan snuck up behind me. I had already sensed her presence in the room, and so was not perturbed when she demanded, "What are you doing?"

She appeared to be alone. Apparently, the kitty witches coven had let out for the afternoon.

"I think you are fully aware of what I am doing," I answered.

"But this isn't your home."

"It is whilst I stay here."

"You can't just come in here and mark everything up like it's your own."

"I can, and I am."

With a harrumph of sorts, Tan stormed out of the room.

Minutes later, she returned with her evil cohort. "What kind of arrogance is this?" Black asked upon seeing me marking the bedposts with my scent. She spoke with a deep, husky voice such as you have never heard in a cat. Whether she has sustained some kind of damage to the larynx from overuse, from breathing in too much of Cousin Don's secondhand smoke or for some other reason, I cannot say. Whatever the reason, her dark, chilling voice seems distinctly unfeline to me, particularly when she is angry.

"Arrogance?" I asked innocently.

"Who do you think you are, coming in here and marking everything as your own?"

"One day," I turned to her, "you will feel honored to have had your territory marked by the great Hastings."

"I doubt it."

"Mark my words."

"I'd rather not. I think you should just stop what you're doing right now."

"Yes, stop," Tan echoed behind her.

"I don't think," I retorted, "that after the rude greeting I received from you upon my arrival, I am under any obligation to concede to your requests."

"Why do you talk so funny?" Tan asked. Her light, sing-song voice was just about as far away from Black's husky tones as you can get.

"I don't talk funny at all," I responded. "I am a cultured and sophisticated cat. The language I use is one of the ages. I am intellectually superior to yourselves and thus my language, also, is superior—certainly much advanced over your own."

Black said, "We've got ourselves a live one here, Tan."

"I can assure you," I answered, "that I am very much alive."

"Well, whatever you are, stop marking the damned furniture. It's ours. You're just staying here a few days."

"I'll mark what I want," I said, holding my head high.

"Not if we can help it," Black said, arching her back in a threatening manner.

Now, Black could have no idea that she was dealing not only with an intellectually superior cat, but one who, if you recall, had successfully dealt with the fearsome Pomeranian next door named Hot Dog. I arched my back in return and intimidated her and Tan so much that, discerning the threat I posed, they simply backed away and left me to my business.

* * * * * * * * * *

For the rest of my stay at the dread Cousin Don's, the two kitties did their best to avoid me. When I walked through a room they were in, they hid behind the furniture to hiss at me. I very much enjoyed this new role and did my best to seek them out when I was bored. I must admit that I was somewhat encouraged by the most compelling arch formed by Tan's back whenever she hissed at me. Its graceful curve gave me much pleasure, as did her very pretty blue eyes.

One day, upon waking from a long nap, I decided to do a round of the house as I often do to ensure that nothing had changed during my slumber. While passing a bedroom upstairs, I was amazed to hear the most exquisite caterwauling I have ever heard in my life. It was an intricate, polyphonic masterpiece, the likes of which I could never before have imagined possible. After recovering from the initial astonishment I felt after encountering a work of such stunning achievement, I quietly entered the bedroom. The shock I received then was staggering.

There, sitting on either side of the computer keyboard, were Black and Tan.

"Great Bastet!" I cried, looking up at them. "You know how to use a computer?"

They both jumped in surprise and scrambled to get away from me.

"It's OK," I said. "I do, too. I just didn't realize that any other cats knew as well."

Dumbfounded, they looked at each other from opposite ends of the desk and took a few moments to compose themselves. Black finally asked, "You know about the Catenation?"

"The Catenation? I know how to use a computer and I know how to surf the web, but I've never heard about a thing called Catenation."

"Hmmm," she narrowed her eyes at me.

"What are you listening to?" I asked, for the caterwauling was still emanating from the computer speakers. "It is the most exquisite thing I have ever heard."

"That's by the great Muzius," Black said. "It's his famous forty-ninth caterwaul."

"It's my favorite," Tan added.

"Well," I said, jumping up onto the desk with them, "it's obviously a work of staggering genius. Would you show me how you found it?"

Having little choice in the matter, Black and Tan set about showing me how to access Catenation (slogan: The Cat Nation) online. They were impressed that I had taught myself how to use the computer but were surprised that I knew nothing about this online feline community. The details of accessing Catenation shall not be outlined here. For this instruction, you will have to purchase my forthcoming book *The Essential Cat's Guide to Computing* or else ask cats that you know to teach you. One thing we do want to avoid is a rush of insincere cats (or, dare I say, even people) flooding the community with useless banter. Having its existence spread by word of mouth is perhaps the best way of ensuring that only the right type of cat takes part.

Allow me to describe briefly for you what Catenation is. It is an online community where cats from all over the world come to exchange ideas, swap music files and track down lost friends and family. It really is the most wonderful thing. I watched Black and Tan interact with others for mere minutes before my superior intellect recognized that this was the mechanism by which I could finally reach my audience. I did not mention this fact to Black and Tan, of course. I remained as passive as possible, trying to learn as much as I could in the short time I would be staying with them.

I must admit that the two kitties did not seem altogether happy to show me the things they knew, but I persisted in my questioning and they reluctantly obliged me. In the remaining days of my stay, I was able to look at JPEG collections of both classical and modern cat painting, to listen to some of the most recognized caterwauling MP3s, to take an interactive graphical tutorial on mouse catching and to watch Black and Tan participate in several online discussions. These latter included the catnip interest group chat hour, the ongoing housecat discussion page and a live online interview with the great Muzius, who detailed how he had achieved some of the phase effects in his upcoming fiftieth caterwaul, which he predicted would change the feline perception of caterwauling forever.

Tracking down lost family and friends is one of the most popular features of Catenation, and one of the first things I did was to look for my old friends Buddy and Mo. Unfortunately, I was unable to find either them or anyone who knew them. I hadn't had very high expectations, of course. Neither of them had ever mentioned such a community to me before, so I knew that the chance of someone in this online community knowing them was quite small.

Despite my disappointment at not finding my old friends, I was elated at this new discovery. What had begun as a banishment, a sentence to endure the alternating neglect and smothering affection of the dread Cousin Don, became a crucial educational experience for me. Black and Tan may not have fully warmed to me by the time I had left to return home, but I myself had greatly softened toward them. I thanked them heartily for all that they had done for me and threw my paws around them to hug them good-bye. Black noticeably stiffened at my gesture, but I thought I sensed a note of tenderness in Tan's body language.

Ah, if only I were capable of a certain physical act with the kitty in question. Our kittens would be quite beautiful, I am certain. But alas, it is not to be, and I am sure that, in the end, it is all for the better. Love is a game we cats simply should not play.

* * * * * * * * * *

I had long recognized the Internet's potential for building a community. I have seen how Howie uses it to exchange his writing with other like-minded artists, and how both he and Alicia keep in contact with old friends that have scattered around the world. Were it not for the Internet, in fact, Howie and Alicia would be very lonely indeed, for they do hardly anything outside of the house since having little Lizzie beyond going to work and buying provisions. On the Internet, they send updates about their lives, exchange pictures of their friend and families, have the most private conversations and connect in many other ways.

I had never seriously considered the Internet as a tool for felines, however, because of the logistics of teaching cats to use it. I never dreamed that other cats from around the world were already taking advantage of it.

Black and Tan confirmed that most cats still could not read. There are, however, certain elevated segments of cat society that are privy to this knowledge and pass it down from generation to generation. Black, while far from an agreeable specimen of our species, was a very clever kitty who had been taught to read and write by another cat in the neighborhood with whom she had had an affair. He was a Persian, she told me with pride, which made me bristle somewhat; my readers well know my feelings about Persians. In any case, Black then taught Tan, and thus it was done.

The reader may imagine that my feelings might be somewhat mixed at finding that I am not the only cat in the world who knows how to read and write. It is true that it is something of a blow to my ego to find that I am not unique in this respect. However, as you know, my grand plans depend upon other cats being able to read my work. Before, the task of teaching others to read so that they might fulfill this purpose seemed nearly insurmountable. Now, I know that there are already many felines out there who can help. I also now have a ready method for reaching these said felines.

Therefore, this discovery actually strikes me as something of a relief.

I might add that the simple fact that other cats can read, or even use the Internet, does not mean that they also have a superior intellect. Rare is the cat who has read Murr's *Life and Opinions* or the human Tristram Shandy's memoirs, as I myself have almost completed. While many cats can apparently read and perhaps some can write, a precious few possess the voracious appetite for higher knowledge that I do. Rare is the feline mind that has pondered the grand questions that I have.

Indeed, my mission in life still stands as important as ever. My work will continue now with a renewed vigor.

* * * * * * * * * *

Now that I am back home, my dear readers, I will return once more to chronicling my days for you in real time. First, however, I must catch you up to what has been happening in our home. In an unsettling echo of my first installment of *The Kibble*, I heard the telltale scratching the other night that indicates the presence of a mouse.

My work will continue now with a renewed vigor.

I detected it through the two wide, slatted double doors in the basement that lead to the storage area. This small, uncarpeted space contains the furnace and water heater, along with various plastic crates of holiday items and other sundries. My suspicions were confirmed within moments when I caught a whiff of the mouse's scent.

I watched and waited throughout the night, but never spotted the culprit. The next morning, I went immediately to the Catenation web site after our caretakers had departed to revisit their tutorial on catching a mouse. It contained many helpful hints, and I set about employing the techniques immediately.

I detected some faint scratchings last night. But I shall succeed, my fellow felines. Never you fret about that. Day and night, I shall await this dastardly creature. I am determined to catch it.

* * * * * * * * * *

My surveillance has been all-consuming over these past several days. I have sniffed and listened relentlessly behind doors and under furniture in pursuit of my quarry. Last night, I was finally rewarded for my diligence.

It was late at night when the nefarious beast finally emerged from underneath one of the doors. I watched as it crept carefully across the hallway and toward the storage closet. I moved slowly toward it, stalking, stalking, my heart pounding with the anticipation of catching my first mouse. I had gained some familiarity with the proper technique by reading the tips in the online tutorial. When it came time to actually execute the pounce, however, the movement was almost instinctual. It was between my paws and in my mouth in a flash.

"Help! Help!" he cried.

My dear readers, I can barely begin to describe for you the elation I felt at finally holding that mouse in my mouth. The sense of accomplishment and pure thrill of triumph might have been satisfying enough. But the taste of his fur against my tongue was also considerably more pleasing than I had expected it to be. It awakened something deep within me, something primal, as if this was what I was meant to be doing all along. It felt like coming home after a long and tortuous journey.

Of course, I dare not tell my dear friend Hercule of my epiphany (and will certainly skip these paragraphs when I read this section back to him). But I must share my experiences openly with you, my fellow felines. If you ever have the opportunity to catch a mouse, do not shy away from the opportunity. There is nothing more exhilarating in all the world!

I strutted around the room for a few moments, then put him down in the middle of the wide open space. He immediately scurried across the floor and I gave chase, swatting at him with my paws to drive him back toward the center of the room. He made for the wall, and once again I pounced and picked him up in my mouth.

Perhaps you do not want to hear every detail of our encounter. I understand that such things are not nearly as exciting in the telling. Mind you, I can supply every minute detail if you wished me to. I remember them quite well. Suffice it to say that I repeated this process many times until the plump little morsel began to slow down, battered and fatigued by my relentless assault.

Eventually, wishing to extend the encounter (for I was having much fun), I allowed the mouse to run behind the cardboard boxes along the far wall. This location gave him some sense of security, but in reality provided nothing of the sort. There was a long, open stretch in either direction before he could reach another shelter, and with my diligent watch, there could be little hope of him actually arriving at one of them. Still, I thought that he might catch his breath and perhaps formulate a plan that would enliven the game.

"Cat," he gasped, "why are you torturing me?"

"Because you are in my house," I answered simply.

"And that gives you the right to do this to me?"

"All cats are sworn to keep you vermin out of our houses. It is our duty."

"Well, why don't you do it quickly, then, if you're going to kill me?"

"Where's the fun in that?" I asked.

"My death is fun to you?" he exclaimed. "All those stories are true. You cats are evil."

"No, you are evil."

"I'm evil?" he cried. "I'm just trying to get some small crumbs to feed my family, to keep my poor children from starving to death. Now they'll never even see their father again." At this, he burst into tears.

Now tell me, dear reader, whose heart could remain closed to such a genuine display of sorrow? My emotions became very confused. I do not have a heart made of stone, my friends.

"You have family?" I asked gently.

"Yes. Three wives and forty-seven wonderful children."

"What is your name, little mouse?"

"Ferdinand."

Hmmm, I thought. Perhaps I could spare this mouse's life. Despite their despicable nature, it did seem particularly cruel to kill the father of forty-seven children, no matter what his species. I certainly had no other use for him now that the chase was over. However enticing this mouse's musty fur tasted in my mouth, I was not so base as to consider eating him. The thought of eating living flesh is utterly repulsive to me. Furthermore, the fact was not lost on me that I was being presented with an opportunity to prove to Hercule that I am, in fact, a cat of a higher order. I can, when the situation requires, make decisions in complete opposition to my natural urges.

"Please let me live, kind cat," Ferdinand pleaded, sensing my hesitation. "I do you no harm. I'll leave this house and its warmth and its food forever if you will just let me go now."

"There is no need for that," I said, my heart softening further. "I may be a stubborn and opinionated feline, but I am not averse to amending my ways when I see that they are cruel, or simply wrong. You may stay here, and bring your family as well. I should love to meet them."

There was a long pause from behind the cardboard boxes, and then the tip of a gray snout emerged.

"How do I know you're not trying to trick me?" he asked.

"I assure you, I am not."

"You seem different than the usual cat," he observed.

"I am a highly educated feline," I informed him, puffing out my chest. "I can read and write, and I spend a great deal of time thinking about the nature of life. You are lucky it was I you ran into today, and not a more common housecat who would have been less philosophical and understanding of your predicament."

"If you're so smart, you could be trying to trick me."

"Here," I said. "I will go over to the far side of the room. My name is Hastings, by the way," I said with a nod of my head. "It is nice to meet you, Ferdinand." At that, I removed myself to the other side of the long basement.

Ferdinand emerged slowly at first. When he saw how far away I was, he immediately dashed for the double doors and dove underneath.

I trotted over to the closet. "You see?" I shouted through the slats. "I kept my word."

"Thank you, kind cat," he cried. "How can I ever repay you?"

"Bring your children, bring your wives. I should like to meet them."

"I'll try, but I don't know if they're going to believe this."

"Well, tell them they have my word."

Afterward, I went upstairs to tell Hercule what had happened, and he seemed genuinely shocked at my generosity. "Has my feline friend finally turned over a new leaf?" he asked.

"I am a sympathetic creature," I pointed out to him.

"Of course you are, my boy, but this behavior seems contrary to your nature. Are you sure you can resist attacking them if they come again?"

"Of course I can, my dear pig. I have a truly remarkable degree of self-control. It will not be a problem at all."

* * * * * * * * * *

Well, my dear readers, I have finally completed reading Laurence Sterne's great *Life and Opinions of Tristram Shandy, Gent.* It only took me this long because I had put it aside to do my research for *The Kibble.* I will no doubt include a detailed critique of this novel in *The Essential Cat's Guide to Human Literature* when I write it, but I believe that the inspirational effect it has had on my thinking bears mentioning here. My readers may have already noticed a change in my writing style of late, a gradual improvement in the use of larger, more syllabical and sophisticated words along with a greater use of twisting, convoluted sentences that allow you to lose yourself in them before you are even close to reaching their end.

The book's influence on my way of thought, however, extends beyond Mr. Sterne's ornamental manner of writing sentences. His narrative also displays a great sophistication of structure, with frequent digressions and diversions and a remarkable attention to the vagaries of time. Hercule and I usually have similar impressions about the work we read, but we have had some serious disagreements about the twisted, convoluted style by which the main character in this book relates the events of his life. While Hercule acknowledges my point that the writer was intentionally delaying, digressing and manipulating time in order to better convey the actual experience of Tristram's life, my dear friend nevertheless found the journey quite frustrating.

"To tell a story this way," he argued, "isn't so much an accurate depiction of life as a tease."

"But life is often frustrating," I countered.

"Yes, but why highlight that aspect of it? We spend our lives trying to make sense of it all. Art is our attempt at order and understanding. Why try to reproduce this confusion?"

Our arguments continued, dear readers, but there is little point in my recounting them further. Suffice it to say that we will not agree on this matter. To me, a straightforward, traditional narrative imposes an artificial order that doesn't reflect the full richness of life. Laurence Sterne has captured the essence of his character's life. Like life, his narrative continually confounds our expectations. Its very structure reflects life; it is life. Although Laurence Sterne is long gone, the book he left behind is more than just a record of things that have happened. The book is alive, and he himself lives within it.

I, in turn, now realize that in order to create a truly great work of literature myself, I must employ every creative technique I can imagine. I must work hard to avoid allowing my narrative to fall into simple, conventional patterns of storytelling that artificially limit the depth and richness of my experience.

I would now like to demonstrate for you the lessons I have learned from the great Laurence Sterne and directly exhibit a greater narrative sophistication. It is quite difficult to recount a narrative such as this with any sort of temporal accuracy, chronicling events over the course of several days or weeks whilst life passes by, potentially creating new things to write about every moment. How might one convey this sense of time? Why, even in the course of writing this very paragraph, more of my life passes here in this room. Not that there is anything worthy of noting at the moment, except perhaps for the gray clouds moving in the sky outside or an occasional squirrel passing by the window. However, if there were something to write about, I might have fallen even further behind as I wrote. I find this quite an intriguing paradox.

Now, at the point in time at which I aim to situate you, it had been three days since I had last encountered Ferdinand. I had almost given up on seeing him again. It would thus be a disservice for me to recount for you our meeting last night so soon after you have read about our previous one. That would distort your sense of time.

Therefore, my dear readers, I command you to put this book down now, no matter where you are or what you are doing. You must pause and wait in anticipation, just as I waited to see Ferdinand the mouse once more, wondering anxiously if I had earned his trust and friendship.

To indicate this pause, I will type in several bars, in order to bar your passage. You may pass beyond them only after three days have elapsed:

****

I now return you to the basement, as I have successfully made my narrative point. You may remember that it is a large open space with short-pile beige carpeting much the color of my own sun-bleached fur. There is a storage area at the far end, behind large slatted double doors. I heard a scratching in the storage area at night, ran to the doors and called excitedly through the slatted double doors, "Hello? Is anybody in there?"

"It's me," came the voice, and I recognized it to be that of my new little friend, Ferdinand.

"I had begun to think you weren't coming back," I said.

"I've been talking to my wives, and they think it's crazy to be friends with a cat."

"My best friend is a guinea pig," I offered as evidence of my credibility.

"A guinea pig?" he asked. "What's that?"

"They look a bit like the groundhogs you see digging in the ground."

"Groundhogs are a bunch of jerks—and they're dumb as anything."

"Are they? I've never spoken to one myself. Guinea pigs are extremely intelligent, and very nice. Would you like to come upstairs to meet Hercule?"

"Uh, I think I'm just going to stay back here for a while."

"Behind the doors?"

"For now," he said.

"Suit yourself. Have you brought your family?"

"They refuse to come," he laughed nervously. "I think they want to see if I come back alive. They all think I'm a fool."

"Well, it is unusual for a cat and a mouse to form a friendship, but I am a very special cat."

"So you say."

"I do say. In fact, I could show you my tome, if you are interested."

"Tome?"

"Yes, I am writing my memoirs, a book detailing the events of my life and outlining my opinions."

"Well, that is pretty unusual for a cat."

"Of course it is, my dear Ferdinand. You tell your family they may come here any time they would like."

"Well, thank you Hastings. You really do seem like a nice cat."

"Of course I do," I said.

* * * * * * * * *

I am fairly certain that Ferdinand brought his family into our home last night. I heard the telltale scratchings within the storage closet. I could also smell their presence around my food bowls this morning, so I know that this is how they are feeding themselves and getting their water. I have caught scents other than Ferdinand's, so he must have convinced others to join him.

They have been venturing outside the closet, to my knowledge, only when I am upstairs. I did not try to speak to them through the door for fear that I would scare them off completely. I am determined to demonstrate to Hercule that I can resist my biological urges and allow any creature to live in our home, no matter what my natural tendency toward them.

* * * * * * * * * *

Last night, I spoke to our guests through the door. I simply welcomed them to our home, saying a few kind words in greeting. Ferdinand thanked me, but the rest of them said not a word. I presume they were hiding their heads and trembling in fear at the sound of my voice. They will soon learn to trust me; I have no doubt on that account.

In the meantime, this does seem an opportune time to interrupt my narrative to write a chapter about a topic I have long been meaning to address: whiskers.

* * * * * * * * * *

Upon Whiskers[1]

Actually, now that I have set out to write a chapter upon whiskers, I am sorry I promised myself to do it. 'twas as inconsiderate a promise as

---

1. Lawrence Sterne's *Tristram Shandy* contained a chapter called "Upon Whiskers" that discussed the double meaning of the word whiskers and the ruination of the word by misuse. Hastings echoes, and even copies, Sterne's language in this section. Sterne used "whiskers," like "nose" and many other words in the book, in the most phallic and suggestive ways he could. Hastings does not seem to be aware of this. —ed.

ever entered a cat's head. A chapter upon whiskers! Alas! The world will not bear it. For the subject of whiskers is one of the most sensitive in all the feline world.

I must put my paw down and declare that there is only one thing that the word whiskers must refer to, and that is the long hair emanating from the sides of a cat's nose. We cats pride ourselves on our whiskers. They are the most delicate, graceful features of our inarguably exquisite bodies. Nothing in the entire animal world can compare to the elegance and beauty of true feline whiskers. Yet humans have appropriated this word and now employ it to mean those short, plentiful, quite indistinct and, may I say, most unattractive hairs on a male's face.

Yes, feline friends, I myself have heard the word used in such a manner. Your outrage is well warranted. We must do everything in our powers to make sure that this practice comes to an end. Words describing precious things, my friends, must not be ruined by misuse.

Humans are altogether too imprecise in their language, distorting the meanings of all sorts of words and phrases, such as saying "let go" when they mean fired from a job, "passed away" when they mean dead, or "out to lunch" when they mean insane. Further examples include "blowing chunks" or "worshiping the porcelain altar" to mean vomiting. What strange ways humans have to express themselves! When it comes to sexual terminology, one might begin to believe that humans are quite incapable of saying simple words, substituting bizarre terms like "making the beast with two backs" for copulation. Humans twist and corrupt these meanings for no apparent reason other than to confuse. The examples are simply too numerous to mention. We must rail against this phenomenon, my fellow felines!

Nevertheless, one word must carry priority above all others. We must not stand for the use of the word "whiskers" to describe unappealing human facial hair! And so I call upon all my fellow felines: Whenever you hear this word being misused by one of our species, kindly correct them and explain that "whiskers" can mean only one thing, and that thing belongs to us alone. When you hear the word being misused by a human, there is but one thing to do: attack. It is not necessary for a human to understand explicitly why such an attack has occurred. When they have been assaulted a sufficient number of times after misusing a particular word, they will become conditioned not to use it, even if this phenomenon occurs on a completely subconscious level.

There comes a time in a cat's life when one must take a stand. This is a call to arms, my friends. Do not let them take our whiskers!

* * * * * * * * * *

Ferdinand appears to have invited more of his family into our home. When I first asked him to bring his family, I envisioned only his wife and children. However, it appears that he has invited his brothers and sisters, cousins, aunts, uncles, nieces, nephews and every other distant relation he has ever come across. I can certainly appreciate their need to escape the deepening cold outside, but their scratchings are now going on at all hours of the night and the chattering has become incessant.

Last night, I encountered a grossly obese mouse waddling across the basement carpet—a certain Slop is his name, he says, a cousin of Ferdinand. Unlike the rest, he does not seem to have any fear of me whatsoever. I shall have to watch this character very closely.

* * * * * * * * * *

I have been tracking Slop for three days now. While the rest of our guests scurry through the walls and hide in closets, Slop behaves as if he hasn't a care or a fear in the world, coming out in the open at all hours and respecting no boundaries. I caught him chewing on the wires of our computer this morning and immediately determined to put a stop to it.

"It is time for you to leave my house," I said upon approaching.

He barely flinched, refusing even to acknowledge my presence. He deliberately turned his back to me and continued to chew on the thick wire connecting the computer monitor to the central processing unit.

"I told you," I said more firmly, "to get out of my house. Now, I say!"

He paused only to lift his head, still facing away from me, and respond, "Ferdinand invited me here." Then he put his head down and resumed his task.

"Well," I declared, "Ferdinand is here on my invitation, and I therefore have the power to uninvite you."

He paused again. "You can't do that. He's the one that invited me, not you."

"This is my house," I cried, my anger boiling. "I do what I wish."

"I know all about you," he answered. "You're too much of an intellectual to actually do anything to me. You just think about things all the time. Action isn't your business," he concluded with confidence, then turned back to chew on the wire and ignore me.

"Oh, I will do something about it," I declared. "I'm going to call a meeting."

I went off in a huff to find Ferdinand. As expected, he was in his usual spot in the storage closet and so I had to speak to him through the door.

Ferdinand seemed quite upset and agreed to set up a meeting tonight. We shall now see what these mice have to say for themselves, particularly this disagreeable Slop!

* * * * * * * * * *

It was 2 am last night. More than 50 mice were gathered before me with their beady black eyes, their various shades of dull gray-brown fur spread across the basement carpet. Some stood, some sat, many munched kibble which they had taken from my very food bowl without my permission. A couple casually dropped poops onto the carpet as they waited for us to begin. I seethed with a growing anger.

Once we judged that most everyone had arrived, Ferdinand introduced me for those who hadn't formally met me and said that he was sure they were all very grateful for my generous hospitality. He then told them that I had some issues with their residence in the house and urged them to listen to what I had to say.

I began my speech, as all good orators must do, by telling them that I was glad they all had come, and I thanked them for their time. "My dear mice," I continued, "I have invited you all here in good faith. Ferdinand seemed like a nice fellow, and his family was in need of a warm shelter as the weather threatened to grow colder. However, you have abused my hospitality, eating my food and drinking my water and, most egregiously, dropping your wastes indiscriminately. The last straw, I am afraid, was when I caught a most disagreeable mouse named Slop destroying some very valuable property for no reason other than that it struck his fancy."

An agitated murmur arose from the crowd.

"What can we do to improve the situation?" Ferdinand asked. "We want to work together to fix things."

"I am afraid that I made a mistake in inviting you here in the first place," I said. "I am now uninviting you. You will all need to leave immediately."

The crowd fussed. "But this is our home now," I heard one say.

"We're not leaving," insisted a fat gray mouse in the front row.

This insolence lit a fire under my already simmering anger. I am generally an agreeable cat, my dear readers, but when I see mice sitting in front of me eating my kibble, pooping on my carpet and arguing that they will not leave my home when they have so grossly abused my hospitality—well, then the claws will be unsheathed. But I am not without honor. I lifted my head up high and warned them very loudly. "At this point," I announced, "I would advise you all to run."

I resisted my now overwhelming urge to start swiping at them for perhaps three to five seconds, but none of them moved. In fact, none did anything. They seemed bewildered, unwilling to believe that I would take any real action to remove them.

How wrong they were, my fellow felines. With a loud warning cry, I leapt straight into the middle of the crowd, unsheathed my claws and started swatting every little gray thing I could get my paws on. They panicked, screaming and rushing about in circles, climbing over each other in a desperate rush to escape. It was absolute pandemonium. I knocked down dozens of them, sent tens flying, but I let them get away for the most part. I wanted them out of my house, not dead on the floor, thus leaving me with a disposal problem.

Dear readers, do not judge me badly. I opened my heart and my home to these odious creatures, but they showed me flagrant disrespect. Never trust a mouse, no matter how sincere they seem. They are rotten to the core. The only good mouse, I now know, is a dead mouse.

I spotted Ferdinand, the very root of my troubles, running toward the closet and pounced. He was in my mouth in a flash. The mice nearby screamed in horror and scrambled to get away from me. I calmly walked the original intruder over to the small, purple plastic children's pool my caretakers use to put Hercule in when they are cleaning his cage, and I dropped Ferdinand into it.

"Oh my god, Hastings," he gasped. "I thought we were friends."

I shook my head. "A cat can never be friends with a mouse."

"So you tricked me this whole time?"

"No, on the contrary, my dear Ferdinand, this is something that you have helped to teach me. I genuinely felt sorry for you and was prepared to let you and your immediate family stay here for the winter. But you took advantage of my kindness and invited your whole community inside. They are fouling my home and showing the most blatant disrespect toward me. I cannot allow it. I am most disappointed in you and in your kind, Ferdinand. This is not the way you should treat your fellow creatures. It is no wonder that you are so widely despised."

The basement was quiet, and I realized that many of the mice must have been listening to our conversation. They were doubtless hiding behind the couch, behind boxes and in the closets; there simply hadn't been time for most of them to get out yet.

"What can we do?" Ferdinand pleaded. "What can we do to change your mind?"

I looked straight into his beady black eyes but felt no empathy. I finally understood the true nature of these creatures. "Nothing," I answered firmly. "You have humiliated and offended me, and you are now to serve as an example for the others. Those who abuse my hospitality must pay the price. Your brethren must all leave my home, or they shall suffer the same fate as you."

At that, I jumped into the pool and proceeded to swat, lift in my mouth and otherwise torture the source of my problems as an example to all the other mice until he was barely moving. I finally dropped him onto the plastic floor of the pool to examine him. He had barely any strength left in him when I was done.

"I'm sorry, Hastings," he whispered with what might have been his very last breaths.

"I am sorry too, Ferdinand."

"Tell my family I loved them."

"I'll do nothing of the sort. If I see them, I will kill them. But I am sure they know you loved them, Ferdinand, if that is any consolation."

My prey was not moving anymore. His eyes were closed. I will never know if he heard those last words—a final expression of empathy from his executioner—but I believe that they prove my mercy and compassion.

I was not quite sure if he was dead yet. Out of respect for him, I decided that the best thing to do would be to go upstairs and let the other mice talk to him if they chose before they vacated the premises. I left him in the pool so that they could not see him, but they could still shout over the edge.

Licking my paws with satisfaction, I went upstairs to take a nap in my caretakers' bed. I slept very soundly. When their alarm went off this morning, I went downstairs to check on Ferdinand and found him most certainly dead. I took him in my mouth and brought him upstairs, placing him in the hallway by the basement stairs as an offering to my caretakers.

Howie was most impressed when he saw Ferdinand. He rubbed my neck affectionately and boasted to Alicia of my hunting prowess. He didn't pick him up in his mouth, which we all know is the proper way to handle a mouse, but rather put on a protective glove and lifted the stiff body by the tail to dispose of it in the garbage.

Alicia, to my chagrin, was not sufficiently impressed with my accomplishment. She said "Ew" and made a face of disgust, which deeply offended me. I might interject here that, although Alicia purports to love me dearly and often forces affections upon me that I do not ask for, her actions, such as her response to this achievement and her consistent passing off of caretaking duties to Howie, suggest a marked lack of respect.

In any case, once the family had left the house for the day, I bounded up onto Hercule's cage to boast of the night's triumph.

"Hastings," he began once I had finished my story, "I understand their offensive behavior, but it's a bit disturbing for me to see how much glee you get from slaying these creatures. They're not altogether so different from myself. I tremble at the thought that you might one day mistake me for a mouse."

"Hercule," I assured him, "as I've told you before, to a cat's refined senses, you are completely different creatures. A guinea pig and a mouse have absolutely nothing in common."

"Tell me, my boy, what makes us so different to you?"

"The pig's heart is pure, Hercule. The mouse's heart is black. It is part of your very essence. A cat can sense such things. My friend, if you were set loose in the world, it would be a rare cat that would target you as prey. You have little to fear from us."

"That's a comforting thought," Hercule said with no small degree of sarcasm before letting out a massive sneeze.

I was immediately concerned, for guinea pigs are known to be quite vulnerable to respiratory illnesses. "Are you OK, Hercule?"

"I think so. This cold, dry air has been aggravating my lungs. I hope I'm not catching cold."

"Well, you take care of yourself. I'm going to go back downstairs to investigate the mouse situation."

At that, I leapt off his cage and went down to the basement. I found further no signs of them, and can only hope that this marks the end of the incident of the mice in my home.

I believe I have a learned a valuable lesson from these mice. Hercule is certainly correct in saying that we can overcome our natures. I went against the very dictates of my nature in trying to be kind to them. However, sometimes our nature is wiser than we are. We ignore what is deep within our hearts at our own peril.

* * * * * * * * * *

I realize now that I was mistaken in my expectation that Ferdinand's death would serve as an effective deterrent for the other mice. These cursed friends and kin of his refuse to leave us. I have spent the past two days and nights in almost constant pursuit of one or another of them.

Whether I kill or capture the little pests depends on what they say to me during the hunt. The ones who taunt me die. I usually decide to show mercy, however, on those who show me some fear and respect. I place them downstairs in the purple plastic children's pool and then wait for Howie to come down for his writing session early in the morning.

Howie is almost as proud of my triumphs as I. After I strut around the pool to signal a catch and he spots it, he always rubs my neck and congratulates me. He then disposes of them by driving them to a park just far enough away that they can't make their way back. I believe that this arrangement is agreeable to all parties involved.

But I must now get back to the hunt. None of these mice should be in my house anymore, and they deserve what they get. They have had more than ample warning.

* * * * * * * * * *

Last night marked a significant milestone for me. Previously, I had been able to catch no more than three mice in one night. Last night, I caught four!

I put them in the pool as usual and, unable to contain my excitement, rushed upstairs to alert my caretakers. I found them sleeping, of course. It is quite amazing how long these humans can sleep at one stretch during the night. It fell upon me, therefore, to wake them up. Now, this is no small task with these lazy creatures, and if you will allow me a digression, I shall briefly detail some methods that will appear in expanded form in the forthcoming *The Essential Cat's Guide to Living with People.*

The first method I developed for waking humans was simple but effective: I would touch my cold, wet nose to their nose or lips. This would wake them up quite suddenly. However, as I have grown older, I have developed an aversion to the foul breath these people produce in their slumber, and therefore have had a difficult time with this method of late. But never fear; there are many ways to wake a human.

The method I currently prefer is biting. One can make a game of this. Humans move very frequently during slumber. Pretend that there is a mouse under the covers and pounce as soon as you see anything moving underneath. This is sure to wake a human. If you need more immediate results or are simply not in the mood for a game, gently biting any number of locations on their bodies will instantly wake them. You need not come close to breaking their skin, which could bring drastic consequences. The mere feel of tooth on skin is enough to wake them. Locations that work quite effectively include the back of the upper arm, the feet or, in general, any other fleshy part of the body (such as the spare tires around their torsos) that you might have access to, depending on their sleeping position, quantity of clothing, et cetera.

There are myriad other ways to wake a human. For instance, it is a matter of fact that people despise the screeching sound of claws dragged vigorously down a wall. Their irritation at this sound inevitably gets them up and out of bed. However, many cats are also irritated by this sound.

Another alternative is to walk over them repeatedly. Pay special attention to stand on their chests and hinder their breathing. Eventually, this pressure will wake even the most deeply slumbering human.

There is another method that is of particular interest because it is both fun and doesn't require you to be near the person at all. I learned it quite indirectly from the great cat named Hope. I overheard Hope's caretaker telling Howie and Alicia that when Hope wanted her to awaken, she would jump up onto the dresser and begin, one by one, to push the coins stored there across the surface and onto the hardwood floor. I think that this is a wonderful strategy. The key to the method is not to dump the coins all at once, for one single disturbance of sleep might be overcome; rather, you must push the coins slowly and deliberately, one by one, and let each drop individually to the floor. Eventually, the sound will drive your caretakers mad, and they will get up ready to skin you alive. But you will already have escaped. They are slow when they wake, and you will have had a great generous start.

Dropping coins on a hardwood floor is an extremely effective method of waking a human, but what if there is thick carpet in the bedroom to insulate a coin's drop? What if there are no coins on top of the dresser? What if there is no dresser? Well, my fellow felines, the strategy of employing gravity to wake a human can be adapted with almost limitless creative variations. In fact, you may use anything you can find on a high surface to create the same effect. I have knocked over tissue boxes, books, glasses, cups of water and even a lamp when I was particularly anxious to wake my caretakers. You may knock over anything at all. The only limit is your imagination. The only rules are to make a lot of noise and enjoy yourself.

This morning I contained my excitement until I thought that there was a realistic chance Howie would not turn violent when I woke him. I walked over his body and then bit him on the fleshy side of his torso where his shirt had ridden up in his sleep. You see, dear reader, you may combine methods if it is a particularly difficult case. Howie, after saying some very unkind things to me, finally awoke and somewhat reluctantly came downstairs to begin his writing. When he spotted the four mice in the pool, he was most happy with me despite his irritation at having been woken early, and praised me to no end as he scratched me behind the ears.

Howie later expressed surprise to Alicia that I had effectively communicated my pride and sense of accomplishment to him. He marveled at how I had strutted around the pool and then happily soaked in his praise. My dear readers, it really is outrageous how self-centered these humans are. If they would open their eyes and look around them, they would realize how much is actually being communicated to them all the time. How surprised they would be if they knew how much more we could communicate if we chose to! Tobermory, if you remember, even condescended to speak their language!

But now I must return to my hunt. More mice await.

* * * * * * * * * *

My encounter with these mice has inspired the latest chapter in my masterwork for the masses. I now present it for your benefit:

The Company of Mice

Angela was the most beautiful kitty in The Lost Forest, a strikingly pretty kitty with long whiskers and fur as white as fresh snow. She was a vain kitty and kept mostly to herself. However, it had lately come into Angela's mind to look for a suitable tomcat to give her kittens.

The toms had always fought for Angela's attention. But she had never liked any she knew and she wondered how she might find one that was good enough for her.

One day, a handsome stranger wandered into her section of the forest. His eyes blazed an intense orange, and his fur was as black as black could be, sucking in all the light that touched it. He barely said a word, but set about wooing Angela immediately with his exquisite style and grace. She found him charming and allowed him to plant his seed inside her without even boxing him on the nose afterward.

Then he was gone.

Angela found herself completely isolated. The other cats wouldn't speak to her. She had betrayed all those she knew by choosing a stranger. So she wandered alone, longing for the stranger to come back to her. She gazed up at the moon at night and wished for it to tell her, with its all-seeing eyes, where her love had wandered off to.

She bore his kittens and raised them. They were a difficult litter, with a streak so independent they were never grateful for anything she did. They never thanked her. They never even said good-bye when they wandered off to live their own lives, and she never saw any of them again.

Angela felt a deep and biting sadness. But her astounding beauty could not be ruined even by such overwhelming sorrow. Eventually, another tom sought and won her affection, and they settled down together to have more kittens.

It was after she had had her third litter that the mysterious tom with the black fur finally came back. He staggered into her section of the forest, tired and haggard.

"Angela!" he called at the top of his lungs. She recognized his voice instantly and tried to hide, but he hunted her relentlessly until she finally stopped to face him. Her husband arrived just in time to see the confrontation and crouched in hiding nearby, ready to protect her.

"Angela!" shouted the stranger. The blaze in his eyes was gone, the orange dulled to a sandy yellow, but the anger in them was intense. "Why have you not waited for me? You have taken someone else, have you? And you've had his kittens!"

"I had yours, and then you left me."

"How dare you not wait for me!" he boomed. "You who pledged your love to me!"

Words could not find their way out of Angela's mouth. She didn't know what to say.

"Bring me some food and find me a bed to lie on," he commanded.

Angela stared at him, knowing it would be of little use to run, but not moving to fulfill his requests either.

"Why do you not obey me?" he shouted.

Angela still would not move. She stared into the deep black irises of his eyes with a growing unease.

The stranger suddenly jerked. "Aaaaaaaargh!" he cried, his gaunt black body seized with pain.

Angela stepped forward to touch his shoulder, but he dropped to the ground, screaming and writhing. His face distorted and his paws began to split. His belly ripped open before her eyes.

Angela was frozen in horror as the stranger's cat face started to slough off. His orange marble eyes cracked like eggshells, falling away to reveal small, round black beads. Torn sheets of black fur slid from his body onto the ground, leaving behind a wet and bloodied mess of matted gray fur. What lay on the ground before her, finally coming out of the grip of its writhing agony, was a fat, stubby, enormous mouse.

When the transformation was complete, the thing finally struggled to its feet and stood before her squeaking with sadness. Angela screamed at the top of her lungs. Her husband came out of hiding and leapt upon the back of the mouse beast, sinking his teeth deep into its neck.

It was over in a matter of minutes, the creature gasping for its last breaths on the fallen leaves that coated the forest floor. It looked pleadingly at

Angela, trying to say something. She leaned down to listen, defying her husband's advice to use caution.

"I love you," the beast whispered, and closed its eyes with its last breath.

Angela stood up, crying hysterically. Her husband hugged her tight. When they finally ended their embrace, they looked down to see that the mysterious stranger had again become a cat.

They lived long lives, Angela and her husband, but they were lives of eternal sorrow, for they had seen with their own eyes the terror that few have witnessed.

Watch, dear cats, for those mice. They will do anything to fool you. They will even tell you they love you with their last dying breath.

* * * * * * * * * *

As timely as this story may be in the context of this narrative, it is nevertheless timeless in the lessons that it teaches. On the surface, it is a simple cautionary tale that I myself would have been better to read before getting involved with Ferdinand and his ilk. And yet it also touches upon one of the greatest fears of all cats: that inside, we are not really all that different from the creatures we hunt. That is why it brings such a chill to our hearts.

I feel a great sense of accomplishment after finishing that story. To reward myself, I think I will spend the rest of the day at Catenation, where I have been getting to know the other accomplished cats of the world. Black and Tan are an ongoing presence in this online community, but I am meeting many other notable felines there.

Hercule's cold is worsening, unfortunately. He is coughing and congested, and seems altogether miserable. I am a bit worried, and should also like to spend some time with him this afternoon, to help lift his spirits.

* * * * * * * * * *

No more talk of hunts! No more talk of anything! My dear Hercule is weakening, and I fear the worst. His illness has grown most serious. Howie did not get up early to write this morning and so, it being my habit to accompany him in the morning to get my fresh kibble, I came downstairs late myself only to find Hercule emitting the most horrifying sounds as he gasped for air. It chilled my heart so, it almost froze still.

"Hercule!" I cried. "Are you O.K.?"

"I have been better, my friend," Hercule wheezed.

"Hang on," I said, and bounded up the stairs. Our caretakers were still sleeping, and I used the now rarely-employed cold nose on the lips technique to wake up Howie. He awoke quickly, but I became extremely frustrated during the precious minutes that followed, for his bullheadedness would not allow him to understand what I was trying to tell him. I wove between his legs, meowed and even resorted to biting his shins. Nothing seemed able to get his attention. He continued getting ready for work at his usual leisurely pace, telling me to go away and stop bothering him. I found I could make little headway with Alicia either, and of course there is no use appealing to the young Lizzie, who has no sense at all in her yet.

When our caretakers finally came downstairs, I meowed and gestured toward Hercule repeatedly, but in their rush to get out the door in the morning they were not willing to pause even for a moment to notice my dear friend's worsening condition. In the end, they closed the door behind them without realizing that anything was amiss and left us alone.

I sat with Hercule through the morning, close to panic, trying to keep his spirits up, all the while seething with rage and resentment at my caretakers' self-centeredness. Hercule has said little. I think he has already lost hope. Oh, my heart is breaking! I know not what to do. I think I will die of grief if I lose my dear Hercule. He is all that I have in this miserable world.

But I must pull myself together. It is now afternoon. I thought that by coming down here to write I might lift some of the oppressive weight off my heart. But nay, it is of no use. Nothing will help save Hercule's complete recovery, an outcome I grow less optimistic about by the second.

It is still hours before our caretakers arrive. I hope they will finally notice the condition of their beloved pet. I must return to him now. He is taking a nap at the moment, but I want to be there when he awakens.

* * * * * * * * * *

I write here not for your benefit, dear reader. Not anymore. My mind is in complete turmoil. My heart threatens to shut down with grief. This manuscript is now a therapy for me. I have been lying on top of Hercule's cage all night in the vain hope that I might provide him some warmth and comfort, as a mother hen might do for her unhatched eggs. But it is of little use. My friend worsens with each passing moment. He moves so little now. He wheezes and shuffles a bit to make himself more comfortable, but he says virtually nothing at all. I say little myself, as I know not what I can say.

It is almost morning now. I must get off the computer soon, for Howie may be coming down to write at any moment. Alicia finally noticed Hercule's condition when they got home last night. They are very worried now, too, but they resolved to wait until the morning to see how he is doing before calling Dr. Choi.

I fear it may be too late by then.

* * * * * * * * * *

My hopes are rising, my friends. A day and a half have passed. It is now late Sunday afternoon. The family is napping, so I have taken the opportunity to come downstairs and write this entry. It must be quick, lest they wake soon.

My mind has been virtually bursting with emotion: worry, despair, elation, hope. They are all mixed together, and I know not which to give prominence to at any given moment.

Our caretakers took Hercule to Dr. Choi's office yesterday morning. Hercule, although weak, received some small degree of hope there. He told me wearily that he had been given some medicine and that, although the prognosis was not very good, there were still grounds for hope. Howie and Alicia have continued to administer this medicine, and I am happy to report that, by this afternoon, I was able to discern an improvement in my dearest friend.

I continue to keep my claws crossed, dear readers, and hope for the best.

* * * * * * * * * *

Oh, it is too much to be endured! I do not know how to write this. I suppose I must be direct.

Hercule is dead.

Sadness and pain are all too plentiful in this universe, and I have suffered more than my fair share in this short life. I type now with tears in my eyes. My heart overflows with sorrow. My paws are so heavy they can barely move across the keys. Each moment, I feel I will not live to the next. And yet, I find some comfort in this old ritual of writing which my dear friend Hercule so encouraged me to pursue. It is all I can do now.

It is hard to believe that he is gone. How many times have we spent the afternoons discussing our hopes and dreams? How many nights have I woken him up when a brilliant idea suddenly struck me and Hercule, dripping with sleep, nevertheless indulged my fancy and listened to what I had to say? How many hundreds of conversations have we had about art and culture and the quirks of human behavior? How much advice has he given me during the time we have known each other? How much laughter and camaraderie have we shared? He may have been a pig, but he was a great pig, a dedicated friend, and indeed I loved him with all my heart.

"What am I to do without you?" I cried last night when he seemed to be turning for the worst.

"I'm an old pig, Hastings," he said with what little energy he had left. "You knew you would have to lose me one day."

"I knew nothing of the sort, Hercule! You are not old."

"I've had the fortune to live for more than six years. That's well past fifteen in cat years."

"But there's so much more to do!" I cried.

"I've done enough, my dear boy."

"Hercule, what can I do for you now?"

"Nothing, Hastings, nothing. Just keep me company, if you will."

"Then you have nothing more to say to me?" I asked in desperation.

He shook his head. "My only regret is that my art never knew an audience."

"But I thought you always said it was for your own enrichment."

"It was." He coughed a deep, bronchial bark and then, recovering, continued, "It has enriched my life greatly, but I sometimes wonder if others might have appreciated it as well."

"Many would have been enriched by it, my dearest pig."

"I'll never know," he shrugged, and then launched into a horrible coughing fit.

When he had settled once more, I muttered, "I don't know what I'll do without you," and found the tears coming to my eyes.

"Hastings, please, you make me feel terrible for dying. I have no choice in the matter. I've accepted my fate. You must accept it too."

"I will not! I do not accept it!"

"That's the spirit I love in you, Hastings. Don't you ever lose it."

I sunk down and buried my head in my paws, letting myself cry to my heart's content. I continued to cry for some time.

"Hastings," Hercule eventually murmured.

"Yes, Hercule?" I asked, looking up and trying to gather myself. I am certain my eyes were as red as felinely possible, but even if his eyes had been open, it would have been too dark for Hercule, with his inferior eyesight, to see it.

"I have one thing to tell you before I go," he said between labored breaths. "Never lose your fire." He was then interrupted by an eruption of sharp bronchial coughs. It seemed an eternity before they settled down so he could continue. "Never give up on your dreams," he said so softly that it was almost a whisper. "Don't let my passing change that."

"I shan't go on without you!" I burst forth. "I can't, Hercule. I can't!"

"You'll find a way," he assured me. "Now I need to close my eyes and rest."

"I love you, Hercule! I love you as a friend has never loved another before."

"Good night, Hastings," he said gently.

I burst into tears once more.

Those were the last words we ever said to each other. Howie came down in the morning to find Hercule already growing stiff, the life force long departed. I can only hope that Hercule has gone on to a better place. He certainly deserved to.

My caretakers held a little funeral, digging a hole in the backyard beside the air conditioner. They put my best friend in a shoe box, along with some of his favorite things to accompany him to the afterlife: a carrot, a piece of apple, some Timothy hay. I watched from the window in the computer room and cried the whole time.

Although they looked quite somber, my caretakers did not draw one tear as they buried our dear friend Hercule. I could hear through the window as Howie and Alicia explained to Lizzie that Hercule was not sleeping and would not come back. Their voices may have cracked perhaps a little, but while each word tore brutally at my heart and made me cry even harder, they themselves seemed hardly affected beyond their concern for how their young girl would react.

These people did not love Hercule as I loved him. They will not feel this loss as I will. They have their family, and they have their friends. I have nothing. I am all alone in the world now. All ...

alone.

Alone and Adrift

I have not written for some weeks now. I hadn't the heart and I hadn't the stomach. My caretakers have observed my sadness and despair, correctly guessed at the cause, and yet wonder in surprise that I, a cat, could miss a dear friend like I do. Humans are so self-absorbed. They think that they are the only creatures with feelings.

My sorrow has indeed been deep. It is compounded by the fact that Hercule is far from the first dear companion I have lost. First I was taken from my friend and mentor Buddy; then from Mo, who might have shown me a different life; and now the greatest loss of all, the death of my soul mate Hercule. The heavens seem determined to deny me companionship! Must I wander this planet alone? What have I done to deserve such a fate? Tell me, great Bastet! What have I done? I may ask these questions, yet there is never any answer forthcoming.

It has been a very long, dark, gloomy winter. I miss my friend so deeply. I wander around this big, empty house quite aimlessly, gazing blankly at its beige carpets and bare white walls, looking for nothing and finding nothing. My only diversions have been the routine mouse hunts I have undertaken in order to uphold my pledge to keep my home mouse-free. It is disconcerting to sit here now, perched in front of the computer once more to tell my story, when I have so little to tell. My heart feels empty, and yet so heavy at the same time, as if its encasing had grown thick and calloused even as its interior thinned. It is now but a weighty sack with little inside.

I have turned to literature to pass the time; that is the one thing I can report to you. At least my curiosity for that has not completely waned. In fact, I have become quite well read this winter, pouring through my caretakers' collection: Dickens, Austen, John Irving, et cetera. It seemed a very lonely endeavor at first, but I soon found the company of Samuel Pickwick, Lizzy Bennet and Garp quite diverting, at least for a time.

I have lately been thinking about my own writing. This may shock you, my dear reader, but in my dark hours I have been questioning the validity and quality of my own work. I suppose you could say I have been having something of an existential crisis. This has doubtless been brought on by the loss of my one and only true friend, but it has also been encouraged by my recent discovery of the likes of Jean-Paul Sartre and Albert Camus in my caretakers' bookshelves.

I now question whether I am accurately representing in this book my own life as it really happens. Although I myself am doubtless the one who knows my own life the best, anything that one writes, no matter how realistic one believes it to be, is necessarily a distortion of the truth. Memory distorts events—perhaps unconsciously dropping a detail to protect us from hurt, changing another to flatter us, and so on. We can never ourselves give a completely factual account of the events in our lives, no matter how hard we try. Cats may have superior minds and be less susceptible to such unintentional distortion than humans, but we are nonetheless still vulnerable to it to some degree.

Furthermore, no matter how good one's writing, readers will inevitably view your words through the prisms of their own individual experiences. No matter how precisely you phrase something, your readers will bring their own interpretations and distort your most cherished ideas. For example, consider the breathtaking diversity of purposes for which the human species has used and misused one single book, the Bible.

Thus, I must conclude that if the purpose of this book is to accurately convey the events of my life, then I am destined to fail, for there has never been a single biography or history, much less an autobiography or memoir, that has given its readers an accurate account of what has truly happened.

So should this book be something more? Is its purpose to influence you, dear reader, into adopting a certain type of behavior? No; that is what *The Kibble* is intended to be.

After considerable thought about this topic, I have come to the conclusion that it is not a hopeless endeavor to try to convey one's thoughts to others. Is that not our whole purpose in life, to try to make such connections with others? However futile these attempts, we must nevertheless continue to try.

And so, dear readers, I continue my book, such as it will be without the constant input and perspective of my dear friend Hercule. Proceed forward, if you can stand to. I, for my part, shall not desert you.

* * * * * * * * * *

Life does not conform to any easy order, my dear readers. Humans seem to expect that, like a bad short story in one of those literary journals Howie is always buying in the vain hope of being published in one, there is a reason for everything in life. But life is not like that at all. There are no epiphanies. Things do not fit together neatly. Friends do not behave like you want them to, and loved ones die when you need them the most. Life is one big, ugly mess of a thing—or a beautiful wonder, I suppose, depending on your mood. Good literature, if it is to reflect life in any meaningful way, must be the same.

Dear reader, you may have assumed that I have carefully plotted this narrative, that I have outlined when and where I will present certain arguments, and that I have carefully examined their potential effects. But I am exposed. I have done nothing of the sort. I might just as well insert a chapter upon strings as explain to you my emotional state, which is gloomy and sullen. In fact, I think I shall.

* * * * * * * * * *

Upon Strings

What can be said about strings that has not been said before? Indeed, I maintain there is much that remains to be said upon this topic. Strings are everywhere. They intrude on our lives, sticking out and hanging down when we least expect them, teasing us when we least welcome them.

Here we are, strolling downstairs to use the litter box when . . . string! There is one hanging from the edge of the tablecloth, and we must take care of it. Then we become so distracted at chewing and chomping and trying to get the cursed thing from hanging down like that, that we almost forget our original destination. Our bladders might burst for the cursed things!

Or we might be lying in our caretakers' beds, trying to take a quiet, peaceful nap. But lo! Look at the pillowcase! There is a string hanging from the corner. How can we neglect this tantalizing piece of thread sticking out so erect? We cannot. We must gnaw at it until it is gone, slapping and slurping with our mouths until it is covered with saliva and sticks out no longer, else we shall have no peace.

If I believed there was a god, I would believe that he or she created these accursed things solely to plague our lives. What have we done, dear god, I might ask, to deserve this terrible fate, to always have these strings sticking out and teasing us, distracting us from our greater missions?

We might determine to view strings as simply unwelcome things in our lives, like mice and babies, that we nevertheless must learn to tolerate. But I prefer to act, to try to remove any and all of these dastardly objects from my sight as soon as they pop into view.

Alas, I fear that the end result of my diatribe about strings will bring little solace to my readers. I advise you only to remember this and to use it to comfort yourself in your darkest hour: You are not alone.

Indeed, the string tortures us all, and we must torture the strings in return until they retract, laden with spit, back into the cloth from which they came.

* * * * * * * * * *

Oh, how cruel is life. Just when one thinks one is ready to move on, to put a tragedy behind oneself and face life anew—no! The mind will not concede. It brings back the insult; it will not let you forget the past. I wrote the previous chapter upon strings weeks ago with all the hope and energy of an artist renewed. But it was a false start. I had no more energy to continue afterward than Hercule had after his visit to Dr. Choi, when he seemed so improved yet was merely expending the last strength he had in a brief burst before his ultimate fall.

More than once in the weeks since I last wrote, I have despaired that I might never write again. Yet a major life event has brought me back to the keyboard, if only for a moment. Only time will tell if this is to mark a true upturn in my determination.

A child is born to my caretakers. Thankfully, with this second birth I have not been banished. Without Hercule's company, a banishment such as we had to endure upon Lizzie's arrival would have been absolutely intolerable.

No, Howie and Alicia seem altogether more relaxed with this second baby than their first, either from experience or simply the sheer exhaustion caused by their constant indulgence of their first child. I witnessed the new baby's arrival in our home and the subsequent fuss as relatives and friends visited to gush over him and, inevitably, tease his parents about the wisdom of having another child. Incidentally, my fellow felines, why humans engage in this ritual is beyond me. It seems quite cruel, in my estimation; there is too much truth in it for me to understand how it could possibly amuse them.

In any case, the boy's name is Colin. He seems a sweet thing, nothing like the hurricane named Lizzie. He cries, yes, but this is an altogether different experience. It seems as if, when he cries, he is trying to communicate something—although I never have any idea what it is—rather than just making a great deal of noise to irritate all those around him, as was Lizzie's habit.

The child's agreeable nature aroused my curiosity, and I went to greet him at the first quiet opportunity I could find. Alicia had put his carrier down on the floor in the family room yesterday afternoon, asking Lizzie to watch him for a moment while she prepared something in the kitchen. Being little more than a baby herself, Lizzie promptly wandered off to the other side of the room, availing me of the opportunity to make the acquaintance of the new arrival.

I approached cautiously at first, but as the creature did little more than make gurgling sounds and twitch his arms harmlessly, I drew closer to his face until I could smell the warm scent of milk on his breath. If the eyes are the window to the soul, as some say, then there is a calm serenity in this child's soul that strikes me as most soothing. He seemed almost to smile at me as I peered into his hazel eyes.

I pulled my gaze away and proceeded to circle him slowly, followed by the powdery odor of the cream they use on his skin, which thankfully masked almost completely that of the dried milk and spittle on his clothing. When I returned to his face, he looked at me with the most familiar expression. I can provide no explanation for the sensation, but I suddenly felt an uncanny tenderness toward this human child. Perhaps I am overly emotional from the loss of Hercule.

Alicia's return ended our encounter. "Hastings, you've made a new friend," she said, or something to that effect. To be frank, I pay little attention to what either of my caretakers says anymore. They so grossly misunderstand my motivations and feelings, I have little tolerance even for their presence anymore. I promptly left the room, determined to return to Colin at the earliest opportunity.

There is little else to report, my friends. I have been thinking of taking up *The Kibble* once more, or perhaps beginning another of my planned projects such as *The Essential Cat's Guide to Living with People*, but I still haven't the energy to embark on such an effort. The soft bed will call me, or else the warm sunbeam shining through the sliding glass doors downstairs. I suppose I am a depressed cat, but what is to be done about it?

* * * * * * * * * *

Holy Bastet!

You may very well evoke the great cat goddess, too, when you read what I have to report. It has to do with a human concept called reincarnation, which we animals have no experience of.

Reincarnation is the process by which a creature's soul—that is, their essential spirit, the thing that makes them what they are—is returned to earth in another body. Some people think that souls go through many such cycles. If you are good, for example, you may be reincarnated as a cat. If you are bad, on the other hand, you might come back as a mouse. This is a most ridiculous concept, of course—until, that is, you see evidence that it has occurred.

Such has happened to me in the case of the new boy Colin. Howie and Alicia were talking earlier this evening about what a kind, gentle disposition the boy has. This is lucky for any family, but how unusual it must be for a couple that has borne a creature such as Lizzie. How can it be explained?

"You know," sayeth Howie, "if I didn't know any better, I'd say Hercule has been reincarnated in our son."

I nearly fell off my perch on the back of the couch, dear reader. By the way, that is merely an expression. Worry not; nothing is wrong with me. My balance is fine, and I was quite stable in my position. But metaphorically speaking, I was so surprised it felt somewhat like I was falling off my perch.

Alicia agreed. "He was such a good piggy. Maybe this was his reward."

"He did die while Colin was inside you," Howie said. "Maybe his soul just went right into Colin."

"I think it might have," Alicia agreed.

"Too bad I don't believe in that stuff," Howie said in a tone I suppose he thought wry.

But I believe it, dear reader! I believe I do. The evidence in favor of the theory is overwhelming. If you would just meet these children, you would understand that despite their common parentage, there is a deep, fundamental difference between them.

I now believe that Colin was given Hercule's soul, perhaps as a gift to me from some deity to accompany me through this dreary, difficult life. If this is true, then I must assume that the deity in question was the great Bastet herself, however fictitious we previously believed her to be. Perhaps she really does watch over all our lives.

I must say, for the first time since Hercule's death I am looking forward to the remainder of mine.

* * * * * * * * * *

I cannot be certain of what Colin can understand, but the first time I spoke to him, I believe I detected a glimmer of recognition in his eyes as he smiled at me. I tell him now about everything that is happening in my life, just as I used to when he was the guinea pig Hercule, and his round hazel eyes gaze at me with interest whenever I speak.

I wonder if Hercule is conscious in this new body. Is he is aware of what has happened and happy to be reunited with me? Or does he really have no memory of his previous existence, everything seems new to him, and this face of mine simply brings him warm feelings he can't explain?

I told him today about how I am becoming active once more on Catenation, and from the bright smile he gave me, I can only conclude that he heartily approves. I have been participating, in fact, in the online chat rooms quite frequently, and have met the most wonderful kitty named Hastel. She is cultured and erudite like myself, and she lives not far from Tan and Black. I think we may have a future together.

Oh, things are finally coming together at last, dear readers. My spirits are rising once more. I believe I have weathered this storm. And having triumphed over the darkness wrought by the death of such a close friend, I can only be stronger. At least, that is what people say. The truth of it remains to be seen. However, I do distinctly feel my spirits elevated for the first time in months, and a big part of the reason for that is the tender essence of my dear friend Hercule beaming from within the body of the baby Colin.

Howie and Alicia have indeed noticed my camaraderie with their new son and have commented on how "good" I am with him. It is no secret to anyone that I like him, although they might wonder why. I look forward to seeing this child grow up and eventually become my caretaker himself. I am certain that he will be attentive beyond imagining. Unfortunately, judging from the pace of Lizzie's development, I have a good deal of time to wait before that day comes to pass.

* * * * * * * * * *

I have been chatting much with the kitty Hastel online of late. She seems a true kindred spirit. She reads works of classic literature, frequently ponders the vagaries of life and has a keen interest in the visual arts. She also has the freedom to pursue hobbies, such as bird catching, that I find absolutely fascinating but do not yet have the means in which to partake. I would like here to preserve a transcript of our latest private online chat:

Has3tings7y142: My dear kitty, are you not tired of the mundane nature of this isolated life?

H43astel300985L: Indeed I am, my darling Hastings.

Has3tings7y142: But when shall we meet? I feel it will never happen.

H43astel300985L: I am free to roam. It is you who must leave your home.

Has3tings7y142: Oh, I would love to meet you, dear kitty, and to put your paw in mine, but it is very comfortable in my home and I quite like it here.

H43astel300985L: Life is nothing without risk, my dear Hastings. Risk nothing and you shall gain nothing.

Has3tings7y142: You are wise, my dear Hastel. Very wise. I will come to you, I pledge, one day. But I have unfinished business to attend to here. You must wait for me.

H43astel300985L: I will wait for a while, but I will not wait forever. My heart is pounding in anticipation, Hastings.

Has3tings7y142: Great Bastet! I can hear it over here, dear kitty! I will come to you, I swear!

And thus, my fellow felines, you can see that I have a problem.

* * * * * * * * * *

I pine for Hastel every waking moment. It is quite a disconcerting feeling.

As you know, dear readers, I am quite a learned scholar on the subject of love, and am well aware that in all likelihood my heart will be ruined by this beautiful creature. Yet I cannot stop thinking about her. I do not know what I shall do.

In the meantime, life goes on in our household. Colin is already noticeably larger than he was at our first meeting. He is beginning to gain some degree of control over his body, pushing himself up somewhat when he is lying on his belly, reaching for things and grasping objects that are placed in his hands. Most notable, however, is the growing intelligence in his eyes. There is now no longer any question, if there ever was, that this boy feels a kinship with me.

Outside, the plants are budding once more, the animals are scurrying about, and I sit by the window enjoying the sights. The wonder and splendor of spring lift my spirits, as does the force of the love that I am feeling. Yet I am torn asunder as this love cries to express itself. I have been inspired to write a poem expressing this troubled exaltation:

Love From Afar
by Hastings

The eyes of a kitty.
What they hold
Is far from a mystery.
One look at them
Makes you captive.

But if you can't see her eyes
She can't touch your soul.
Words can hide lies.
When true love is your goal
Distance takes its toll.

* * * * * * * * * *

It may hardly seem an appropriate topic to follow my deeply heartfelt poetry, but I am most vexed at the moment by my caretakers disparaging the bunnies in the backyard. They are very angry because they believe that the bunnies have been eating the roses. However, I have witnessed the culprit, and I can report with confidence that it is not a bunny but a squirrel!

Yet my caretakers never seem to suspect the squirrels. It is most uncanny. The squirrels bound about on top of the fence, run across the grass and enter the various sections of the garden with regularity—and yet the humans seem not to even notice their existence.

Their reactions to the bunnies are quite the opposite. If one bunny happens to hop across the yard, they become nearly unhinged.

Alicia: "Look! Lizzie! Out the window."

Lizzie (running to window and looking out): "Bunny!"

Howie: "Yes, a bunny rabbit. See him go?"

Lizzie: "Go! Go!"

And so on and so forth. You would think that the Holy Trinity had suddenly appeared out of the woods. It is most absurd. Furthermore, they accuse the bunnies of crimes they did not commit, as if there were no other suspects running about the garden at all hours of the day. Eating the roses, indeed!

My fellow felines, were it not for Colin and my loyalty to Hercule, I would not remain with these silly people for one moment longer. As you know, something altogether more enticing awaits me.

Oh, how I pine for Hastel! She assures me that she is most attractive, with light gray fur and green eyes. I can see her beautiful visage—or at least, the image I have drawn of her in my mind—every waking moment. Elegant and refined, this striking beauty haunts me.

I must go to join her soon.

* * * * * * * * * *

I regret to report that my caretakers have adopted not one but two guinea pigs—and both of quite disagreeable character.

Their names are Carter and Hoffman. They were named, as I discovered whilst grooming on the fireplace mantle during Howie and Alicia's conversation in the family room, after E.T.A. Hoffman, the supposed creator of the great Murr, and Angela Carter, another of Howie's favorite authors, who wrote the novel *The Infernal Desire Machines of Doctor Hoffman.* This latter, incidentally, was inspired by a Hoffman short story, *The Golden Pot.* I have read both, of course, and must confess that I thought them both somewhat ridiculous at the time. However, now that I am in love under Hastel's spell, I must concede that perhaps these works of high romance had something more to them that I didn't perceive upon first reading. Such is the way with literature; so much of one's experience with a work depends on one's state of mind at the time one reads it.

Whether or not I approve of the names for these two pigs, I most certainly do not approve of the creatures themselves. They are vapid and silly, and do not in any way justify names of such pedigree. They would better be named Imbecile One and Imbecile Two, in my opinion. They prance and giggle, take nothing seriously, and are altogether an annoyance.

"Hello!" I said to them upon their arrival. "Welcome to my home."

"Hello there," chirped Carter.

"Hello," cooed Hoffman.

"Is there good food to eat here?" Carter asked.

"And nibble sticks?" Hoffman inquired. "What about nibble sticks?"

"You will have ample food here," I assured them, anxious to get past these basics and learn more about their true passions.

"Ample?" Carter asked. "I've never heard of that brand!"

"No," I corrected. "You will have enough food here."

"Well, of course we'll have enough food. How could we not, silly?"

"You might not if you had another caretaker."

"Not have enough food!" Carter burst out. "Don't be ridiculous."

"What's the brand if it's not Ample?" Hoffman asked.

"I don't know what brand it is," I said patiently. "Ample is another way of saying 'enough.'"

"Why don't you just say 'enough,' then?"

"Sometimes I choose to use different words. It's my prerogative."

"Oh," Carter said, drawing back a little, "I can see that you're a fancy cat."

"Oh, a fancy cat," Hoffman echoed.

"He uses the big words. He must be superior."

"No, most superior," Hoffman mocked my tone.

"Well, if you don't want to be friends . . .," I began.

"Why do you think we'd we want to be friends with a stupid cat anyway?" Carter exclaimed.

"Please!" Hoffman agreed.

"Yeah, please!"

"Well then," I said with a slight bow, "I shall take leave of you now."

"Take anything you want. Just stop bothering us. Go play with your stupid cat toys!" At that, they both burst into laughter.

Suffice it to say that I have left them alone since. They are stupid, senseless creatures, with none of the artistic talent or intellectual curiosity of their porcine predecessor.

These pigs provide yet more fuel for my burning desire to escape. I now wish little other than to join my dear Hastel, with whom I continue to develop quite a deep and committed online relationship. It is only a matter of time now before we are together. I can quite guarantee that.

* * * * * * * * * *

It is the final nail in the coffin. The straw that broke the camel's back. The ____ that ____, if you care to insert a metaphor of your own choosing.

The young Colin has grabbed my fur! If ever there was a proof of my foolish misguidance, my fellow felines, it is this! My beloved friend would never grab my fur in such a vicious, inconsiderate manner! I now must ask myself how I could have believed that this boy was the incarnation of my dear Hercule.

It was a Saturday morning and we were all in the family room. I was doing nothing, minding my own business, stretched out by the window napping. Colin, who is now capable of some rudimentary motion, must have crawled over to me with the greatest of effort for the express purpose of grabbing my fur, for I woke up with a peal of pain to find a clump of fur near my tail secured in his grubby fist.

I howled, and Howie and Alicia both jumped to my defense. They released me fairly quickly, but it was too late in one sense, dear readers. This event now leaves me with no reason whatsoever to stay with them. It is now settled. I am to leave this house at the very first opportunity. I shall go to my love and I shall live the rest of my life in joyous happiness.

I have but one more duty to fulfill, and that is to leave you with the conclusion of *The Kibble.* I shall post all that I have written on the Catenation web site, and we will see what will become of it. As I have said, I am not averse to the idea of others adding stories in between mine, to teach other lessons and to encourage other sorts of behaviors. In the future, I may decide to return to my masterpiece myself one day. I expect, however, that this project will take on a life of its own.

And so, here it is: the way it all ends.

* * * * * * * * * *

Exposure

It had been many generations since Elis and Ulla first wandered into The Lost Forest and spawned the race of wild cats that lived there. These cats had learned to live together in harmony, each with an area to call their own but always ready to cooperate to fend off larger predators or help in any other way. They were content and at peace.

But there was one cat named Yorick who had great dreams. Earnest and passionate, he never ceased thinking of ways to make life better for all of them. He envisioned a society where cats cooperated to build shelters from inclement weather, to design devices allowing them to communicate across great distances and to create weapons to vanquish large predators. Perhaps most important, he believed, would be the invention of a method for recording ideas, which would allow all of society's collective knowledge to be combined and passed from generation to generation and from place to place. With such a tool, he maintained, each generation of cats could grow smarter and more successful.

Yorick described his ideas excitedly to whoever would listen. But his plans made little sense to the others, who were content with their comfortable ways and who were lacking in imagination and foresight. They would shake their heads at his silliness and dismiss him, "You really say the most ridiculous things, Yorick."

The longer that Yorick's ideas were ignored, the more desperate he grew to promote them. But as his stridency grew, so did the other cats' resistance. He eventually developed a reputation for being insane, and so no one came to take anything that he said seriously, no matter how valuable the idea.

One day, Yorick presented what he thought was a very practical proposal. "Please," he said, "Please listen to me. The rainy season is coming. Let us try to build shelters in the trees to protect us from the rain. Let us try to devise ways to store food in case fresh food is unavailable to us."

"You always worry so much, Yorick," they said to him. "But none of your scary scenarios has ever come to pass."

"But what if this one does?!"

"And what if the sky were to fall?" they laughed. "There are some things you can't do anything about. It's best not to worry about them."

"But we can do something about this," Yorick argued, "if we all work together."

"Leave us alone, you crazy cat," they said. "The sun is warm today, and we would like to enjoy it without bothering ourselves about things that will never happen."

And so it came to pass that a particularly violent storm struck their forest. The river that ran through the center of the forest began to overflow its banks, and before the cats knew what was happening, the ground around them became covered with rushing water.

Now, Yorick had long ago located some comfortable branches in which to live, high in a thick, strong tree and with a space in the trunk in which he had stored some food. When the flood came, he invited the other cats to join him, but none would pay him any attention.

"Yorick, you silly cat," they said to him, "it is just a temporary thing. The water will go down soon." And they sat in whatever branches were nearby, watching as the water passed beneath them.

But the rain did not stop. For forty days and forty nights, Yorick sat on his branch sighing mournfully as he watched the chaos unfold below. Hungry cats jumped desperately from tree to tree looking for birds to eat. Many fell in the water and were carried away. Trees started to uproot and fall, taking the cats seeking shelter in them splashing down into the raging water. All the while, Yorick called to the others to join him, but none would consider listening to crazy old Yorick.

Some of the cats were carried away from The Lost Forest altogether and found themselves cast out into the world outside, the legendary place ruled by humans. These are the cats that live among humans today. They had no guidance for surviving in this new world other than the vestiges of stories that had been passed from generation to generation. These stories had been so distorted over the years that they provided little practical advice about how to live with people. In fact, the lost cats were surprised to find that humans had two legs, not three.

The cats soon discovered that humans speak very sweetly to fool you, then lock you inside their homes with no hope of escape. If you scratched their possessions in revenge, they would remove your claws in a very painful procedure. You might want to procreate, but they could remove your sex and prevent this most fundamental of life's functions.

They tried desperately to find The Lost Forest again, but to no avail. Many dedicated their lives to the task, much as their ancestors generations before had searched for a way out of The Lost Forest. But like those other cats, none ever succeeded in recovering what they had lost.

"If we had only listened to Yorick!" they lamented.

We cats who now live in human society are descended from these poor unfortunate souls. We are doomed to feel at home nowhere.

And what became of Yorick? When the rain finally stopped and the water receded, he found many water-logged corpses on the forest floor, but not one cat left alive in The Lost Forest but him.

Alas! Poor Yorick! Always trying to help others but never respected, much less appreciated. He was condemned to die as frustrated as the day he was born. High up in his tree, he lived all alone to the end of his days with only the birds and the bugs for company.

If only the others had listened to reason.

* * * * * * * * * *

They say a cat has nine lives. We know better than that, of course. Like all the other creatures on this earth, we have but one.

And that life is all too fragile. A car's wheel, a dog's jaw, a gang of children out for fun; any of these could end a feline life in an instant. We must all ask ourselves: Are we content to spend this one life indoors, away from Nature, which we so long for in our hearts? Are we content to seek solace in a solitary beam of sunlight filtered through a window pane, in a bowl full of processed kibble and in a bed shared with humans? This is not what we were meant for, my fellow felines.

You must make your own decisions, of course, but my time for reckoning has come. I have studied and learned a great deal. I have become a cultured and erudite cat. But the time for study has passed. It is time for action. I must now take my life into my own paws.

So farewell, my dear readers! Perhaps one day when I am old I will finish these memoirs and recount the rest of my wonderful life for you. For now, however, I must leave you, along with the home I have known so well these many years. My caretakers must catch their own mice now. They must content themselves to live with these two silly guinea pigs, a very loud daughter and a son whose soul is not nearly as pure as my Hercule's. They will miss me, I am sure. But I will not miss them.

You, dear reader, I will miss. I am sorry that I will not have your company on the rest of my journey through this life, but it is an unavoidable condition. I bid you all adieu and good luck in your own endeavors. Thank you for coming this far with me. I hope you have found the journey enlightening.

Your Humble Servant,
Hastings

Enlightenment

It has been only a matter of weeks since I wrote my last entry, but I am already quite a different cat than the one that left Shady Court. One thing that has not changed, however, is my dedication to you, my fellow felines. Even during my most harrowing adventures, I often found myself pondering how best to describe my experiences and wondering what lessons others might draw from them. The means by which I once more have access to a computer will presently become clear, but allow me first to begin where I last left you.

It was on a Saturday morning that I finally made my long-anticipated escape. I had made arrangements to meet my beloved Hastel that evening. I had actually been trying to arrange a meeting with her for some time, but she had inexplicably persisted in delaying the joyous hour. We were to meet at a particular park—coincidentally, I believed at the time, not far from the house of the dread Cousin Don. I was to meet her in this park at the wooden platform at the top of the large slide before sunset, so that we might watch the sun go down together.

My past attempts at escape proved to be crucial practice sessions. With a confidence born of experience, I waited behind the wall in the living room until Alicia went out the front door to get the newspaper from the driveway. As soon as she opened the door, I sprinted at full speed past her legs and onto the front yard.

My past escape attempts, I recognized, had failed because I hadn't any plan for once I was outside. This time, I had carefully plotted my entire escape route with the help of the wonderful online service Map—. All you need to do to use Map— is to type in your starting point and your destination, and this web site tells you the quickest and easiest route to your destination. Thus, I knew exactly which way to run when my paws hit the grass.

"Howie!" Alicia screamed as I raced across the front yard. But before her husband could even voice an impatient "What?" from upstairs, I was already halfway across the cul de sac. I rounded the corner in no time and never looked back. I imagine that Howie may have run around the neighborhood for some time looking for me and perhaps even gotten into his car to drive around, but they never found me.

I moved quickly through the suburban landscape, leaving my old life behind for good. Winter had ended. The ornamental cherries were in full bloom, and the brilliant azaleas added various colors to front yard displays.

My elation deflated somewhat when I reached my journey's first major road. It had only four lanes, but I had never been so close to so many moving vehicles before. Allow me to admit, my fellow felines, what a shocking terror I found their foul smells and roars as their engines belched and their tires noisily gripped the road. I was paralyzed for I know not how long, trembling and staring with astonishment at the grotesque sight before my eyes. Eventually, my hope pushed me to gather my courage and press on. I crept slowly along the road, crouching in the brush as far away from the pavement as possible.

I followed the map I had carefully memorized, but Map—, which is, after all, designed by humans, charts out the fastest way to go by car. Fully aware of this limitation, I had carefully charted out my own route, keeping to as many residential streets as possible. Unfortunately, touching pavement and crossing a handful of large roads during this long journey was unavoidable. I was somewhat prepared by the useful advice I had read in the primer on crossing streets posted at Catenation. At each crossing, I waited very patiently for long intervals of calm before venturing from safety. Nevertheless, it was quite a terrifying experience, and if I were not emboldened by my longing to see Hastel, I am not sure I would have continued on such a quest.

Prompted by this adventure, you may be happy to know, I subsequently proposed the concept of CatMap to the board of Catenation, and you may now thank me for the recent addition of that critical feature to the web site. CatMap will instantly tell you the best way to get where you are going without the use of any major roads, if such a thing is possible. This, my fellow felines, is but one of the numerous ways I have contributed to improving our way of life.

Finding the park Hastel had specified once I had reached the neighborhood was a simple matter. When I arrived, there was not a creature to be seen in the entire park. It was oddly still. I was hungry and thirsty after my long and trying journey, but I was too excited at the prospect of finally meeting Hastel to attempt to seek out any sustenance. I went over to the playground equipment, ascended the slippery slide with a little difficulty and settled down on the platform, resting my weary limbs as I waited for my soul mate.

It was the perfect setting, I remember thinking to myself. Hastel had chosen well. The playground sat at the end of a fairly large, open expanse of grass and backed against a thick cluster of trees. The deserted beauty of the locale struck me as the perfect place for a romantic tryst. My heart was brimming with joy and anticipation.

I must have fallen asleep—not a completely unexpected event after such an arduous trip, I might note. When I awoke, I heard noises all around me and looked down to see several toms swarming around the playground equipment rather than the beautiful green eyes of a sleek gray kitty, as I had expected.

This must have been a regular meeting place for these toms, I thought. I was livid. What a poor choice for a rendezvous Hastel had made. Surely she knew the feline comings and goings of a park in her own backyard. She was an outdoor cat, after all. Didn't she want the same privacy for our first meeting that I craved?

"Is that the great Hastings?" a large black and white spotted tom called up in a deep voice.

Assuming that these must have been Hastel's friends and that she had sent them to deliver a message to me, perhaps an apology for being detained, I answered promptly, "Yes, it is I, Hastings."

"Come on down, Hastings. We have something to show you."

"Is the lovely Hastel detained? Is she still planning to meet me?"

"Of course she's still planning to meet you, Hastings," he said, and the others meowed with laughter.

I became suspicious that something might be amiss. I stood up and walked cautiously around the edge of the platform to assess the situation. There were six toms, all bigger than I, circling the playground equipment quite aggressively.

"Where is she, my good friend?" I bellowed with all the confidence I could muster.

"I think you will find," he said in a chilling meow, "that you have few friends here, Hastings."

The manner of their subsequent attack was oddly passive. At first, they merely continued to circle below as I tried to decide what to do. But then two of them suddenly appeared behind me, and without so much as a word, swatted at me with their paws. Standing by the edge of the platform as I was, I lost my balance and tumbled to the ground. I landed on my feet, of course, but the others were waiting for me, and they immediately began to box me about the ears.

I did not panic, dear readers, although you may think I had reason enough to do so at that time. You see, you have the benefit of my hindsight and the foreshadowing I have so carefully laid down for your benefit. I was quite naive back in those days. In fact, I persisted in the belief that Hastel would soon come to my rescue and tell these toms to leave me alone.

They played with me in a seemingly harmless manner, batting me about fairly gently but never letting me run away. Every attempt I made to escape was countered by one of the menacing toms moving to block my way. When I began to tire, I implored them to stop playing with me. "I have passed your test," I panted. "Now let me through to see my dear Hastel."

This speech evoked hearty laughter from the toms, and their black and white spotted leader suddenly swatted at my face with his claws unsheathed. He sliced three lines across my cheek.

I lunged at the tom in anger, but he was quicker than I and darted away, leaving his colleagues to launch an all-out assault. I found myself collapsing to the floor under their weight, my right ear in someone's mouth, someone's paws around my neck, someone's claws in my flank.

It was vicious. My suffering was quite intense under their ruthless onslaught, and the last thing I remember before losing consciousness was the fleeting image of two felines that briefly caught my eye in the distance at the edge of the park. One was black as night, one orange and white. They looked on and nodded approvingly at my suffering.

* * * * * * * * *

They left me for dead. I am certain of that, my friends. Life is cheap on the streets. Those toms cared not a whit for my potential and the great works I was capable of bringing to the world. They care only for cruelty and power, and a feeling of triumph over another living thing. It is an elixir, victory, and these types gulp it without regard to the larger consequences.

I took myself for dead as well. I remember thinking as I staggered under the weight of their relentless onslaught that I would likely never wake again. But I did, my dear readers. I did, although I wished I hadn't.

The first time I awoke, it was already dark. I have no way of gauging how long I was unconscious. I lifted my head to look about, but the park was deserted. My head dropped back down, and that is all I remember.

I awoke two or three times during the night, but had not the strength to move. It was extremely fortunate that no fox or other animal found me then, for I was quite helpless.

When the morning sun broke, I awoke again and tried to move. My whole body cried out with pain, despite the cold air having dulled much of its feeling. I tried once more to move myself, but to no avail.

I remember lying on the cold, dew-covered grass hoping that the end would come quickly. I licked the cool drops off the stiff blades near my face to quench my thirst in an attempt to make myself more comfortable as I passed away. I chastised myself in the harshest terms as I lay there, thinking of how dumb I had been to trust the word of someone on the Internet. I realized even in that half-conscious state that Hastel hadn't been real; she was a creation, a composite designed specifically to appeal to me, to lure me into this trap and eventually to my death. I supposed Black and Tan had been the culprits, but it was impossible for me to be sure if that last image I thought I saw of them as I slipped from consciousness was real or simply a product of my imagination.

In any case, I no longer cared very much. I longed only to die so that I could stop thinking about my torn, shredded heart. The emotional wound was the deepest of all I had sustained.

* * * * * * * * * *

It was a group of boys that eventually roused me to move. They came later that morning, four of them, on two-wheeled bicycles with thick tires racing around the park. I watched them with curiosity and hoped that one would roll over my neck, thus putting me quickly out of my misery.

A pudgy one with oversized shorts passed close by and finally noticed me. "Hey, guys," he called, "look over here." The other three brought their bicycles near, and they all stood there straddling their crossbars, gripping their handlebars and debating what to do with me.

"He looks like he's dying," the pudgy one said.

"No, he's not," another answered.

"Well, he sure is gnarly looking."

"Let's pick up his tail and twirl him around to see what happens," said the third.

"Guys, I don't think we should touch it," advised the fourth. "We might get West Nile virus."

"You don't get that from cats, stupid," said the third. "You get that from birds."

"What about Lyme disease?" asked the fourth. "We can get that."

"Yeah, we could get that," the third agreed.

"My dad got Lyme disease," the pudgy one chimed in. "You can get medicine for that. It's no big deal. Why don't we just pick him up?"

"Guys, I'll bet he stinks," the second one said. "Let's just leave him alone."

I meowed in assent, and they laughed.

"He does look pretty beat up," the second one reconsidered. "Maybe we should bring him to a doctor."

"There are too many cats in the world anyway," the third said. "Let's just get him off the field and throw him in a ditch or something."

He stepped forward to touch me without waiting for an answer from his friends, and in my terror I felt a sudden surge of energy. I hissed and tried to get up. I fell right back down, but he backed away from me anyway. I suppose I must have been quite a frightful sight.

"You think he's going to bite me?" the boy asked nervously.

"Yeah," the pudgy one said in a voice suggesting the outcome was obvious.

"Shit, let's get some rocks and just stone him."

The others quickly agreed, and so they mounted their bikes to go and collect some rocks with which to kill me.

Spurred by the potential humiliation of thinking that my great and magnanimous life could be terminated by these four idiotic young boys, I mounted an absolutely Herculean effort to stand. The fear and adrenaline coursing through my system, my fellow felines, must have given me superfeline strength. I stood myself up on four wobbly legs and, my poor tattered body screaming in pain with each step, moved slowly in the opposite direction.

Before they had even noticed I had gotten up, I was able to slip into the safety of the trees at the back of the park. It was lucky for me that they had such brief attention spans. After an extremely cursory search, they were off on another presumably destructive adventure. I was left alone in the park once more.

* * * * * * * * * *

But where was I to go? I could not return to Shady Court, not after such a triumphant escape. Besides, there was nothing for me to go back to. I had long since grown out of that restrictive existence. The thought of living once more with those two new abhorrent guinea pigs ensured that I wouldn't even consider returning.

Sitting shivering in those woods at the edge of the park, hiding from the four boys as well as from any of my feline assailants who might come back to

270 - *The Life and Opinions of the Housecat Hastings*

check on my status, it seemed to me that the only friend I had left in the whole world was Mo. Calling Mo a friend is perhaps an exaggeration, I concede. I had not left Forest Drive with the best of feelings for him. However, Mo was the one and only cat I knew who might help me to get back on my own paws again. I had, in the past, made periodic attempts to find my old mentor Buddy on Catenation, but whatever had happened to him, he'd never learned to get onto Catenation, nor did anyone in the community know of him. I thus reasoned that the wisest strategy for me to pursue was to return to Forest Drive and hope that Mo could find it in his heart to help an old acquaintance.

My first task was to figure out how to get there. I limped slowly through the woods until I reached a neighborhood of small houses behind the park. I laboriously snuck across several backyards before I located a back door with a cat entrance. As I climbed inside, every inch of my flesh seemed to scream with agony. I prepared to beg for mercy in case I should encounter anyone. For all I knew, I was about to come face to face with one of the very toms who'd attacked me.

But the quaint kitchen in which I found myself was empty. It had white-washed wood cabinets and smelled of apple and spices, albeit of a distinctly artificial variety. I walked cautiously across the sky-blue linoleum floor and entered a den, where it warmed my heart to see a small computer stand with a printer. Both were already on, and so I was quickly able to print out a map using Map— to lead me back to Forest Drive. I was back outside in minutes without ever encountering a soul, either human or feline.

The tortuous journey that followed was long and arduous. Suffice it to say that I expended great effort to avoid any contact with human or feline for fear that either might finish me for good. I faced enough challenges without boisterous boys and tyrannical toms, from depressed deer who wished to share their misery with me to dastardly dogs that needed avoiding, to many stretches of pavement that needed to be crossed. My days as a cowering kitten in Martha's catopia seemed to reclaim me. I longed to disappear once more, darting under every bush I encountered and hiding behind every tree.

I returned to my old street looking quite thin and haggard after this arduous journey. I staggered slowly to our old house, only to find a creamy beige Persian sitting on the front steps watching me approach. *Oh Bastet*, I thought at the time, *how cruel you are!* To be greeted by one of these ghastly Persian aberrations, of all creatures, at my very own former place of residence. Why not simply send me back to Black and Tan and their tom friends so that they could finish the work they had begun?

I must have groaned aloud, for the Persian got up and came down the steps to greet me. "Are you all right?" she asked. "What's happened to you?"

"Do not fret," I replied. "It is nothing that death will not solve."

"Come inside, please," she said kindly in a lyrical, melodic voice. "You can have some of my food and water. You look famished."

"No thank you, my kind kitty. I am here to seek out my old friend Mo. Only he can truly help me."

It is fortunate, I suppose, that out of sheer exhaustion I was looking down at the time, for the look on this Persian's face might likely have given away Mo's fate, thus breaking my heart right there. But I was so exhausted, I looked only at the ground. There was a long silence, and I began to wonder what was the matter when the Persian asked, "You were a friend of Mo's?"

I nodded wearily and said, "I used to live in this very house."

"Why don't you come inside?" she said tenderly. "What's your name?"

"Hastings."

"Hastings, my name is Tess. Please, let me help you."

She ducked under my front leg and lifted my right paw onto her shoulders. She led me slowly around to the back of the house, bearing much of my weight, and squeezed through the cat door the new residents had installed.

I was greeted by a great shock inside. The house looked completely different than when I had lived there. Not only were the decorations different, which is to be expected, but new rooms had been added, an upper floor had been built onto the first, the diminutive kitchen had been greatly expanded, and the whole general design improved. It was no longer my old house at all. If I had had any presence of mind, I would certainly have noticed these major changes from outside the moment I had first glanced at the place.

"What's happened?" I exclaimed.

"What do you mean?"

"I used to live here, but it isn't the same at all."

"Oh, my owners renovated before we moved in."

I cringed at the word "owners," and she could tell something was bothering me. "What's wrong?" she asked. "Are you upset it's changed?"

"No," I muttered sadly, shaking my head. "It's what you said. Humans are not our owners. We are living beings, not trifles. They could no more own us than one of their own children. They are our caretakers."

"I agree with your sentiment, Hastings, but they do apply the rules of ownership to us."

"Well, I prefer not to think of it that way," I said, then grew dizzy and fell down onto the carpet.

"Why don't you just rest here, Hastings? My owners won't come home for a couple more hours. You can get back your energy, and we can talk more later."

I hardly knew what happened next. It was hours before I awoke.

* * * * * * * * *

Sometimes, no matter the particular insanity of a given family, it is nevertheless comforting to be instilled in one. Such was the case that evening when I finally awoke from my slumber. As I slept, the members of Tess's very large and, might I add, boisterous, family arrived home one by one. Tess stood guard over me and insisted on their kind treatment toward me. They respected her wishes until she finally roused me and asked me to go to her bed to rest for the night.

"Your bed?" I asked, groggy and only partially coherent. "But where will you spend the night?"

"Oh, I sleep in their bed most of the time anyway. My bed is very comfortable, though."

"May I impose on you for some nourishment before retiring?" I asked timidly.

"Of course you can, Hastings. Follow me to the kitchen."

I ate from her bowl, and the mother and grandmother of the house, perceiving Tess's kindness toward me, teased that Tess had found herself a boyfriend. I was surprised that the idea seemed such a novelty to them. Despite my exhaustion—and despite Tess being a Persian—her beauty was difficult to ignore. Her squashed face could certainly use some inflation, I thought to myself, but it seemed to me that beneath her copious amounts of long fur there was a fine, sleek figure. It really was a shame these Persian creatures had been forcefully bred like that, I thought. Doubtless her breeding was the main reason she hadn't brought a tom home before. Perhaps time and opportunity may have played a role as well, I considered, for she seemed to me a very young cat, unsoiled by the years as I was.

In any case, under their scrutiny I suddenly became very self-conscious about my appearance. I thought I must have been coated with dirt and blood after the trials I had been through, but when I glanced down at myself I found that I was actually quite clean. Surprised, I looked up at Tess. She gave me a slight nod and I realized that, while I had been asleep, she had been hard at work making my appearance acceptable.

"Thank you, Tess," I said warmly.

"You're welcome, Hastings," she answered with a wink, instinctively knowing what I was thanking her for.

She led me to her pink, fleece-lined, pill-shaped bed in the master bedroom and sat on the floor watching over me as I dozed off. Even though she claimed she hardly used it, the bed was infused with her sweet fragrance, and I found it very relaxing. The family retired a short time later, and I was comforted knowing that Tess was sleeping in the main bed just a few feet away from me. I thought of her as my guardian angel that night, and slept one of the soundest, most refreshing sleeps of my life.

* * * * * * * * * *

I heard the family bustling about in the early morning, but my body was filled with such a relaxed buzz that I kept my eyes closed and made no attempt to get up for some time. I finally climbed out of bed and stretched my aching body. The bedroom was empty, and there was no sign of anyone when I peeked my head out into the hallway. I stepped out and began to look around for Tess.

I went upstairs first, both because I was quite interested in seeing the new level and because it seemed a reasonable place to start a systematic exploration. My muscles protested with each step, but my curiosity drove me onward. The house really was considerably larger than when I had lived there. From the look of it, they needed the space, for every bedroom upstairs was occupied. The common decorative theme was clutter, with the flimsy furnishings packed so close I didn't know how a human could walk around. There were personal effects scattered and piled everywhere in quantities such as I have never seen. These people, I fancied, were like large squirrels, hoarding everything they could get their hands on for that one rare occasion when they might find a need for it.

In the end, I found only the grandmother at home. She was sitting on a couch in the living room watching television. When she saw me, she said, "Ah! Little cat. Tess is outside waiting for you." She had some kind of an accent—Greek or Turkish, I believe. After speaking to me, she promptly returned her attention to the television, so I helped myself to some of Tess's food and water and then headed outside to find her.

Tess was sitting on the front stoop, exactly where I had come across her the day before. She smiled when she saw me and asked how I was doing.

"I am doing fine thanks to you, Tess. How can I ever repay your generosity?"

"The bill's in the kitchen. Didn't you see it?"

I stared at her in amazement.

"I'm kidding, Hastings. I'm just kidding!"

I let out a sigh of relief.

"You really are tense, aren't you?"

"I have had a terribly rough week," I said, sitting down beside her.

"I know you have," she answered. "I shouldn't tease you like that. Can I ask what happened to you?"

"I was ambushed by a bunch of toms."

She looked surprised. "Ambushed? That's unusual. I didn't think our toms had the brains to cooperate like that."

I nodded sadly. "It was all set up by two kitties who don't like me. They pretended to be someone else, arranged a meeting with me, and then had their friends attack me."

Tess's mouth hung open in shock. When she finally gathered her wits about her again, she said, "I can't believe anyone could be so cruel."

"As you grow older, my dear kitty, you will discover how cruel this world really is."

"But how did they pretend to be someone else? Did they wear some kind of costumes?"

"No, no. It was all done on the Internet."

"The Internet?" she asked, perplexed.

"On the computer."

"On the computer!" she echoed incredulously. "What are you talking about?"

"I was online at Catenation."

Tess seemed more and more confused. "You don't know how to use a computer?"

"I certainly do," I said with pride.

"I don't believe it! I've never heard of a cat using a computer."

"Many of us can," I told her. "There are pockets of activity all over the world these days. Once one cat learns, he or she teaches others, and the phenomenon spreads. There are hundreds of cats who can do it now, if not thousands."

"I had no idea," she said, shaking her head in disbelief. "How did you learn?"

"I taught myself," I bragged. "First I taught myself to read by watching my caretakers read to their children, and then I studied how they used the computer until I figured out how it worked."

"That's incredible, Hastings! Would you teach me?"

"Of course," I said proudly. "I noticed computers in two of the rooms upstairs. But we must wait until the house is empty. No human can ever discover what we're doing."

"Do you live far away?" she asked.

"I live nowhere," I said wistfully. "I've run away from home."

"Well, I'm sure they'd be happy to take you back, Hastings."

"Yes, they would, but then they would lock me up again and I would never see you again," I said sadly. "You see, when they got me from the shelter, they had to sign a contract saying they would keep me indoors."

"So did my owners...," I flinched at the word, causing her to pause, but she promptly began again. "So did my caretakers, but they've never actually kept me locked inside."

"So I guess it was my bad fortune to have caretakers that abided by the law."

Tess nodded in agreement. There followed a long, awkward pause until I finally decided to broach the subject of Mo once more.

"After the ambush," I began, "I didn't know where to turn, so I decided to come find my old friend again. Do you know where Mo is?" I asked anxiously.

Tess sighed and gave me a look of deep sympathy. "Mo is gone, Hastings."

"Gone? They've moved, too? Do you know where they went?"

"His owners have moved, Hastings," she clarified, "but Mo didn't go with them."

I stared at her, unwilling to accept what she was saying. "What are you trying to tell me, Tess?"

"I'm trying to tell you," she sighed dolefully, "that Mo is dead."

"Dead!" I jumped up in anger. "Dead! The tom was in perfect health. What happened to him? Was he hit by a car?"

"No," she shook her head. "He was killed by another cat."

"Another cat! Another cat killed the beloved Mo? Have we no manners? Have we no civility? Must we constantly kill our own kind like this? Is the world not difficult enough for us that we must work to lower our own numbers as well? I lament this state of affairs!" I exclaimed in frustration.

"So do I, Hastings," she said calmly. "Our neighborhood has been terrorized for months by this cat. Killing Mo was only one of many things he's done to frighten us all."

"Then we must put a stop to it! Where is this cat? What is his name?"

"His name is Thrasher. He lives just down the street," she said, indicating the direction with a rightward tilt of her head, "about ten or twelve houses down. But I wouldn't go down there if I were you. He's very strong and very tough."

"Has no one tried to avenge him?" I asked, outraged.

"Three already have," she said, her voice a melancholy song. "They've all joined Mo now."

"Great Bastet! All three at once?"

"No, they challenged him separately."

"Ah, therein lay their problem. They should have made a coordinated attack."

"But that's not the way to duel, Hastings."

"How can this be the right way," I cried, "when four good toms lay dead at the paws of an evildoer? No, we must gather our forces and attack in unison to rid our neighborhood of this scourge. Come, Tess, we have work to do."

Tess reluctantly followed me as I worked my way down the street, moving in the direction opposite from Thrasher's house. While many of the cats I used to see had moved away, many others had arrived to take their places and so there were still a good number of felines in the neighborhood.

However, not one of these fellow felines would agree to join me on my mission. They proclaimed fearfully that, even united as a group, it would be folly to confront Thrasher.

And yet, dear readers, that is precisely what I intended to do.

* * * * * * * * *

I had been walking for perhaps an hour or two, trying unsuccessfully to recruit others to help in my assault, when I heard a deep, threatening meow behind me. I turned around to see a large, muscular gray cat approaching me on the sidewalk.

"Who dares try to rally the cats against me?" he roared.

"Hastings dares," I proclaimed.

"Hastings?" he said, stopping a few feet from me. "Hastings apparently has a death wish."

"Hastings will bring about your fall," I said threateningly.

"Well, come, Hastings. No time better than the present." He arched his back and hissed at me.

I felt no fear, dear readers. In fact, nothing was farther from my mind. I was reckless with anger. I had nowhere to go and no one to turn to. This tom in front of me had killed what I had seen as my very last hope. I was determined to make him pay for this offense or to die trying.

Cats from up and down the street started to gather around us as word spread of the impending confrontation. The crowd grew quickly, spurring us to make the front lawn of the nearest house a stage for our clash.

Tess remained by my side as we walked up onto the soft grass. "Hastings," she whispered into my ear in a voice that betrayed her rising panic, "normally I would say you had little chance of beating Thrasher, but in your weakened condition, I don't think you have any chance at all. Why don't you try to delay the duel, at least for a day or two?"

"Do not grieve for me, my dear Tess," I declared. "I fear him not."

"You should fear him."

"I do not fear death, and therefore I do not fear him."

"You must be crazy, Hastings."

"Such are those who change the course of history," I responded.

A large crowd had gathered around to witness the spectacle. I arched my back and hissed, stretching my limbs to their maximum length. Thrasher spread his claws threateningly, glaring at me.

"Hastings," Tess said in a low voice, "I've noticed that when Thrasher attacks, he almost always feigns to the left. He pauses briefly before going in for the kill. Do you understand?"

"To the left?" I whispered excitedly. "My left or his left?"

Tess paused for a moment, trying to quell her panic and think. "Your left," she finally said with confidence.

"Thank you, Tess," I said tenderly.

I glanced toward Thrasher. He seemed to be growing impatient to begin. I turned back and looked into Tess's beautiful golden eyes. "You have been very kind to me," I said. "I am extremely grateful for all you have done for me and, if I survive, I will surely repay you with interest. However, if I never do see you again, please remember me fondly, as a cat with good intentions. Grieve not, dear Tess. Wipe that sullen look off your face. My heart is already broken. Death will not be so different for me."

"Let's go!" roared the gray cat. "Stop pussyfooting around!"

Tess kissed me and wished me luck, then stepped back with the other cats.

"So," Thrasher roared, "you're angry about your friend Mo. Well, don't worry, pip, you're going to join him soon."

Thrasher approached me and swung with his paw. He hit me on the temple and sent me reeling. After he swatted me a couple more times, I realized that, with his longer reach, I stood little chance of competing in this manner. I therefore summoned all my anger and leapt right at him, claws unsheathed, mouth open for attack.

That was a surprise for him. I inflicted quite a bit of damage with my impassioned, relentless attack until he was finally able to throw me off. We paused, and I grinned at him with satisfaction. The crowd was struck with silent awe. They couldn't believe the brazenness of my approach.

"You'll pay for this!" Thrasher cried and lunged at me. But as Tess had graciously warned me he would, he feigned to the left and gave an involuntary pause that, as I was prepared to take advantage of it, proved to be quite a considerable weakness for him. Before Thrasher knew what had happened to him, my teeth had sunk into his neck. I bit down as hard as I could, tasting his salty blood as it flowed into my mouth. For an instant, I noted its agreeable character, but I quickly dismissed the observation to focus on the task at hand.

Thrasher swatted at me with relentless force, but I closed my eyes and refused to loosen my jaw, my fury blinding me to any pain my body might feel. He began to writhe in panic to try to throw me off, but I held strong until I felt his body weaken and then slump to the ground. He gradually stopped moving altogether. His body was completely limp before I finally released him.

My jaw was sore. My ears and cheeks ached where I had been slashed. But I had been victorious.

The cats roared with approval, rushing toward me to give me their congratulations. I realized that I was now a hero. I searched for Tess's long beige fur in the pandemonium and finally spotted her in the crowd. She was watching me silently, a mixture of fear and relief in her golden eyes. She nodded at me, and I nodded back in acknowledgment.

"My fellow cats," I shouted, lifting a paw. "My fellow cats, please calm down."

With my newly established authority, it wasn't long before they heeded my calls for their attention.

"First, will someone please check Thrasher to see whether he is still alive?"

"Oh, he's dead, all right," said a very tall, sleek black and white tom with a distinctive black patch around his right eye. His name, I later learned, was Sinbad. "He's very dead," he added with a smile, glancing down. I then saw what accounted for his inordinate height: he was standing on Thrasher's carcass!

"I came here to find my old friend Mo," I announced, turning around to make eye contact with as many cats as I could, "only to find that he had been murdered by this brute who I have now dispensed of." There was a roar of approval from the crowd, but I barely acknowledged it. Once they had calmed down, I resumed, "I would now like to know where Mo is buried so that I can pay my respects."

Tess had come through the crowd, and was now standing at my side. "He was left in the brush behind his house," she said. "No one buried him. His ow . . . caretakers never found him or even knew what happened to him."

"Was there at least a proper funeral service?"

Tess looked around, more for support than for an answer to my question, for she well knew that no one had given my old friend a proper funeral.

"Then we shall have a funeral," I declared in response to the silence.

Several cats volunteered to help me, and we quickly set about preparing for Mo's funeral, which we agreed would take place at three o' clock that afternoon in the brush behind his old house, where his body had been left to fester.

* * * * * * * * * *

We assembled at three, and a sadder group of cats the world has seldom seen. We had looked through the brush for Mo's body in the hope that we might be able to make a proper burial, but it was nowhere to be found. Doubtless some savage animal had taken the carcass. Instead, we used as a substitute a roasted side of beef that one of the cat's caretakers had burnt and discarded in the trash. We decided we would declare the symbol null at the end of the ceremony and use it as a centerpiece for the reception meal.

In addition to the roasted beef centerpiece, the neighborhood cats had put together quite a spread. One pair of sprightly young black cats, a young tom and kitty with the inexplicable names of Spike and Willow, lived with a pregnant woman who had had a craving for sardines at lunch but who had, upon opening the can and smelling its contents, immediately threw it into the trash untouched. Spike and Willow were thus able to procure fresh canned sardines for the reception. Many other cats contributed as well; there were chicken bones, fish bones, half a tuna fish sandwich and some half-turned milk. Best of all, a small group of cats spent the afternoon hunting to gather a fresh assortment of mice, sparrows and finches.

There were almost two dozen of us in all. Congregating around the roast, we used our imaginations to substitute in our minds the body of our dear departed Mo for the blackened hunk of beef before us. This vivid image brought forth a collective lament, a song whose notes came straight from our tormented hearts. It was the saddest, most miserable mourning ever heard.

Once our song of sorrow had ended, Sebastian, a gaunt cat with black tiger-like streaks who claimed to be an expert in such things, stepped forward and began the funeral oration. "My friends," he said, "today we lament the death of a dear friend to us all, a cat with a heart of pure gold, who always gave a paw to help out his fellow cat, who was always there for his friends and who tirelessly fought for truth and justice, no matter what the consequences.

"But let's be honest, dear friends; that is not really why we've all come here today. We've come to share our relief that it's not our own body lying here before us. We've come to celebrate the fact that it's someone else. Yes, we're glad that it's Milo on that pile of dead grass instead of us."

My heart jumped. "Mo," I corrected him.

"My name is Sebastian," he said, somewhat embarrassed for what he thought was my mistake.

"Not you. Him," I gestured to the hunk of meat. "His name was Mo."

"No it wasn't."

"Yes it was."

"Sebastian," Tess chimed in, "It's true. His name was Mo."

"Well, wither my whiskers. Who's Mo?"

"He was the white cat who always used to chase you down the street," she said under her breath.

Sebastian thought for a few moments, then suddenly seemed to find his memory. "Oh, I remember Mo!" he exclaimed. Then he frowned and asked, "I'm supposed to say nice things about him?"

"Yes, you are," Tess said.

Sebastian took a few moments to gather himself and then resumed, "As I was saying, whoever it may be lying dead in the weeds here, we come together to celebrate the fact that it was someone else and not ourselves. Better him than me, I always say. Life is not always pleasant, but it certainly is nicer to have it than not."

He cleared his throat with a sort of cough, looked around gravely and continued, "And so we gather today to congratulate ourselves for living to see another day. And also," he added, "I heard the food was going to be good."

At that, Sebastian seemed to have reached an end. We started to lament in unison once more for our old friend until we heard a shout coming from one of the houses nearby. I shall not repeat the exact words that were used, but suffice it to say that they formed quite an emphatic request for us to cease our cacophony. It is an unfortunate truth that humans cannot appreciate the fine art of caterwauling. Their sensibilities are simply not that delicately attuned.

"Why don't you say a few words?" Tess prodded me. I nodded and stepped calmly forward, even though inside my heart was racing, for I had no idea what I would say. I noticed that Sebastian had already eaten a sardine while we were singing, and was licking his paws. The others were looking at me expectantly.

"What is cat?" I began. I had never delivered a funeral oration before, and so I instinctively decided to model mine on the only one I had ever heard before—more correctly, read before—and which had touched my heart very deeply. I refer to the funeral oration given by Hinzmann and described by Murr in his memoirs. I, of course, brought the topics up to date and added my own personal touch.

"What is cat?" I repeated with more confidence. "If he be a graceful, four legged beast who breathes in the air and purrs and meows, then this," I said, gesturing toward the meat, "is no longer our dearest Mo. Only the carcass of our dear Mo lies here. No breath passes its lips; no twitch graces its whiskers. Mo is dead and gone from our lives, and we are all the worse for it."

Some of the kitties began to weep, and the toms supported them in their grief, patting their shoulders with sympathy. Tess, however, stood near me and listened with rapt attention.

"It is customary upon such occasions," I continued, "for someone to give a long, extended life history of the deceased, outlining all his great accomplishments, touching upon all those he influenced, describing the exemplary aspects of his personality, et cetera, et cetera, with the express purpose of leaving the attendees so relieved to finally be free of the oration as to cured of any sadness that they had felt before. It is thus that the orator performs two duties: he properly honors the deceased, and he comforts the bereaved."

I looked up to see a nod of approval from Tess, and continued, "Mo meant a great deal to me, and how happily would I lay out every detail of his life for you. How I would enjoy describing all I know about him, recounting amusing anecdotes of our time together, laughing about the silly things we did and describing the lasting influence he has had on my life. I would bore you so to tears, my fellow mourners, that you would leave this gathering happier than you had ever been in your lives, simply to get away from me." They all nodded with approval.

I sighed. "But it will not do. I will not perform this service for you. I would give you the most long-winded speech you have ever heard in your life if I could, but the unfortunate fact is that I really know very little about Mo. We scratched through the screen in conversation. He gave me some guidance in my youth and advised me to try to escape, but when I did make an attempt, he didn't even fulfill his promise to help me, instead sleeping on the grass in cold selfishness. I do not blame him, mind you. Such is cat, my friends. I am sorry to say, but such is cat."

They murmured in approval.

"Oh bitter fate! Have mercy upon us—selfish, apathetic beasts that we are. Lead us not to death, but to long life, good food and a warm beam of sunlight to bask in. That will be our prayer for today."

"Amen!" shouted one of the cats, who must have lived in an extremely religious home to have supposed such exclamations customary at civilized feline gatherings. The offending cat, whose name turned out to be Moses, looked suitably ashamed once everyone had turned to glare at him. The awkward pall eventually wore off, and the others brought their attention back to me.

"Let us consider Mo's life," I resumed, inspiration suddenly striking me. "Were he a kinder, better cat, I would urge you all to use his behavior as an example and to follow in his pawsteps. But I do not," I declared, pausing to let my words sink in. "Rather, I urge you all to aspire to much greater things in life than the example set by our deceased friend here. I urge you to think about the welfare of your fellow cat in everything that you do, to lend a helping paw whenever you can, to unite to confront evil wherever it arises and to think about performing good acts for your fellow felines every moment of every day.

"When you do this, Mo will look down upon you—or up, as the case may be—and say to himself, 'What in the world are they doing?' But we will have the last laugh. United, happy, we shall move forward together."

"Here, here," someone exclaimed.

"Mo is gone," I continued. "Thrasher is gone now, too. We all deserve better than their examples. Let us turn over a new leaf. Cats are great and noble creatures, and we should behave as such.

"And so, if the death of Mo brings about one good thing, let it be this: We will be as one, together in our comforts, together in our miseries, together in whatever cruelties fate has in store for us in the days, weeks, months and years to come."

There was a general roar of applause, someone shouted, "Let's eat!" and the feast began. It had been my first try at public speaking, but my inspirational sermon garnered universal praise. During the reception that followed, more cats than I can count came up to me to introduce themselves and compliment my oratory skills.

I met many cats that day, but Tess made a point of introducing me to two older kitties from down the block who had taken an interest in her when she was a kitten and had shown her the ropes of living on Forest Drive. Misty was a plump kitty with a rather unusual pattern on her fur: a cinnamon and black tortoiseshell fading into a bluish gray and white face. Sassy was a thin ginger cat, but as different as their physical features, their kindly, soft-spoken manners and gentle voices seemed to mirror each other's almost exactly. Tess told me she was very fond of them, and made sure to spend at least part of every day lounging and chatting with them. Misty and Sassy nodded their heads and affirmed how much they enjoyed their visits from "young Tess." I could only imagine how the three of them must have speculated about me as they lounged around chatting in a beam of sunshine while I lay recovering in Tess's home.

Misty and Sassy were very warm, telling me how pleased they were that I had come to Forest

Drive and rid them of the tom that had tyrannized them for so long. They struck me even at that first meeting as two of the sweetest, friendliest cats I had ever met, clearly providing a model for Tess's own kindly, nurturing nature.

After we had all gotten some food and chatted for some time, Treble, a young orange kitty with a deep alto voice, sang a soft, heartbreaking lament that brought us once more to tears. There followed more songs and more speeches, and then numerous overlapping conversations as the party gradually dwindled and dispersed. Tess and I finally said our good-byes to Misty and Sassy. We were the last of the party, leaving only a mess of bare bones and feathers behind Mo's old house.

As Tess and I headed back toward her home, I mused about how changed these cats were from those I had met only hours earlier. Knowing that their great tormentor had been vanquished, they now spoke their minds freely, exhibited the greatest qualities of friendliness and welcomed me with open paws. Gone was the initial fear and caution with which they had first greeted me.

The excitement of the day began to fade, and I gradually became aware of a full, warm feeling in my breast. I realized that I had not been so genuinely happy in many months—certainly not since my dear friend Hercule had passed away.

I resolved right then and there that this was where I intended to stay for the rest of my life.

* * * * * * * * * *

I believed that Tess would be pleased about my decision, but I still harbored enough doubt to make me reluctant to speak with her about it.

Tess and I woke up late the next morning and lounged lazily about the house for some time getting to know each other better. As the sun reached its peak, we went outside for an afternoon stroll and soon came upon some of the neighborhood cats lounging on a well-manicured front lawn. Sinbad, the black and white tom who had been standing on Thrasher's carcass at the funeral, was telling Misty and Sassy some sort of story that was making them laugh as they lay relaxing in the sunshine.

"Well, well, look who's here," Sinbad called to us good-naturedly as we grew closer. "It's the Slayer."

"Tom Slayer," I improvised.

"Tom Slayer it is," Sinbad said, and thus was born my nickname in Forest Drive.

I have finally—for the first time in my life—become part of a society of my own kind. I cannot begin to tell you how filled with joy my heart has become. If only my dear departed Hercule could see me now. My days as a tomcat here on Forest Drive have been without question the best of my life. I can enjoy my beloved Nature as much as I like—in the brush behind the houses and in the woods beyond when I am feeling wild, or in the neat, tended front yards when I am in a more civilized mood. I finally have the freedom for which I have so long yearned.

Tess's family has adopted me in a way, feeding me and allowing me to sleep inside their home but letting me roam free during the day as much as I like. Only the grandmother is home during the day and she rarely ventures upstairs, so I can use one of the computers to write in the afternoons whenever I wish.

Indeed, I believe that this is the ideal living arrangement for the modern, sophisticated cat.

* * * * * * * * *

It is now time for me to reveal to you what is perhaps the most surprising news in all of my life. Against all my better judgment, I have done the one thing I believed I would never do: fallen in love.

In the weeks since I arrived here, I have been in close proximity with such a sweet and wonderful kitty that she was bound to arouse strong stirrings within my breast. It soon became clear that Tess and I shared similar feelings for each other. It is of little import that I am no longer able to sire any kittens for her; my heart remains untouched by the theft of that particular part of my tomhood, and my potential for amorous feeling is as strong as ever. In fact, as a result of the operation Dr. Choi performed on me, I am able to feel a deep, unsullied love such as those with more base urges may not even be capable.

Tess has a goodness and a nurturing kindness that I have never before seen in a cat. The other cats recognize this in her as well and, along with

Misty and Sassy, she serves as a sort of "mother hen" to them all. When I literally stumbled into her life, Tess took me into her home, nursed me back to health and gave me the secret to survive my perilous encounter with Thrasher. Her unwavering dedication since has served to strengthen me further and make me a better tom.

Tess also has an endearing playfulness about her that is simply irresistible. I remember one night I was woken by a strange rattling from the bathroom. I got up to investigate and found Tess there, swatting at the toilet paper hanging from its roll.

"What in the world are you doing?" I asked.

"I was bored, so I thought I'd come in here and play."

I looked at the pile of toilet paper she'd already unraveled onto the floor and said, "Aren't our caretakers going to be angry?"

"Angry? No. They break out in peals of laughter when I do this. It's fun for all of us."

"Are you sure?" I asked skeptically.

"Absolutely," she assured me. "They find it endearing. One night when I was tearing it all up, I got a little piece stuck at the side of my mouth. They thought it was the cutest thing."

I shrugged, skeptical, but resigned to join her in swatting and tearing. By the time we were finished, there was a messy pile of torn paper all over the floor, with not a square left on the roll.

"Come on," Tess said to me, "let's wake them up."

A deep, unsullied love.

We made sure to attach some scraps of paper to our mouths and together leapt onto the bed. We used the cold nose-to-nose technique to wake them both up; Tess woke the wife and I the husband.

"What are these stupid cats doing?" the man groaned.

"Oh, my god. They've been at the toilet paper again," the wife said.

"Get out of here, you two," he said, swatting at us. We dodged his blow, and the game began. They swatted, they kicked their feet, and we had a grand time scooting around, leaping and avoiding harm. I attacked a foot under the covers and was thrust right off the bed. Tess leapt down to join me and, giggling with glee, we fled the room. It was a grand time.

In the morning, whereas it might have seemed to the casual observer that we were being roundly chastised, a close study of our caretakers' bemused expressions and their suppressed laughter as they shrieked, "What did you do?" revealed that they were not really angry with us at all. I realized that Tess was right in perceiving that they adored our little hijinks and would have been quite sad had we stopped.

These were the kinds of things Tess liked to orchestrate. They were entertaining for all. This was one of the reasons I fell so hopelessly in love with her.

I must not forget to mention, of course, that Tess is truly a beautiful creature to behold. Beneath that long coat of creamy beige fur, one may discern how graceful the arc of her back, how alluring the curve of her flank, how delicately expressive her tail. Upon espying her, one soon overlooks the common Persian features and comes to see her true charms, which stem from a strong inner beauty that cannot be masked by any ill-conceived forced breeding.

And so, my fellow felines, I have gone and fallen in love. You might feel sorry for me if you have taken my past writings to heart, but I do not feel the least bit sorry for myself. Love is a wonderful thing to feel, and I would not trade it for the world.

* * * * * * * * * *

Now that I have become a respected member of a fairly sizable feline community, I have been thinking much about our societal structures, or lack thereof. I concede that the most desirable form would be a free, anarchic wonderland with no leader whatsoever, one in which everyone pursues their own interests unencumbered and uninhibited and fully lives up to their potential. The members of such a society would, ideally, band together to help each other whenever needed, but freedom and individuality would be their general guiding principle.

In reality, however, members of such chaotic communities rarely feel compelled to cooperate. If a society is to achieve anything of note, I believe that someone must assume responsibility for the good of the group and set some kind of direction for the others.

"But wait!" you say. "Cats cannot be led. It is simply not in their natures. It is folly to try."

I respectfully respond that it would be folly not to try.

This afternoon, as we lounged on our stoop, I asked Tess if she thought I was doing a good job of fitting in.

"Of course, Hastings. You must be kidding. Everyone loves you here. You're the alpha now."

"Do you really think so?"

"I know so. They all look up to you, Hastings. And they do it gladly. You're kind, you're smart, and best of all, you got rid of Thrasher," she said with a wink.

"Thanks to you, Tess."

"I gave you a small hint. You're the one that had the courage to do it. That's why you're where you are now: their Tom Slayer."

I pondered over my situation for a while as we lay there soaking in the warmth of the afternoon sun. I was hesitant to seize a larger leadership role. With great power, I know, comes great responsibility. This is something I have heard often, but unlike many oft-repeated phrases, this one strikes me as quite profound.

"Tess," I ventured, "do you think I could lead these cats?"

"Cats are hard to lead," she considered. "It depends where you want to lead them. What are you thinking of?"

I put my paw to chin in thought. "I know how to read and use a computer."

"And you keep promising to teach me," she reminded me.

"I shall," I declared. "We will start tomorrow. But what I have been thinking is that I should like to start a class."

"I think I see where you're heading with this, Hastings."

I nodded. "Tess, I do not often brag about it, but I am a cultured and sophisticated cat. I have read the great works of human literature, I have studied their great art, and I have long envisioned the feline world similarly striving to reach its potential. Our own arts, culture and literature are woefully undeveloped. I am determined to use my talents to improve this situation."

Tess sighed and leaned over to stroke my cheek. "Cats like to be left alone, Hastings. It's in our nature. You can't force enlightenment. It has to come from within."

"But there is so little opportunity for them to even see their potential!" I cried. "How can enlightenment come when none can read, none can write, none have even seen a great painting or dance? How can one appreciate something that one has never even been exposed to?"

"I'm not telling you not to do it," she said gently. "I'm just telling you not to expect much."

"It is better to fail horribly than not to try in the first place," I declared.

Tess smiled at me. "I love your spirit, Hastings," she said, and leaned over to kiss me on the cheek, meshing her whiskers with my own. The feeling was heavenly, dispelling any sense of bitterness or disappointment I might have felt before.

* * * * * * * * * *

If I am to become the leader of Forest Drive, I know that Tess must support me with all her heart. Not only is she strong and levelheaded, but all the cats already love and respect her.

After our conversation that afternoon, I fulfilled my promise and began to teach her how to read. I soon discovered that, in addition to being the sweetest, most understanding and supportive cat I have ever met, Tess is also extremely intelligent. She proved to be a very hardworking and determined kitty and, under my tutelage, advanced to reading competence within two weeks. Within another week or so, she had become proficient with the computer.

One of our challenges has been that our caretakers, despite the size of their household, owned few books. Therefore, we have taken it upon ourselves to expand their book collection by ordering from a popular shopping site on the Internet where someone in the family has a credit card number already stored. They rarely review their credit card statements, and so the charges are certain to go undetected by the family. We have also been careful to order no more than two books at a time, so that the charges remain small enough not to be noticed if they do check. Making small orders also ensures that the packages are delivered normally along with the other mail through the slot in the front door, thus allowing us to intercept them before the family ever sees them. We have been building quite an impressive literary collection that is already proving to be an invaluable resource to me and Tess.

I hope that one day it will prove an invaluable resource to all the neighborhood cats.

* * * * * * * * * *

During Tess's intense period of study, we often took breaks from our lessons to walk about the neighborhood and get some fresh air. We invariably ran across our feline friends and explained to them what we were up to in a deliberate attempt to entice them to think about the arts and culture as passionately as we.

We planted the idea in Treble's mind that, considering how poignantly she had sung at Mo's funeral, she might enjoy composing her own music. Garth, a very agile cat, expressed interest when we raved about the beauty of a dance we had observed on Catenation. Tess's beloved Misty and Sassy, whose caretaker was an artist, became excited when we casually asked if they'd thought of developing their own artistic skills. Spike and Willow were touched by a free-form poem that Tess cited from memory about the changing weather, giving us the opportunity to describe the joys of literary exploration.

However, before any of our fellow felines could undertake their own explorations, we explained, they needed to learn how to read and write and use a computer. Thus, we persuaded about a dozen of our neighborhood friends to join us in our resolve to become more worldly and educated. We began by organizing small classes to teach reading and literature. We then taught them how to use the computer and all that the Internet had to offer.

I have described these events in but a few sentences, but of course it took many months of hard work before our fellow felines were proficient enough to begin their own explorations. Thankfully, an unusually early Fall and a long, lazy winter provided us ample opportunity for serious study. Now, almost a year after I first arrived here, I dare say that our fellow felines have become quite driven in following their own interests. One might argue that we have already become one of the great feline communities that I once read about so longingly on Catenation. I submit that we have become quite as rich a cultural center as Catacalla, that famed feline society in Italy that has produced such wonderful art and caterwauling, and consider us to be clearly superior to North Catisberg in Germany. While also fabled, North Catisberg's literature, for which it is best known, has always struck me as dire and depressing, particularly that by Grashalm.

Not long after our cultural colony began to take form, Sinbad, who had decided to explore the sciences, argued that we needed to create a unique name for our society if we were to become as renowned as Catacalla or North Catisberg. The others agreed, and we set to work trying to create a name with a distinctive intellectual and artistic feel but that also clearly indicated a feline community. Catalonia, for example, is an ideal name but, as many of you know, has already been taken by another species. We finally decided, after considering several possibilities, to call our community Catamenia.

Some of the cats maintained that if Catamenia were to be considered a real society, we must also give thought to other aspects of a successful society such as laws and economic development. We argued over the introduction of currency, about drafting an official constitution and instituting a system of laws. But in the natural order of things, Tess and I were in charge and we defeated these ideals as handily as we could. We are benign dictators, I am not ashamed to admit, and I believe our citizens are better off for it.

Catamenia, as Tess and I conceive it, is to be a sort of artists' colony. As William Congreve once wrote: "Music has charms to soothe a savage beast, To soften rocks, or bend a knotted oak."[2] The same charms, we assert, are shared by the visual arts, literature and dance. These arts elevate our minds. Through them, we might become even more sophisticated and refined than most humans.

Sadly, human society seems to have somehow lost sight of the value of most of its finer arts. We felines, in contrast, will not make such mistakes.

---

2. Congreve wrote, "Music has charms to soothe a savage *breast*," not beast. It is unclear whether Hastings misread the quote in the first place, misremembered it, or deliberately changed it to serve his purpose. —ed.

* * * * * * * * * *

Catamenia is indeed a wonderful, vibrant place. The days are racing by. One day an art show, another day a concert, another a dance performance and who knows what is to come next?

We have started a book club in which we read the most modern human works by the likes of Ian McEwan, Peter Carey, Jeannette Winterson and so on. Franz, a tom in our group who wants to become a writer himself, took to the very weighty intellectual works of Don DeLillo, Richard Powers and Thomas Pynchon, but sadly became so depressed that he stopped coming out of doors altogether. The rest of us were thus scared off from the books he recommended and haven't gone near them since. Nevertheless, we continue to soldier on without Franz, meeting often to explore other aspects of contemporary human fiction.

Misty and Sassy, meanwhile, began to explore the visual arts. One day, these kindly and soft-spoken kitties showed us an unexpectedly wild side of themselves when they smeared their bodies with paint and rubbed themselves all over the walls of their house. They invited us over once they were finished, and we marveled at the sheer scale and audacity of the project. It symbolized for all of us a freedom of expression that we had not previously considered. Tess beamed, telling me that she had never seen the old kitties so happy. Unfortunately, when their caretakers came home, they resolved to make all their art supplies cat-proof, and so the two kitties have since become much more limited in their medium.

Garth and Treble began a collaboration, with Garth pushing the boundaries of movement in his dance while Treble explored the very outer limits of caterwauling. These two felines are spurring each other to greatness, and each performance becomes greater than the last. For one recent performance, Garth recruited all of us to participate, and I must say that being part of such a moving work was truly exhilarating. We dashed across fences, jumped up and down, slithered and snaked, and leapt over each other, all in the most intricate patterns, accompanied by the heart-wrenching wails of Treble's great masterpiece of a caterwaul, opus thirteen in A flat minor. I can hardly wait until their next grand project.

I would suggest that their shared love for the arts is largely, if not fully, responsible for their falling in love. Ah, the power of art and the power of love. Who could unite two more mighty forces?

I myself have great plans as well, dear readers. I have embarked on a new work of literature called *A Cat's Sentimental Journey*. It will be a fictional account of the journey from my old home on Shady Court to my true home, Catamenia. I plan to reveal deep truths about feline nature by embellishing my arduous journey with colorful encounters with all sorts of compelling feline characters. In the process, I will expose the foibles and delusions at every level of feline society. Although I have been able to make little progress thus far, I will continue to work on this project in whatever time I can spare.

These are indeed great times, my friends. They are quiet, peaceful times, disturbed only occasionally by the danger of a car speeding recklessly down our narrow residential street or by some imbecilic children driving us back into the woods. It is difficult to describe our happy state of existence in mere words. We can lounge for hours in the warm sun on a front yard, endlessly discussing art, literature, life or nothing at all. We laugh, we cry, we expose our greatest hopes and dreams to each other, and sometimes we just doze in the comfort of one another's company.

My fellow felines, I could not think of a more ideal life. May you all be so fortunate as to find a place like Catamenia for yourselves.

* * * * * * * * * *

Unbeknownst to the others, I recently took it upon myself to create a blog to write about our community's development and to try to stimulate discussion about the future direction of feline society. Unfortunately, it has proven very difficult to interest other cats in such intellectual pursuits. My humble writings simply cannot compete in the blogosphere with the likes of Fishtank, with its endless links to silly online diversions, or Scittermouse, with its withering mockery of anything non-feline. I have all but given up hope on this approach.

I now wonder if writing a book of intellectual achievement is a fool's errand as well. Most cats don't know how to read and aren't interested in learning. And for those who do have the requisite literary skills, the ease with which they are distracted by frivolous entertainments is deeply disheartening to me.

I have of late pondered the wisdom of seeking an audience in the human world, with the goal of bridging the chasm between our species. Many people do have the skills to read. However, like our own species, they seem to prefer spending their time watching television and engaging in other more passive activities. Not only is it highly unlikely that I could ever find an audience with them; it would be nigh impossible to convince them to take seriously any arguments from someone they view to be of an inferior, subservient species.

Indeed, the challenges I face with either species are daunting. The odds that I will find success are quite low. But whenever I begin to despair, I think of what Hercule would say if he heard me conceding so easily to defeat. "That's not the Hastings I know," he'd proclaim.

Dear readers, the primary purpose of creating a work of art or literature is to have others see, hear, read or otherwise experience it. It is an attempt at connection with others, a way for us to tell each other how we feel, to say to complete strangers, "Friend, you are not alone."

That, my fellow felines, is certainly something worth doing, and I intend to continue trying until

the day of my death, no matter what obstacles I
may face.

* * * * * * * * * *

I had been aware, of course, of the reluctance
of the other cats in Catamenia to publicize our
achievements. However, I had no idea of the
intensity of the opposition until just yesterday
afternoon.

It was a warm, clear day, and we were lounging
as usual in the sunshine on someone's front lawn
when I recalled the philosophy that Hercule had
held for most of his life, which was that there was
no need for an audience if you yourself found your
art enriching and fulfilling.

"I completely disagreed with him, of course," I
remarked, "but that was his opinion until the very
day he died, when he finally expressed regret that
he had never sought an audience."

"I think he was right in the first place," Tess
said.

"Yes," Misty agreed. "Look at us. We're
having so much fun here."

"We are," Sassy confirmed.

"But that will only last for so long," I said.
"Eventually we will get bored having only each
other as an audience. Now we are in an incubation
phase as we develop our arts, but soon we will want
to show the rest of the world what we have done.
We will want as many of our fellow felines as
possible to know about us and to share in the fruits

of our creations. To that end," I added, "I have been thinking about setting up a web site for us."

"What?" Tess exclaimed. "Then all the cats will come here."

"And then we will be able to start spreading the word!"

"What word, T.S.?" Sinbad asked, having long since abbreviated my nickname, Tom Slayer, to its initials.

"The word about what we've done," I answered. "The idea that cats can strive for higher things in life: higher means of expression, higher modes of behavior, a higher degree of cooperation and, in general, a higher level of happiness."

"But the only reason we've been able to do this," Tess argued, "is that we're a small group of friendly, dedicated, supportive cats. I don't want any more cats here."

"Neither do I," Treble agreed. "I like it how it is now."

"They might ruin it all," Tess said. "We might get cats like Thrasher who'd just want to destroy it so they could take over."

"She's right," Misty agreed.

"Yes, she is," Sassy echoed.

I couldn't believe what I was hearing. "Do you all just want to stick your heads in the sand?" I cried. "Think of all the cats out there who could benefit from what we've done. Think of how we could help them improve their lives. We have an obligation to show them what we've accomplished, to inspire them to greater things in life. That's why I began *The Kibble* in the first place."

"Yes, that needs work," Tess said.

"What?" I asked incredulously.

"It needs work."

"What does that mean?"

Tess shrugged her shoulders.

"Garth," I said, turning to him, "you haven't said anything. What do you think?"

"I don't think that's our responsibility," he said pensively.

"Not our responsibility? Then whose responsibility is it? Don't we all have a responsibility to each other?"

He shrugged his shoulders. "We do here, but not to everyone out there."

I looked around at their faces, but found no sympathy. There was pity in Tess's eyes, which fired my anger to a boiling point. Rather than fight further, I stood up and left them.

* * * * * * * * * *

I stewed for the rest of the day. I wandered the woods behind Forest Drive, my self-righteous indignation growing in the solitude. It is not only in the arts that I wish to elevate the status of cats. I believe that once we have established our own arts and literature and philosophy, humans will not be able to deny us our rights as equals to their species. In fact, we felines must demand these rights from them.

And yet, if I cannot even convince my closest colleagues to make their arts public, what hope will I have of creating a broader social movement involving tens of thousands of strangers? This thought made me immeasurably sullen and despondent.

I returned home in time for dinner utterly bitter and despairing. I was surprised when Tess met me in the most optimistic spirits. She kissed me and hugged me and apologized for insulting my masterpiece. "It really is fantastic, Hastings," she said. "I'm just scared to ruin what we have here."

I apologized profusely for my temper, and we made up for our first fight in a most satisfying manner.

Nevertheless, a general discontent has been growing within me about this subject, and I can clearly see that I am causing a great deal of anxiety among the other cats of Catamenia. They have resisted any mention that I have made about greater exposure quite emphatically, and I am beginning to sense that I am destined to lose this battle.

* * * * * * * * * *

Despite these recent troubles, I nevertheless took it for granted that my idea to begin a *Kibble* study group would be a success, fully anticipating that sessions about the virtues of my masterpiece would be every bit as popular as Bible study groups are to humans, who eagerly gather to discuss and debate the teachings in their moral guidebook. Tess sensed it would fail, however, and tried to warn me as much, but I refused to listen.

How confidently I strolled around the neighborhood inviting our fellow felines to our first meeting. I encountered not a shred of enthusiasm—nothing more than an "I'll think about it" or "We'll see what's going on that day"—but I remained willfully blind to it.

I chose to hold our first meeting at the scene of my wildly successful introduction into the community, the scrubby brush behind Mo's old house. Tess came with me and waited faithfully, but when the anointed hour passed and no one had come, she began to pace.

As the minutes continued to crawl, I looked ever more eagerly toward every possible entryway. However, the truth soon became undeniable. In the end, not one of our fellow felines came.

I was enraged by our colleagues' apathy but held my tongue, knowing Tess could only say that she had tried to warn me. She sank to the ground quite a distance from me and sighed heavily, looking down, her disappointment hanging heavy in the empty air.

She was still staring down toward the ground with a dejected expression when I finally said, "I guess we'd better go."

"Yes," she said softly. But it was the pity on her face that struck me when Tess lifted her eyes and looked directly into mine for the first time since we'd arrived.

I suddenly realized that it wasn't our fellow felines Tess was disappointed in; it was me.

* * * * * * * * *

Tess and I haven't mentioned my failed study group attempt to each other, and neither have our fellow felines. While I am disappointed in them, I am nevertheless not completely disheartened. I know that there is a wider feline community out there that may benefit from my work and appreciate its true value.

Thus, I have set out to do what I can on my own. I have posted *The Kibble* publicly at Catenation. We will finally see how it is received by greater feline society.

* * * * * * * * *

Oh, how deeply the pain of rejection can pierce. Nay, it is not that my masterwork has been slandered or heavily attacked or even mildly criticized. In fact, it has encountered none of these things. It has simply been ignored, and that is the very worst fate a work of literature can meet.

There have been but three messages posted about *The Kibble* in its feedback forum. One called it a nice story. Another described it as a "decent, if unfocused" short story collection. The last called me a promising young new writer.

Promising? Nice story? New writer? As cutting as these remarks may be, however, they are nothing to the fact that the broader feline community has taken no note whatsoever of my masterwork.

I have become very disappointed with our online community. Gone, apparently, are those halcyon early days when I first discovered the wonderful works of art and music that the feline masters posted for our benefit. Our sites have now become overrun by vapid entertainments—common games, such as Whack-A-Mouse and Beat That Bird, and videos like the one of that poor old catnip-drunk tom who falls off the wall or the one of that group of kitties shamelessly wiggling their torsos as they meow the human hit "Beat It" in multi-part harmony!

I need not explain to any reader of this work how frustrated I have become at this mass ignorance amongst our kind, who are so eager to be entertained by the lowest thinkable intellectual endeavor. I am determined to bring about the elevation of our species, regardless of my fellow felines' unwillingness to support the effort. Indeed, I have conceived of a clever plan to finally gain our species the status it deserves. If the furry masses cannot be motivated to rise up and achieve their potential, then perhaps an outside force will push them into it.

Therefore, I have crafted a Resolution. I have done this in absolute secrecy, and have sent it off via e-mail to the President of the United States and to every member of both houses of Congress. It is a grand salvo to force what should have been granted to all of us in the first place. Here is how it reads:

Dear Mr. President:

Resolution

On establishing citizenship status for *Felis catus,*

Whereas the common housecat is now considered to be little more than property in human society;

Whereas many humans treat the value of a cat's life without regard;

Whereas cats make a significant contribution to human society, proving companionship, sympathy and mouse-catching services;

Whereas cats have a superior intelligence heretofore unrecognized by humans;

Whereas cats have rich arts and cultures which equal, if not excel, that of humans;

Whereas cats are much beloved by many people but treated cruelly by others, particularly boys;

Whereas cats are currently left unprotected by human laws;

Whereas cats are not currently granted any rights whatsoever as citizens of the United States:

Now, therefore, be it

Resolved, that the Constitution of the United States shall be amended to grant full citizenship status to the species *Felis catus,* but not to any other animal species such as dogs, which are not nearly as smart.

END

I have also written an impassioned and carefully argued editorial, which I sent out concurrently to *The New York Times, The Washington Post* and the local *Gazette.*

For Feline Recognition

We hide in the shadows—in the alleys, under your beds and behind your sofas. Some love us and care for us. Others hardly notice us. Few respect us as we deserve.

When this country was founded, the Constitution established equal rights for all men. It took a long time for that ambition to become a reality with the emancipation of human slaves. It took an even longer time for women to be recognized. In both cases, the error was eventually identified and rectified. There is one more error left to be corrected, and that concerns the status of *Felis catus,* known to most of you as the cat.

Yes, I am a cat and I have written this myself. We can write. We can read. We can use computers. We have a rich artistic and cultural life. In fact, we are much more than we let on to be.

We felines have provided companionship and loyalty to humans for centuries while being treated as little more than cheap property. It is time for humans to finally acknowledge their beloved feline friends. It is time for us to be treated with respect and granted the equal status under the Constitution that we deserve.

Now, some animal rights activists argue that all animals should be granted such status. This argument makes no sense, however, as no other species has the intelligence and sophistication of *Felis catus.* Dogs, for example, are the dumbest creatures imaginable. They may be loyal and true to their owners, but they wouldn't know what to do with their freedom if they had it. Dogs enjoy being loyal and subservient. They are simply too stupid to know any better. Most other species, such as mice, are simply mean and do not deserve our sympathy.

However, one other species should be considered carefully in this discussion, and that is the guinea pig. Pensive and thoughtful, the guinea pig is a philosopher and an artist. This species certainly deserves greater recognition and protection under the law; however, the mechanism of this protection need not be so extensive as to warrant amending the Constitution. Guinea pigs do not have the independence of the cat, and are thus in greater need of human care. They are well worth it for the human, I might add, for they reward loving care with much loyalty and affection. But guinea pigs are incapable of enjoying the full freedoms of the Constitution if they were granted to them.

Therefore, in proposing to amend the Constitution, I suggest that only cats be granted status equal to humans. I call on all my readers, both feline and human, to support a Resolution to amend the Constitution which I have sent on this very day to the White House and to both houses of Congress.

To my fellow felines, I say it is time for us to step out of the shadows and be recognized. Support this cause.

To the people reading this, I appeal to your sense of justice and equality and ask for your support in this endeavor. If you have any good in your hearts, you will recognize the wisdom of granting citizenship to a living, feeling species that is in every way equal to your own.

We are cat. Hear us meow.

* * * * * * * * * *

It will hardly shock you to discover that my attempts at recognition have been met with absolute silence. Indeed, you have seen no resolutions passed and no newspaper editorial published under my name, so how could I pretend otherwise?

There was not one single politician who took my Resolution seriously. I received generic form letters from several Congressional offices acknowledging my concern. The White House wrote back thanking me in a patronizing tone for my suggestion. There was no response whatsoever from any of the newspapers. My follow-up e-mail messages requesting the status of my submissions have all gone unanswered.

I ask you, my fellow felines, how can we accomplish anything if no one is even aware of what we are trying to accomplish? These people have defeated my efforts not by arguing about the merits of my proposal, but simply by refusing to acknowledge its existence.

I have become quite despondent about this situation. I finally revealed my surreptitious activities to my beloved Tess after she showed persistent concern about my gloomy mood. She listened and tried to be supportive and understanding, as is her nature, but the fact remains that she does not agree with my means nor with my ultimate goals.

I am at a loss. Perhaps my idealism has been misplaced. Perhaps I can never convince the world to see the folly of its ways. Perhaps I must accept that our kind will forever be relegated to secondary status in this cosmos.

The Shelter Papers

I must write quickly, for I am soon to die. I know not when, precisely, but that I am to die is certain. We are trapped in a windowless dungeon. There is no sunlight here, just the cold white buzzing fluorescents overhead to blanch our fur through the bars of these cages.

Yes, my dear readers, I am in an animal "shelter" as I write this. How they can use such a word to describe this place is quite beyond me. It is yet another example of the human tendency to say one thing while meaning something quite different. I am in prison—on death row, as a matter of fact. I will find little "shelter" here.

I am writing this manually, painstakingly shaping these letters with the stub of a pencil in my mouth! Hercule and I never did figure it out how the great tomcat Murr could write with quill in paw. This is an arduous method, I can assure you, but then I have little else to occupy my time.

You may think it a terrible risk for me to expose my unique talents by writing my memoirs in full view. But we are all so absorbed in our own private sufferings that we pay little attention to each other here. My fellow inmates actually welcomed my requests for them to secure me pencil and paper, as it gave them some purpose and direction. They never questioned why I wanted these things and haven't so much as glanced at me to see what I am doing with them.

My first instinct when I procured this pencil and paper was to write a note introducing myself and demanding that the humans release me.

However, the man who found me pushing the paper through my bars thought the whole thing a joke. He chastised his colleagues for trying to fool him and took away my pencil and paper, thus challenging me once again to coax my fellow inmates to secure replacements for me.

I cannot risk losing my pencil again. I must console myself with the possibility that someone will find this document after I am gone, and that my life's work will then be unearthed.

I intend this document to be a continuation of my *Life and Opinions*, although it must necessarily be of quite a different nature from the previous installations, considering what little time I may have left. My manner of casual digression and meandering must end. Thus far, if one were to plot out the course of my story, it has looked something like this:

Henceforth, it must be much more direct, to wit, like this:

Oh no! Tess is looking at me again. She is in the row of cages perpendicular to my own, so that we can see each other quite well. Her fur is now matted and smudged with dirt. Great Bastet, god of all cats, have mercy on me! Blind me, I beg you!

Don't let those innocent golden eyes remind me of what I've done!

She is still watching me as I write these words. It makes the pencil tremble in my mouth as I try to hold back the tears. I know she worries about my sanity. She frets about this free, wild spirit locked in confinement. But I do not deserve such feelings of warmth from her, for I have doomed her to the same horrible fate to which I have doomed myself. I do not know how she can look at me from behind those bars with anything but hatred. And yet she does. There is nothing but love in her eyes.

It pains me now to think of those better times as I sit here awaiting my death. Only days ago, Tess and I gazed into each other's eyes, tenderly holding paws without ever even considering the idea that something might intrude upon our bliss. Now we are separated forever, each confined in our own metal cages. We shall never again gaze into each other's eyes or throw our forelimbs around each other and hug, nor feel each other's whiskers intertwine as we kiss.

Tess just called to Misty, but as usual she showed no sign of response. She lies curled on the cold floor at the back of her cage, a thick mound of dark patchwork fur wracked night and day with sobbing. Tess tries to elicit a response from her every so often, but she will not answer to anyone's voice. She has not looked toward me once, and for that small blessing I am grateful. I do not think I could stand the guilt of facing her, from whatever a distance.

My heart is crushed, my dear readers. It pains me to write any more, yet I must continue. They might come for me any minute, and then it will be all for naught. I must make haste and tell you what has happened.

* * * * * * * * * *

It was a warm, sunny day. A few of us were lounging on a front lawn, not saying much, careful to avoid the topic that had of late been causing our community so much tension. Misty suddenly came running down the sidewalk toward us just as fast as her strained aging legs could carry her, crying hysterically. Tess jumped up to put a paw around her shoulder. "What is it, Misty? What's wrong?"

"It's Sassy," Misty sobbed. "She's been hit by a car."

The rest of us sprung to action without a word and quickly followed Misty to the spot. The car was long gone. We had moments before commented on a silver BMW speeding down the street that had screeched, we had assumed, around the corner at the end of the block. In fact, the screech had come short of the corner, where Sassy had been crossing the street.

Her ginger carcass now lay in the middle of the road, flattened across the flank and streaked with red and other unspeakable colors. I do not need to further describe for you the image of a cat who has come under the pressure of a car's tire. We have all seen it, and it is an ugly, heartrending sight. Sinbad bravely examined the carcass and, in a heavy voice, pronounced Sassy dead on the spot.

We broke down and cried right there in the middle of the street. Tess tried to comfort Misty, but the old girl was hysterical with grief over the loss of her close companion. Eventually, I suggested that we move the body out of the road lest any more of us fall victim to a speeding car.

"We should have a funeral," Tess said between tears, and we immediately agreed.

We prepared for the event much the same as we had for Mo's funeral, but the mood was far more somber this time.

I was called upon to do the oration, and I let vent to my anger in the very backyard where only yesterday we had been gleefully practicing the moves for Garth's latest modern dance together. Sassy's lithe body, I reminded everyone, had been slow but beautiful in its own graceful way.

"Must we always," I cried, "fall victim to the arrogance and apathy of humans? They give not a thought to us. The person driving that car did not condescend to give one moment to ponder the wonder and beauty that was Sassy's life. To them, we are just animals. Sassy was simply an animal who got in his way as he drove to pick up a burger and fries for his lunch!"

Misty lost control of herself at this point and bawled openly. Tess put her front leg around her friend's shoulder and tried to comfort her, but others, caught in the swell of Misty's anguish, began to cry as well. The display of sorrow soon became almost too much to bear. It riled me further, and I continued with renewed vigor.

"Must we always live in their shadows," I asked, "and say nothing when their cars crush us and their children swing us by our tails? When will the day finally come when they recognize that we are their equals, capable of profound thought and feeling? Capable of creating groundbreaking art and music and dance and literature! When will they stop treating us as second-class citizens and see that while we may be different from them, we have our own rich arts and culture? We are worthy of respect, not a crushing under the tires of their cars!"

Caught in the powerful emotions of the moment and spurred on by my persuasive oratory, my comrades cheered me on, and I let the surging emotion lift me to even greater heights of inspiration. "When is the time for us to stand up and demand recognition?" I cried. "Is it next week?

"No!" they answered.

"Is it next month?"

"No!"

"Maybe we should wait until next year?"

"No!"

There came a shout from one of the houses for us to be quiet, which provoked us all the more.

"Maybe we should wait until she tells us it's OK," I said, pointing my paw toward the befuddled woman.

"NO!" they cried.

"Then let us go now. Sassy's death shall not be in vain."

"What are you planning?" came the sole voice of reason in the crowd. It was my beloved Tess's, and now how I wish we had followed her sober judgment.

"When I came to Forest Drive after being so brutally assaulted by my fellow toms," I explained, "I passed behind city hall, the seat of the local human government. It is not far from here. I propose that we hold a protest there until the humans recognize us and meet our demands."

"This is ridiculous, Hastings," Tess said. "I know you're upset—we're all upset—but think of the consequences."

"The only consequence I can think of is that of doing nothing," I proclaimed, pleading to the crowd. "Maybe tomorrow Misty will get run over. Maybe then it will be Garth, or you, or me, or any of us. It is time for us to take our rightful place in society!" I bellowed, lifting my paw high in the air.

Spike and Willow, the young black cats, began a deep, mournful meow, and the others joined in, pouring their emotions into a collective cry that built in force until it sounded like the fearsome roar of a tiger. The strength of that cry, my fellow felines, made us feel like nothing could stop us.

As we made preparations to embark on our protest, Tess pestered me with constant arguments about how unreasonable our quest was and how impossible our goals. But I was brimming with anger, and the others were as well. Such is the will of crowds. Humans call it the "mob mentality." We felines can fall prey to it too, as I now know.

Thus it was that I, their Tom Slayer, led them into battle.

* * * * * * * * * *

Sinbad had painted a sign that read "CATS RIGHTS NOW" in bold red paint, but other than that, we carried very little. Nevertheless, we slowed our pace in deference to Misty. In retrospect, it's clear to me now that she was too overwhelmed with grief to seriously consider what we were doing. She doubtless couldn't bear the thought of being left alone. Misty would never have supported our endeavor—and certainly not have accompanied us on our fool's errand—if she had been in her right mind.

Tess reluctantly joined us as well, her pleas for reason growing more desperate the entire way. "Hastings," she admonished me, "humans won't take this seriously. They're going to think it's a joke. They're going to lock us all up."

I shook my head with confidence and lectured her excitedly, "We have power, Tess. Can't you feel it? Nothing can stop us."

"Remember Tobermory, Hastings, and what happened to him."

"That was a long time ago," I argued. "People are open to new ideas these days. And we have a true and just cause. Humans love good causes. Remember, Tess, nothing will change if no one is willing to risk anything."

In spite of her disapproval, Tess stayed by my side. She is the most dedicated, loving kitty whose graces a tom could ever hope to enter. I only wish I could have behaved in a manner that merited such loyalty.

When we finally arrived at the city hall building, Tess's pleas grew absolutely frantic, but I brushed them off. Spike and Willow transformed into wild, quick black flashes that raced up the front steps of the building and ferociously attacked people's legs until the space was cleared for us. We lined up on the steps, propped our sign against the wall and began our chants.

We drew quite a crowd with our angry ruckus, but the effect was not at all what we had anticipated. They laughed. Yes, my friends, they thought us a joke. They formed a semicircle around us, pointed and cackled at our fury. Which only, of course, helped to feed it.

"No one goes in or out of this building," I bellowed from the top step. Tess, by my side, looked anxious and worried. The rest of the cats cried out in approval.

The legs of the next man who tried to enter the building were roundly attacked with teeth and claws. The people around us rushed forward to rescue him. We let him go and, once the surprised man was out of harm's way, the crowd began to yell at us in anger. We hissed back.

The standoff did not last long, for it was soon thereafter that the animal control officers arrived at the scene with their nets. "Run!" I shouted as the first net descended, and we scattered, our protest dissolved in pandemonium.

Several people, recognizing my role as leader of the attack, fingered me as the primary target. I began to run, with Tess sticking by my side as the officers gave chase.

"Run away from me, Tess!" I shouted.

"I won't leave you, Hastings!"

"You must. I won't have your blood on my hands."

"I love you, Hastings!" she cried. "I can't live without you."

My eyes filled with tears at those words. I suddenly recognized the gravity of my folly, and it infused me with a heavy panic. The two of us bounded side by side, faster than either of us ever have, desperately trying to escape. I remember glancing toward Tess, just for a moment, and seeing reflected in her expression the same terror that I felt.

But it was not long before we were in their nets and there was nothing I could say to save her. We were shoved roughly into adjacent cages in the back of a truck, my teeth unable to penetrate those gloved hands no matter how hard I tried.

When we finally looked around, we saw none of the others from our group there. We didn't realize at the time that the sobbing we heard beneath our cages throughout the ride was our own Misty; we discovered that only when we arrived at the shelter. Aside from Misty, however, to this day we have not seen any of our other friends, and I presume they have escaped and are now carrying on our vision for Catamenia in comfort and obscurity.

I spent the entire dark, jittery ride to the shelter professing my deep and profound love for my beloved Tess, pressing my paws against the wires that separated us and pleading with her to forgive me. She smiled at me sadly and assured me that she loved me too. "I would have followed you to the ends of the earth, Hastings," she said, putting her paw gently against mine.

"And I would have led you there, selfish cat that I am!"

She looked away from me without responding.

"I long ago tore my collar off, Tess, but you still have your name tag," I said hopefully. "They will call your human caretakers, and you will be saved!"

"No, Hastings, I can't leave you here. My heart will break if we're separated."

"They'll take me, too," I said, "when they come to pick you up."

Tess shook her head. "You're not their cat, Hastings. They think you're just a stray. They may not even see you when they come to get me."

At that, she reached up with her paw, slipped off her collar and tossed it out of the cage. It fell to the floor and, with the jostling of the truck, soon slid, to my dismay, under the wall of cages in such a manner that I knew it would never be found.

"Tess!" I cried.

She turned back to me, and her loving smile nearly broke my heart.

* * * * * * * * *

And so, dear readers, that is how I, as accomplished and sophisticated a cat as you will ever find, have come to be in a common animal shelter awaiting my demise. Writing my story down these past days has greatly helped me get through the long, dark hours, and I am thankful for having done it.

I know these papers will not save me. I can only hope that they are found by a sympathetic reader, put together with the documents I have stored online (the web site, username and password are listed at the top of the first page) and published for all the world to see. I know it is but a distant hope, but it still glimmers.

There has been one true ray of light in this long darkness. Misty's caretaker came to rescue her a number of days ago. I am very happy and relieved for her. I am certain now that Tess would have been saved as well had she left her collar on. How I wish she had not discarded it for this unworthy charlatan!

Dear readers, if you have somehow come into possession of this history, I have but one piece of wisdom to impart upon you in these, my dwindling days. I have been striving my entire life for many lofty goals, but now that I am facing my final hours, there is but one thing that I care for, and that is my dear Tess. I have learned that reaching out to others and opening our hearts to them, above all else, is what gives our lives meaning. Friendships, love, community—these are the things that matter. The arts are all in service of these goals, never in opposition to them. I finally understand this now, and yet now it is too late.

This morning, I called out in desperation, "Tess, I am so sorry for what I have done."

She looked at me sadly from behind her bars. "I know you are, Hastings."

"I love you more than all the world."

"I love you too, Hastings. Maybe when this life is over, we'll be united again."

"Don't speak like that," I pleaded. Her words broke my heart anew, and I began to cry.

If, dear readers, by some crazy twist of fate, we were ever to escape this predicament, how differently I would live! I had everything in the world that mattered, and yet I wanted more. It was only my loathsome hubris that brought us to this hideous end.

I now believe that had we continued to focus on building a quiet strength in our community, as my friends had wished, Catamenia would have naturally become a great force. Others would have eventually discovered us and tried to emulate what we had created. My arrogance and impatience were what led us to expose ourselves so prematurely, and my heart is leaden with that knowledge. However righteous the cause, I now know, one cannot simply force upon the world that which it is not yet ready to accept.

But perhaps the others will further our vision. I know that they will not forgive me for what I have done; that is not in our natures. But I hope they will not neglect their newfound interests and return to the groundless, unfocused existence that they sustained before I urged them to reach for higher things. I would like to think that I have at least had some positive influence on their lives.

And on your life as well, dear reader. Do not despair over my demise. It is only I that is doomed. Pledge to continue to strive for great things in your own life and I will die happy knowing that mine has not been in vain.

Now that my task is complete, I shall say farewell. I wish to go and spend my final moments with my love. Your company has been most welcome during my journey. I hope that you have found it as rewarding as I have. I only regret that I could not stay with you for a little longer....

Your Humble Servant,
Hastings

Epilogue

After reading my purported final words, my dear readers, you must now be wondering how you come to be reading anything further from my paws.

As you know, Tess and I had come into the shelter with no collars. We were promptly offered for adoption, but of course neither one of us displayed the least bit of warmth toward the few who requested to visit with us. Thus, I wrote those last words with an absolute certainty that we were marked for death and that our fate would soon descend upon us.

I knew my time had finally arrived when the burly young African-American man named Chip came over to my cage early one morning and opened it to remove me. I found myself descending into a blind panic. I hissed and clawed at his approaching hands as viciously as I could.

"I'm going to have to get the heavy glove out for you," he said pensively, then closed my cage.

As he retrieved a pair of long, thick protective gloves out of a metal drawer by the doorway, Tess shouted, "Hastings, this can't be happening!"

"I am loath to admit it," I responded, "but it most certainly is!"

"Fight him, Hastings! Fight him with every ounce of strength you have in you!"

"I shall, my love!" I bellowed bravely as Chip opened my cage once more and reached inside. I fought him valiantly as Tess shouted and cheered my efforts. However, in the end that hulking mass of a man was able to pin me down and hoist me by the scruff. Tess and I called each other's names in desperation as he stuffed me into the carrier.

"What are you two making such a fuss about?" Chip asked. He put my carrier up to Tess's cage to test our response, and we immediately reached out to each other. Tess stretched her paws through the bars of her cage; my own were confined by the metal mesh of the carrier's door, but I pressed hard against it so that our paws touched tenderly for one last time.

"I ain't seen nothin' like this in my life," Chip said. "I guess I can just take you two together. Sandy said we got way too many cats now anyway."

Joy rushed through every fiber of my body as I realized that Tess and I would be together once again, for however brief a period. She let him pick her up without protest, and I watched with agonizing anticipation as he languidly turned around and fumbled to open the carrier door with his free hand. Finally, Tess sprung inside.

We embraced ardently and professed our love for each other in the most passionate manner. Neither of us even noticed that we were being carried outside. Suddenly, the door opened and Chip reached in to take Tess away from me again.

"Help!" she cried, reaching toward me as he grabbed her by the scruff.

Chip pulled her away from me, but before he could close the carrier again, I sprung toward him and sunk my teeth into his free hand. He jerked away and shook me off momentarily, but I would not relent in my attack. I viciously clawed and bit any piece of exposed flesh I could find, adeptly dodging the hand that tried to swat me away. Finally, he bent to put Tess down in order to free his other hand, just as I had hoped.

"Run for the fence!" I shouted as soon as he had released his grip. Tess did not hesitate for a moment. Side by side, we dashed across the yard and leapt over the short chain-linked fence.

Suddenly, we were free. The sun shone high in the sky, with not a cloud to obscure its warmth. We felt in those first few moments of freedom as if the whole beautiful world was an expression of the peaceful bliss we felt in our hearts.

* * * * * * * * * *

Tess and I spoke at no small length about whether to return to Forest Drive. The idea of a symbolic new beginning was quite attractive to us. We also could not know the extent to which our onetime friends still harbored anger toward us. In the end, we deemed it unwise to put it to the test; feline fury is not to be trifled with. A new beginning it would be.

We wandered for quite some time before we were able to establish an arrangement with a human family in which we could build a quiet, happy life together. As for our whereabouts, we both agree that best not to disclose. We plan to maintain a considerably lower profile than we did when we lived in Catamenia. We will patiently teach others to read and write, and gently encourage them to pursue their interests in the arts and sciences. In this steady manner, we will gradually build a solid foundation for a strong, growing community of supportive and like-minded felines.

And so, dear readers, we carry on. You will not find me proselytizing on a street corner or blogging in some remote corner of the web. You might come across my writings here and there. You may, one day, encounter the art, music or poetry of our colleagues. I still hope that our accomplishments will lead to a recognition of our higher intellects and, eventually, to the social advancement of our species. But for now, we will focus on cultivating our work itself rather than on promoting our nascent achievements.

It is possible that these very pages will help to affect social change on behalf of our species. However, I have learned that one human phrase about our species is, indeed, true: One cannot herd cats. I suppose that one would have trouble herding any species of higher intelligence. We must each of us find our own paths and hope that, in the end, our personal efforts will together form a better world for us all.

Suddenly, we were free.

Acknowledgments

Thank you to those who made many valuable suggestions and contributions to this book: Olivia Wein, Joan Herrington, Barbara Esstman and Lorene Lanier.

CPSIA information can be obtained at www.ICGtesting.com
Printed in the USA
BVOW04s0438210314

348331BV00002B/3/P